In Red Blood

by

Bernard Pearson

Published by Leaf by Leaf Press 2022
www.leafbyleafpress.com

ISBN 978-1-9993122-7-5

Cover art by Reg Turrell
Printed and bound by Clays Ltd, Elocograf S.p.A.

About the Author

BERNARD PEARSON: Lives in Oswestry, he is married and has two grown up children. Before turning his hand to writing, Bernard had a long career working in social care. In addition to his novels, he has been published as a poet, biographer and short story writer.

Acknowledgements.

There are so many people to thank for their help in writing this book, in particular my fellow Leaf by Leaf writers, Ron Turner, Trixie Roberts, Vicky Turrell, John Heap, Wendy Lodwick Lowdon, and Kirstie Edwards for their tireless support and advice. I would also like to thank Kirstie for her brilliant copy editing and for keeping me on the straight and narrow throughout. I am once again indebted to my friend and wonderful artist Reg Turrell, for the books front cover.

This book is dedicated to my late father John Pearson.

1
Different Stations

In the picturesque town of Stamford, The Right Reverend Nigel Osgood, was in a reflective mood as he sat in his conservatory with Grizelda, his Siamese cat, listening to Bach's Mass in B minor. He had a passion for baroque music which had stayed with him most of his life. Where it had come from, he wasn't sure; his father liked martial music and his mother had a penchant for light operetta, but Bach did it for Nigel every time, and apparently for Grizelda who, usually of an incredibly anxious disposition, now lay abandoned in bliss, on the old clergyman's lap.

Nigel was a little nervous as he was at heart a very private man, but he had received a call from a very personable young man called Callum, asking whether he might consider being the subject of a television series for which Callum was the producer. The show was called *Family Matters;* it appeared to be a kind of *This is your Life!/Who do you think you are?* hybrid.

'Well Grizelda, have I been a wise or foolish virgin?' He enquired of his feline companion. 'There's no need to give me one of your looks, now is there.'

For several months now, Osgood had been undergoing radiotherapy for an obstinate tumour in his back passage. He faced the prospect of meeting his maker with calm resignation, as his death had, in his own mind, seemed somewhat overdue. He had after all escaped the Grim Reaper many years before and now it appeared, it might finally have its man. It was during 'the summer of love,' when he had first been recruited to spy for the Soviets. He had been up at one of the smaller Oxford Colleges, studying Classics. Julian Markovich, a beautiful young man, had befriended him after a performance of 'The Dream of Gerontius.' Julian was tall, athletic, with turquoise eyes and a tumble of blonde hair. He was one of those types one met around Oxford with no visible means of support. Nigel was never sure whether

Julian was studying anything much at all. Their affair was consummated the night after the limited legalisation of homosexuality. For Nigel, his life had begun at this point. To his surprise, he gained a first-class honours degree and with a little help from his father, who had been a junior minister in the Macmillan government, he got a job in the Foreign Office as an undersecretary of state.

He and Julian had set up home in a little, muse flat, in South Kensington. They would spend their days in the antique shops around Camden Passage and the burgeoning boutiques of Carnaby Street. Life for a time could not have been sweeter. Some few weeks into their relationship, Julian would begin enquiring about Nigel's day; it was lovely that he took an interest, thought Nigel, and the little snippets of information he shared with Julian about government foreign policy seemed a small price to pay for coming home to the love of his life, who in other circumstances Nigel would have considered way out of his league.

The earlier brush with death, had come when he and Julian had gone swimming off the Cobb in Lyme Regis. Nigel had been a strong swimmer and had left Julian to wade back to shore. He was about 100 yards out, when a riptide grabbed his legs and pulled him into an upright position; he could free neither his arms or his leg's but was swept round and round as if in a centrifuge. He had a strange sense of peace, waiting to pass into unconsciousness, when for a few moments the turbulence subsided and he was able to get his hands free and managed to doggy paddle a few yards to a buoy, to which he clung until help, in the form of the local inshore lifeboat, arrived.

Detective Inspector Nic Mycroft, known to his friends as, 'Swot,' sat at his desk watching the world and his wife go by, wondering as he often had during his career whether he was, in reality, cut out for the police force, coming as he did from one of the oldest, established, underworld families of the East End. His office sat next to the fire escape on the second floor of Lincoln's police station, a large, modern building, which, if it wasn't for the regular police sirens coming from the car park, one could easily mistake for a largish comprehensive school.

Downstairs there was the constant hustle and bustle coming from reception and the custody suites but Nick's office although dark and pokey was well away from the hubbub.

Mycroft was tall and sparse in build, with a slight stoop, dark hair greying at the temples, with a somewhat, hunted look. He was now in his early fifties but could pass for ten years younger.

Crime fighting in Lincolnshire had gone through a bit of a lull in the last couple of weeks. In Sleaford, a lawn mower had gone missing, but had turned up a little later none the worse for wear in the garage of its owner rather than its usual place of residence in the garden shed. However, things were about to change.

Mycroft had counted the number of paperclips in his stationery drawer and had just created the illusion of a man running, on a pad of post it notes, all in an effort to distract himself from a particularly nasty murder case that he had been involved in investigating. The case revolved around the surgical removal of body parts of young women. He was relieved when his boss, Detective Chief Inspector Stella Kingsley called a section meeting.

'Okay, thank you, if we can have a bit of hush, I'd appreciate it. As some of you will no doubt have heard, this morning the body of a young man was found in a little used lane, on the outskirts of the town. The post-mortem will take place this afternoon, but early indications show that he was severely kicked and beaten. In all probability, he had died from strangulation. Although it's early on in the investigation, we also believe that that Hanif Singh may have been the victim of a racially motivated hate crime. Any questions so far?' asked Kingsley.

'Yes Bob.'

Kingsley turned to the water cooler. Detective Sergeant Bob Coombs, a man in his sixties with a face almost as crumpled as his suit, was pouring himself a drink.

'Ma'am two, if I may?' said Coombs. 'What leads you to think this was a hate crime? And secondly, will this mean our leave being cancelled again?'

'Well to answer your second question first, Bob, yes; any leave due will be honoured but it will have to be taken at the end of this inquiry. As to a racial element to the crime, we believe Hanif was strangled with his own turban. And there was a note saying, "Death is too good for your sort."'

The DCI allocated each in the section with their tasks, door to door enquiries, witness statements, family liaison duties, and then turned to Nick.

'Can I have a few minutes with you, Nick?' said Stella Kingsley.

'Hey up, extra homework for you, my lad!' said Bob, straightening Nick's tie for him.

Although Coombs was senior in rank, Nick had never been able to establish a proper, professional relationship with the man. Coombs treated him more like a son than his superior officer. In reality, Nick was never happy with hierarchies where everyone knew their place, as he'd never really known his. He had been attracted to the police and in particular detection, by the puzzle solving element of the profession, and had served his time in uniform purely as a means to an end.

'How can I help Ma'am?' said Mycroft.

'Nick, I need you to be my eyes and ears on this case.'

'I'm not with you, Ma'am, you mean you want me to be your nark.'

'You are direct, at times Nicholas aren't you,' teased Kingsley.

'Sorry, but it's taken me months to be accepted as one of the team Ma'am.'

'Do you think I'm not aware of that, DI Mycroft? said Kingsley. 'Now what I'm asking you to do is just feedback to me, if there's any slacking or back sliding on this case.'

'As I thought, Ma'am, a spy in the camp.'

'Look Nick, the evidence such as it is, points to Hanif's murder being a racially motivated one,' said Kingsley, walking across her office to open a window. 'The team will be under a lot of scrutiny from the media, and I do not want the usual suspects screwing it up for the rest of us.'

'Okay, Ma'am.'

'Thanks Nick, I really appreciate it,' said Kingsley, putting her hand on his shoulder

Nick could never stay cross with his boss for long. Stella Kingsley had the appearance of an intelligent toad, accentuated by wearing horn rimmed spectacles of the type that were the height of fashion in the 1950s. She was short and squat, with dyed blonde hair and pale, green, watchful, eyes. Her world-wariness rarely tipped over into cynicism; however, most under her command knew she was no push-over. As a detective she was Nick's first boss and he felt he owed her a favour or two.

She had been in his corner when his underworld family connections made him a subject of some barely concealed suspicion among some at the station. Stella Kingsley, however, saw Nick's upbringing as an advantage in trying to understand the criminal mind.

At The Right Reverend Nigel Osgood's handsome town of Stamford, there was a knock at the door. Expecting only to see one caller, Osgood was surprised to find he had two visitors: a young man dressed in a rather infuriatingly, casual manner to Osgood's mind like an under employed, lumberjack, in a check shirt, with too much facial hair and showy-off glasses, and a girl, who was much more his cup of tea, with her gamine, Audrey Hepburn eyes and touching, street urchin haircut.

'Your Grace, it's very good of you to see us, and sorry it's getting on a bit.'

'Hope we are not delaying your evening meal,' said Callum.

'It's Nigel. I'm in civvies today, and don't concern yourself over my appetite. When you are cooking for one, supper is always a moveable feast.'

Osgood peered over his half-rimmed spectacles.

'And who might this be?'

'This is Chloe Whiting. She will be the researcher on the project,' explained Callum.

'Oh, so I'm a project, now, am I?' said Osgood somewhat acidly. 'You'd better come through. Sorry if I'm a little tetchy. It's a trifle early for Grizelda and me.'

'Oh, I'm sorry. I hope your wife will forgive us,' said Chloe.

'I can't help thinking you must be new to the research game, Ms Whiting,' said Osgood. 'Do come through. As I say, I'm afraid you will have to take us as you find us.'

2
The Pickers

For Alexei Shalikov this, he had decided, would be his last job. He had grown tired of it all. He was only there because people back in Moscow had very long memories; too long Alexei thought, while he tried to work out how best to dispose of 'this traitor of Mother Russia.'

As a he sat in the draughty caravan that he called home these days, wiping the strawberry juice from his hands, Alexei began to consider the progress he had made so far. Once he was free of the sticky residue of his day's work, he picked up the photograph of his target. Nigel Osgood was a tall, cadaverous, figure in his late seventies, a man with quite a reputation in the English popular press, particularly in *The Daily Mail*, in which he was always referred to as the 'Red Bishop.'

Shalikov had found it quite easy to be assimilated into the workforce of Killpeck Farm. The manager, Mr Lomax, had been desperate to find pickers for this season's crop, Brexit was looming large, and many of the men and women who had been employed in previous years were now drifting back to their east European homelands. The farm ironically was set in countryside which, at a push could have been mistaken for the Russian steppes, with vast skies, long straight roads with nothing much more on them than an occasional tractor and a perpetual, often bone chilling, wind. Home sweet home, thought Alexei bitterly. He had joined the FSB straight from The Red Army. 'Travel the world,' they had said. Well the bits of the world he had seen were shitholes for the most part: Afghanistan, Chechnya, the Kola Inlet, you could keep them all as far as he was concerned. Once he was in the GRU, as a senior security officer, however, things markedly improved. Stints in the gulf states had been followed with jobs on the Europe station in Vienna, and then latterly in Talin. He had earned a reputation as a fixer, someone who without a fuss solved problems for mid-ranking, Kremlin officials and latterly even for some within the President's inner circle. So, it had come as an unpleasant surprise when he was assigned to a job in the UK that would involve few of the perks he had become used to. It wasn't that England was a bad place: after all, it had produced Elton John and his personal favourites, The Smiths. Another advantage was you could go any place and get a Mac and fries. It was just that most of the people, he found boring. The men were generally very stupid and the ones that weren't, that you could have conversations with about great art, or the history of the novel, for instance, turned out to be homosexuals. Alexei had nothing against homosexuals. In fact, some of those he had had to kill as part of his job, he felt sure were gay, but nice people.

The Skripal poisonings in Salisbury, had certainly made it a little more difficult to operate in the UK. But with the expertise of the GRU, gaining a visa and a fabricated passport meant the start of his mission had still proved relatively simple.

Alexei and Lizzie Rimmer had met one Saturday at the end of Alexei's first week at Killpeck Farm in The Shirings, the only pub within ten miles of the farm. Now normally, Alexei didn't get involved with women when he was on an assignment, but there was something earthy and irresistible about Lizzie, and she'd certainly made herself very available.

It was perhaps Alexei's vulpine appearance that made women's hearts melt on meeting him. He was tall and angular, with a mop of dark hair flopped over heavy lidded, light green eyes.

Lizzie had a place out near the A417. It was two years since her former husband, Kyle, had had a heart attack and dropped down dead, right in front of her. Lizzie described to him how she still saw the event in her mind, unfolding in slow motion before her several times a day. But as Alexei was to discover, grief had had a peculiar effect on Lizzie's libido.

She was a tall, raven-haired woman, who looked older than she actually was. They had got into conversation about invasive species ruining the countryside, moving from mink to Japanese

Knotweed and American crayfish. As the alcohol flowed, the conversation became more domestic and intimate. Lizzie was wearing a tight-fitting little black dress; her hair tied loosely fell in wisps about her shoulders, and her eyes were dark and luminous. Alexei was aware that the other men in the pub were looking at her with their tongues practically hanging out. The only people Alexei despised more than himself, were other straight men, particularly westernized men emasculated by their veneer of political correctness: their testosterone seeped uselessly out from them, like piss in the snow.

Alexei lied easily to Lizzie about how he was yet to meet the right woman, making up some yarn about having been at sea all his adult life. She took him back to the farm. Despite being several times over the limit, they weaved down the lanes, in between deep reens, which should Lizzie have veered off the road, would have more than likely seen both of them drowned. Almost as soon as they got through her front door, Lizzie pulled Alexei to her, hungrily lifting his t-shirt off, pushing him to the ground and climbing on top of him. Such passion, thought Alexei, she could almost be Russian.

Killpeck Farm was a considerable affair. The old house was a massive, square, red brick building, with a flat roof and numerous, multi-pained windows, some real, others dummy windows, to maintain the property's symmetry. Most of the house was surrounded by a high privet hedge. Spreading out in all directions were great, snaking, polytunnels for the growing of soft fruit. The land the farm was built on rolled and swelled gently to the north of the dead calm of the Lincolnshire plains. Here, what villages there were, had been spaced out as if deliberately, so as not to have to speak to one another, apart from on market day, or the great Christian festivals, which in past years had seen the spired churches full to overflowing.

Killpeck Farm was Lomax's domain, and such was its geographical isolation that until recently, he had held sway over everything that occurred there with very little interference from the outside world.

Alexei cleaned the sticky, fruit juice from his hands, he was busy cooking a meal for the other men who shared his caravan. The accommodation could best be described as spartan. Each small bedroom was shared by two people; the living area had seen far better days. The curtains drooped, half on, half off their rails, like leaves on a storm damaged tree. What carpet there was, was worn and covered in various stains of uncertain origins. The drab environment was completed by an odour that hit the back of the throat in such a way that for the uninitiated, it had the effect of making them want to gag.

Alexei made goulash and rice with a side salad, and everyone was helping themselves from a huge saucepan and then taking their meal outside into the fresh air to sit around a rickety old trestle table. Those present consisted of: Nat Van Troon from the Netherlands, enormously tall and gangly, with horn rimmed spectacles, who when not fruit picking, could always be found with his head in a book; Dave Cheung, who said very little and kept himself to himself; Sean from County Mayo, dark haired and good looking, in a 'poor man's George Best' kind of way, who spent much of his time romancing the local female population; and then there were Jason and Drac whose trust Alexei had been carefully cultivating over the last few months.

'Why is it you cook us this shit? Was your mother whoring when you were a kid? Did you never know what proper food was?' This was Drac's usual response to Alexei's cooking, before wolfing down what was put in front of him.

'Yes, you're right, Drac, no better than pig swill.' Jason would say in support of his hero. The contrast between the two men could not have been greater. Drac Kranovich was six and a half feet tall, with a mane of curly, greying hair, tied back in a ponytail. He had the frame of a retired, middle weight boxer and the eyes of an intelligent, raptor. Jason, on the other hand, was skinny and baby faced with a receding hairline. He walked with a slight limp caused, reputedly, by a riding accident which had thwarted him in his ambition to be a jockey.

The two men were both members of 'New Glory' set up to fight for an 'All White Nationhood' espousing both an introduction of apartheid in Britain and the phased programme of eugenics. New Glory's twitter feed claimed to have over ten thousand followers. Among the pickers, only Alexei knew of Drac and Jason's involvement in far-right politics. For Alexei, the two appeared ripe for recruiting to his operation. Drac had grown up during the civil was in the Balkans. His father had been involved in the Srebrenica massacre, but had then got himself killed when a military vehicle blew itself up on one of the mines which its own side had planted. Jason seemed something of a lost soul; he had been in and out of trouble as a teenager, never held a job down for more than a month, and he was also, Alexei decided, someone he could definitely use, because although of little intelligence, he had a modicum of natural cunning and it also appeared he had very little to lose, no family, no home. He could disappear off the face of the earth and no one would really notice at all.

'I think it is okay,' said Nat Van Troon.

'It's just like the goulash me mammy used to make back in County Cork,' said Sean.

'How about you, Cheungy?' No chopstick's I'm afraid,' said Alexei.

'It's good, I think,' said Dave Cheung. Dave was slight with thinning hair; his wiry frame was distinctive due to a long scar right up the left-hand side of his body. He could have been any age. His eyes darted around their sockets like those of a small fish in a bowl. In respect of the facial disfigurement, Sean had once asked him whether it was from an operation.

'Something like that,' Cheung had replied.

The review of the meal Alexei had prepared continued.

'And posh boy, what's your take on it?' asked Drac.

'Fine, a bit heavy on the paprika perhaps, but perfectly edible,' said Nat without looking up from his Noam Chomsky.

Alexei had been given a few other duties while undertaking his assignment in the UK. They were more in the way of general instructions to all Russian operatives to take any opportunities that arose, to assist in creating division in Britain, using existing, extremist groups, of whatever persuasion, to further disrupt the national discourse, concerning Brexit, immigration, and community integration.

He had been told by his boss, an elderly ex KGB man, that cyber disruption had only a limited effect and feet on the ground could still achieve a great deal in keeping Russia's enemies occupied with their own, silly, internal political infighting. While they were doing this, they couldn't threaten the country from the west. The spectre of both Napoleon and Hitler remained as strong as ever, a reason for paranoia even in modern day Russia. So, Alexei, despite his dislike of Britain, accepted there would be consolations. As well as being very well paid on the completion of his mission by a particular Russian citizen, he would also see his star rise within the GRU.

Alexei had no one left back home now to whom he felt any attachment. His mother had died when Alexei was ten, after many years confined to a wheelchair due to Multiple Sclerosis, and his father, who had only showed a passing interest in him as a child, had remarried several times, his present wife being thirty years younger than him. They now lived in St Petersburg, where his father wrote books on Peter the Great and his fascination with ship building. It was the Russian state for the most part, who had been responsible for Alexei's upbringing and what little nurturing he had received.

Nick Mycroft had been tasked with the job of a follow up interview with Hanif Singh's parents in Wigston on the outskirts of Leicester. They lived in a modest, turn of the century semi, in a quiet, suburban part of the city. Hanif was Vasander and Som Singh's only child. Vasander worked at a local garage as a mechanic, while Som had a part time job as a seamstress in one of the large clothing factories in the town. Nick sat at the Singh's dining room table taking notes, while the Singhs huddled together on the sofa. He pondered on how grief seemed to physically shrivel people. Photographs on the window showed a tall, well-built man, in cricket whites, who bore little resemblance to the man on the settee, as he sat trying to hold himself together.

'Hanif, was our reason for living, you see Inspector; our Prince,' said Vasander. He was a thick set man, with solemn, brown eyes, and a long greying beard.

'It's a terrible thing and we will find whoever did this, Mr Singh. I can assure you of that,' said Nick.

Hanif's mother let out a low, guttural, wail.

'This country is rotten, I tell you; godless, gone to the dogs. Its only hope is people like my Hanif, good people, not scum. You catch them Inspector, please.'

'We'll do our very best, Mrs Singh. Did Hanif have a computer or a laptop?'

'Who doesn't these days? Yes, it's upstairs,' explained Vasander.

'Would you mind if we took it down the station?'

'No, no, but if you wouldn't mind collecting it.'

'Neither of us can bear to go into his room at the moment. I hope you understand,' said Vasander removing his glasses to wipe a tear from his eye.

The Right Reverend Nigel Osgood had provided his two young guests with refreshment in the form of a can of beer for Callum, which he was sipping at suspiciously and a small glass of dry sherry for Chloe, which was doing anything but hit the spot for her. Chloe couldn't work out why she was feeling so nervous. She was after all now a seasoned professional who'd undertaken research assignments all over the world, so why was this elderly cleric giving her the jitters.

'So, tell me about *Family Matters*. I so rarely get the opportunity to sit down and watch tele these days,' lied Osgood. In fact, he was an avid BBC4 watcher and partial to the odd binge watch of the latest Nordic noire.'

'Well, it's human interest stuff really. People love to see the face behind the mask,' said Callum absently and then wished he' hadn't.

'Oh, I see,' said Osgood coolly.'

'Some people say it makes their careers for them,' said Chloe. What was it about this man that made her feel so gauche?

'So, you think the Church of England, now let me see... what is the expression? Ah yes, needs a makeover,' said Osgood, smiling thinly.

'Oh no it's not like that. It's the person's story we are after. What makes them tick.'

'Tell me are you both people of faith yourselves?'

'Well... er... I'm... I'm a bit lapsed these days, actually,' admitted Chloe.

''Fraid I've never been one of your flock,' said Callum.

'In my father's house, there are many flocks, to misquote Our Lord,' said Osgood pouring himself a large, single malt.

Nick Mycroft was relieved to have finished his shift. It was only the second time he had had to deal with newly bereaved parents. On the first occasion, he had made such a cock-up of it, he wasn't sure he would be able to do it again. He'd had to tell a single mother that her son had been electrocuted while trespassing on the railway line, and among his consoling remarks to the grief-stricken woman had been 'This must have come as a dreadful shock.' Her reaction was more terrible than tears. a kind of mirthless laughter, but the look in her eyes would stay with him for ever.

Hanif's computer had thrown up very little apart from the usual games, and a huge back catalogue of Bhangra music.

There were few clues to his private life. There had been no phone found with the body but there was no sign of it in Hanif's room either.

3
Crimes and Misdemeanours

Nick Mycroft's home was a two-up, two-down, cottage in Shappington. It was an isolated spot, surrounded by acre upon acre of fields. About a mile away, lay RAF Shappington, an abandoned Second World War air base, one of many that haunted that part of the world. A few of the locals swore that on some nights you could still hear running footsteps and propellers cranking into life. Lincolnshire more than any other county still maintained a vestige of the feel of wartime Britain over seventy years after the end of the war. The little village itself seemed to be dying. The only shop had closed six months back and the pub only opened a couple of nights a week and on Sundays, when one could get a micro-waved meal for under a tenner. These days, it suited Nick fine as he had had his fill of city living. The house itself was – to the exclusion of most other things – full of books; every spare nook and cranny was filled with them, mostly classic literature and law books. His only companion now was a ginger tom called Bodkin Adams, who disported himself wherever he could, amongst Nick's vast library.

The irony was not lost on many in his family when Nick got a first-class degree in criminology at university. 'Following in the family business after a fashion, I suppose,' had been his Uncle Jimmy's comment. Mycroft's fast streaming into plain clothed policing had followed a short stint in uniform.

He'd worked as a DS in Nottingham for a while, mostly on cybercrime, internet fraud and money laundering, which for a while he enjoyed, for most of the people involved were faceless and this suited Nick fine. After all he knew what criminals looked like; he only had to thumb through his mother's photograph album. There was great Uncle Tommy, the safe cracker Cousin Cyril, well known for handling stolen goods, and his Aunt Minnie, who was done for running a disorderly house, between the wars, and then, of course, there was his maternal grandfather, who had been kingpin of the Collins Family's nefarious activities.

Whether it was this background that had made Nick love criminology he was not sure, but his knowledge of all the great cases of the Old Bailey was second to none. He had just settled down with a book about the Jeremy Thorpe affair, when his mobile rang. It was Jake, his father, and the news was not good.

At Killpeck Farm, Drac and Jason were busy making plans. They would often take themselves off to some deserted part of the farm with a few tins of beer and start dreaming of how they might change the world, so it was more to their liking.

Drac seemed almost apolitical in his nihilism. For him, it was as if any cause would do, to kill and to die for. He was in total thrall to the brutality that had been imprinted on him as a child and instead of reacting against it, as one might imagine, he had embraced violence as a familiar friend. It was his currency in the same way as over intellectualising; banality was the currency of the British middle class, one of the many groups Drac particularly despised.

So, the two men were drawn together, one steeped in violence and the other steeped in hopelessness. Drac and Jason had given up their idea of holding a 'Spectacular,' but instead had drawn up a list of potential targets. Royals were, of course, off limits but MPs, particularly Labour MPs were definitely on the list, along with all Muslims. Jason had at various times been a member of The National Front and The English Defence League.

'Giv' 'em a bit of their own medicine! See if they like it ain't that right, Drac?'

'If we don't make a stand, my friend, we will all be overrun. I'm telling you.'

Then there were the luvvies shooting their mouths off about gay rights, benefit cuts, and Europe. They wouldn't know a day's work if it got up and slapped them in the kisser, thought Jason, and as for fruit picking, a morning would see them crying off to their nearest Chiro… sodding… practor. All vermin were to be taken off the street, as Drac would say, and he agreed wholeheartedly. If only things could go back to the way they were in the fifties. The fact that the fifties ended twenty years before Jason was born was irrelevant. People knew what mattered then, before they let in who knows what from who knows where.

As Drac and Jason huddled over an ancient laptop in what had once been a cattle shed at Killpeck Farm, there was a knock at the door.

'Piss off!' shouted Jason.

'It is me, Alexei.'

'I said Pi…'

'No, it's okay, but shut the fucking computer down though, Jason,' instructed Drac.

'What is it that you want Alexei?'

'Hey, you know I've been thinking to myself what if I join your group, Glorious Days?'

'It's called "New Glory,"' corrected Drac.

'How do we know we can trust you?' said Jason. 'For all we know you might be one of those anti-fascist tossers, sent to infiltrate us.'

'You don't know you can trust me,' said Alexei, but I could be very useful. I too hate the way this country is. People need real leaders not the London elitists. Gone to the dogs, if you ask me.'

'Then why you don't you go home, wherever the fuck that is?' said Drac.

'Why don't you do the same, Drac? said Alexei, staring directly at Drac.

'Listen, if you're serious, we will have a think about it. We'll get back to you, okay,' said a conciliatory Drac.

'Good. Anyway, listen. I'm so bored,' said Alexei. 'There's nothing to do in this god forsaken dump.' He kicked at the shed wall. So, I was wondering whether you wanted to come shoot some rabbits? Lomax, though he doesn't know it, has lent me the keys to the pickup.'

'Where are we going to get guns from then, shit-for-brains? Lomax will have them all locked up,' said Drac.

Occasionally Lomax would organise a party of men for 'pest control' duties around Killpeck Farm but these were carefully choreographed affairs and always within the bounds of the Killpeck estate.

'I have gun,' said Alexei.

'How the hell?' said Drac, looking at the point 22 rifle Alexei had produced from an old potato sack.

'Can't you see, we are busy?' said Jason, who was possessive about his and Drac's friendship and suspicious of Alexei.

'Sorry, I go on my own.'

'No, no, we come. Only playing stupid video game,' lied Drac.

'Good, I thought we might try Nipton Wood. Will be good, you'll see.'

'That's not Killpeck land,' said Jason.

'I know but it will be better sport, you'll see,' said Alexei.

'Now tell me how you have gun?' said Drac.

'I have friends who fix it for me,' explained Alexei.

The three men climbed into the pickup.

4
A Bump in the Night

Nick Mycroft looked at his birdlike mother propped up on hospital pillows, her wasted legs protruding from the blanket like twigs from a magpie's nest.

'Now Nick, you're not to worry about me, you hear darlin',' ordered Nellie Mycroft.

'And how do you propose I do that, Ma?' said Nick.

'Listen Nick, you are not the only family I've got, you know. I don't want you thinking you've got to drop everything whenever there's a tiny little problem. There are a lot of people who owe me a favour and can come and lend a hand. There are loads of us Collins, you know.'

Nick was only too aware of this.

'Then there's your dad of course.'

As a carer, about as much use as a chocolate tea pot, thought Nick.

'And don't forget Uncle Jimmy. Now he's had a lot of experience of taking care of people,' said Nick's mother.

Oh yes, Jimmy "the Stick" Collins certainly knew how to take care of people, thought Nick allowing himself a mirthless grin.

As for Nick's father, he could hardly take care of himself these days; he was short and vastly overweight, resembling a ten -pin bowling ball, rolling slowly down the hospital corridor.

'Alright Nicky boy, just been trying to find some decent grub but the cafeteria's full of 'ealthy option shite. How's your mother doin'? Do you know she hasn't had a shit for a whole week? And they call this place a hospital.'

Congenital heart failure was the diagnosis, a terminal prognosis: three to six months.

'You got any good murders on the go, Son,' asked his mother.

'Well, as a matter of fact, I can't tell you anything about it, but we've got a pretty interesting one on at the moment.'

'Oh, that's just the sort I like,' exclaimed Mrs Mycroft.

As Nick drove home that night from the hospital, his mother remained on his mind. She had always lived something of a fantasy life, where television replaced the reality of what was going on around her. Surely, she must have known while growing up that her family's money mostly came from nefarious means. But if she did, she showed little concern or interest, busying herself instead with shopping, lunches out with girlfriends and keeping up with her soaps.

Nick's father had for many years been a bookmaker, but quadruple bypass heart surgery had put an end to that. He had met Nellie through her brother Jimmy, who had taken a 'business' interest in Jake's betting shops. The two men barely tolerated one another. Jimmy thought Jake was a lazy, fat, slob and Jake had Jimmy down as a psychopath. But business was business and always best to be kept in the family. Nick's parents were married in 1970 and Nick came along two years later. He was Nellie and Jake's only child and Nick, although aware he was the apple of his mother's eye, he was also aware he was a great disappointment to his father.

His mother's words in the hospital 'That's the sort I like,' kept rolling around in Nick's head for some reason. What had the note found with Hanif said? 'Death is too good for your sort.'

There were six bodies laid out on the bed of the truck. Not a bad haul. The method of such hunting, if it could be called that, was to drive up near to where the rabbit warren was, turn the lights off, wait twenty minutes and then switch all the vehicle lights on full beam. Dazzled and unnerved, their quarry, which mostly this consisted of rabbits, would stand stock still for a few moments confused by the sudden illumination of the world.

Alexei and Drac were beginning to lose interest in the shoot, but Jason had got a real taste for it now. 'Oh, come on!

Just another twenty minutes? I'll tell you what, I'll drive the truck, you pop the rabbits, Drac.'

'Sounds good,' said Drac, who was swigging vodka from a half empty bottle.

'What shall I do?' asked Alexei.

'Piss off, for all I care,' said Jason. 'Come on, Drac. Show us how it's done.'

Jason drove further down the tiny lane that led to the other side of Nipton Wood. It was a moonless night and there were no other cars on the road. The copse of trees ran to about 10 acres in all. It was ancient in origin, but unmanaged now. Many of the trees had come down in storms over the years, while others were having the life throttled out of them by great tendrils of ivy. Here and there, small tracks enabled vehicular off-road access. Jason drove up onto into a small clearing

On previous such expeditions Lomax had led on Killpeck land, the rabbits had been supplemented by Roe deer that had the misfortune to be in the wrong place at the wrong time. Lomax was an excellent shot and made sure any money from the venison accrued went into his pocket alone. The business was suffering from a lack of pickers and sometime ago, Lomax had begun to realise he would need to diversify to survive.

Jason didn't see the fallen beech tree until it was too late; the truck shuddered and lifted off the ground hurling Alexei against the window. Unbeknownst to Jason, Draco had been thrown off the back of the truck. A set of car lights flashed through the wood from the lane at which point Jason panicked and threw the pickup into reverse.

'Bastard trees!' screamed Jason as he slowly backed the truck over Drac lying prone and semi-conscious in the mud of Nipton Wood.

The lights were still on at the offices of Janus Films. Barry Goldwing, the chairman of the company, had called a meeting to discuss progress with the series *Family Matters*. Chloe and Callum were still in something of a state of shock that Goldwing had decided to resurrect the programme after the episode regarding celebrity Chef Tom Bradshott had been hurriedly shelved eighteen months previously. They had both been kept busy with other smaller projects. Callum had recently directed a film called *Britain's Best Young Beekeepers*, while Chloe had been assigned a research project concerning Winston Churchill's role in the Gallipoli fiasco. Chloe was still hurting after the final breakdown of her clandestine love affair with Mr Upstairs.

'So, what did you make of our clerical friend, then,' Goldwing enquired of Callum and Chloe.

'Oh, he was very old school,' said Chloe.

'Rather pompous as well as being something of a bore, if you ask me,' said Callum.

'Well keep digging! There's a lot more than meets the eye, believe me,' said Goldwing.

'Prickly prelate doesn't come close,' said Callum.

'Barry, can I ask, what made you decide to start the series with Bishop Osgood?' queried Chloe.

'Yes, it's all a bit *Brideshead Revisited*, isn't it?' said Callum.

'Look, the geezer's always on the telly or in the papers spouting off about this or that.'

'You're the boss.' said Chloe Whiting who needed her job more than Callum, who had moved to the country and could comfortably have lived on the one wage of his partner Oliver coming into the household.

'Look the thing is, Janus Films needs *Family Matters.* I reckon it's our flagship show. Genealogy is really taking off, I tell you, after that bloke from the soaps found he was related to Henry VIII. Now there was a man, who knew how to handle women,' said Barry, who was still feeling a little embittered by his fourth divorce.

Chloe gave Callum a puzzled glance and hoped that Barry hadn't seen it.

'Okay, you're the boss,' said Callum.

'He comes from gentry stock and joe public likes nothing more than a bit of 'black sheep of the family' stuff. You know, like we had with Tom Bradshott.'

'But the plug was pulled on that,' said Callum.

'Well, whatever, we need this show badly and I'm looking to you two to shake the closet and see what comes out. Oh, sorry Callum, that came out a bit wrong, as the bishop said to the actress,' said Barry patting Callum's knee.

'Chloe, I want you to go up to Stamford. Book yourself in somewhere local for a couple of nights. Have a dig around in the town. We are looking for more of a Louis Theroux vibe to this programme, you know like that one with *Joe Exotic* and the tigers.'

'Not much call for tigers in Lincolnshire, boss,' said Callum, and then wished he hadn't.

In Nipton Wood, Jason was fighting back the tears.

'How the hell?' he sniffled.

'I tried to warn you, but you had your headphones on,' said Alexei.

'Is he?' whimpered Jason.

'Hey look, it was an accident. He was probably dead from falling off the back of the truck.'

'But I must have bloody reversed over him,' said a dazed Jason.

'It'll be okay,' said Alexei.

'I suppose we better call the cops,' said Jason, for a moment discovering he had a conscience.

'Is that what you want?' queried Alex.

'Oh Christ! He was my best mate, and I've gone and killed him.' The reality of the situation was slowly dawning on Jason.

'Jason, listen to me. It can all be okay. Not for Drac, unfortunately, but for you, yes,' said Alexei.

'How do you make that out? I've been inside twice before, You think the cops are going to believe any stinking story I come up with, even if it is the truth this time?'

'Okay, listen to me Jason. I can make all this disappear.'

'Oh yea?'

'Yes. Now you go back to Killpeck, clean yourself up, and wait till you hear from me. You will have to walk, I'm afraid, not on the road, though, across the field.'

'And what are you going to do?' snivelled Jason.

'I will do what is necessary. Now help me get the body onto the back of the truck and then how you say, scram!' said Alexei looking directly into the terrified boy's eyes.

For Alexei, Drac's death was, of course, an inconvenience. There was no question that Drac had far more potential as an assassin than Jason. But he was something of a loose cannon. Jason would be more malleable in undertaking Alexei's instructions with very little questioning. For a start, he was quite a stupid boy in many ways. Alexei then turned his mind to a more immediate problem: how to dispose of Drac's corpse. Back home in Russia, there were usually people around to help make bodies of – for instance, political opponents of the Kremlin – disappear, but here it was different. He was very much on his own.

5
The Evil that Men Do

DCI Stella Kingsley paced up and down her office, playing absent -mindedly with a gold pendant round her neck. She had just come back from giving evidence for the case of Betsy Mulligan. Betsy had been fourteen years old and had disappeared from a children's home in Lincoln. She had had a history of absconding but would usually return the next morning or be brought back by a patrol car. The case involved her being groomed by a number of local taxi drivers, who had passed her around as a commodity. She'd been bribed, cajoled and sweet talked by men three times her age, a sadly not unfamiliar tale. The horror for Betsy had only just begun, for into this group of pathetic, paedophiles, a super predator arrived, Rex Priday. Priday was the only person she had come across in all of her thirty years of service, who should the death penalty be in place, she would quite happily have tied the noose round herself and watch him drop. Hopefully, the evidence which she, amongst others, had provided would be enough for him to get a whole life tariff and given the state of some of the UK prisons, he would actually rot in hell. The case had disturbed Stella in a way no other had, and she found it hard at times to focus on her current investigations.

The post-mortem on Hanif Singh had thrown up very little in the way of fresh information and the pressure to make progress in the case was coming from all sides. There had been no witnesses coming forward and it was likely there was no one other than the perpetrator or perpetrators about, at the time of the offence. The body had been found at 4.00 am by a milkman while doing his round and answering a call of nature down a quiet lane that led nowhere, apart from the municipal rubbish dump, a bit like her inquiry, Stella thought to herself. They were well out of what detectives called the 'golden forty-eight hours' during which time most murders often produced apart from several confessions – the work of fantasists and self-promoters –

the most reliable of witnesses; after this, people's recollections became flaky and they were easy prey at any court hearing, for a defence team worth their salt.

There was a knock at her door and Stella beckoned for Nick Mycroft to come in.

'Sorry to disturb you Ma'am.'

'It's okay. Have you got anything for me?'

'No, I'm sorry Ma'am, but I have been thinking.'

'Dangerous, Nick.'

'It's just that...' Mycroft hesitated.

'Go on spit it out!'

'Well, are we focusing too much on one line of enquiry?'

'What do you mean? A racially motivated crime? Well, as far as we know, nothing was taken, so robbery can be ruled out. According to his parents, Hanif was a clean living, studious young man. This cuts down possible motives.'

'Should the love life angle of things be being considered, Ma'am?'

'I'm presently between relationships, Nick,' teased Kingsley.

'The thing is Ma'am...'

'The thing is Nick, we have had a number of assaults in recent months, along with numerous threats on the internet. It's nasty out there, really nasty! It's only a couple of years ago that a lovely young MP was killed in her own constituency. Anyway, I'm doing an appeal on *Crimewatch* this week to see if we can flush out anymore witnesses, though who'd want to be on that lane to nowhere in the middle of the night, god only knows!'

'How did court go, Ma'am, if you don't mind me asking?'

'Pretty unpleasant really, Nick. Priday was there in the dock, with that supercilious grin still playing across his chops.'

'Surely, we are going to get a conviction?

'One would hope so, Nick, but there's still more evidence to be heard. The defence's case is still built around the fact that several men had opportunity and a possible motive for her murder.'

'Yes, but Ma'am, to do what he'd...?

'You know, perhaps you're right about focusing too much on one motive. After all, in Betsy Mulligan's case, in the early stages we got a bit fixated on it just being another Rotherham or Telford case, a group of men, pimping local girls around their peers and then something going wrong and them covering their tracks and murdering poor Betsy.'

'Only to find the truth was even more depraved than that,' said Nick. 'I still have nightmares about it, Ma'am.'

'I know, Nick, so do I. Now let's get back to the matter in hand, catching villains, and try not to worry too much about the machinations of the judicial system.'

'Of course; you are right, Ma'am.'

'Hanif Singh... we've had the post-mortem findings.'

6
The Passion

Alexei drove slowly away from Nipton Wood. He had not fully formulated a plan as to how to dispose of Drac's body, now under the tarpaulin in the back of the truck, but he knew he had several advantages over the police and that he only required a short-term solution, as he would be out of the country within a month, if all went to schedule. As for the hapless Jason, Alexei had big plans for him.

For now, there was only one place he was heading, Lizzie Rimmer's Farm. He drove up the potholed drive to a ramshackle group of buildings. Since her husband's death, Lizzie had let things go a bit. The hay in the hay barn was strewn about like children's building bricks, bits of farm machinery littered the field, a few bedraggled hens pecked at the grass at the back of the farm. Lizzie came to the door wearing a grubby, grey, dressing gown. A cigarette drooped from her full lips and she looked as if she hadn't slept for a week.

'And where the fuck have you been?' she snapped at Alexei.

'Busy! You know how it is.'

'What's her name then?'

'We are fruit harvesting. I told you. Now you go make yourself beautiful. We go out. No, you beautiful already... but you need bath though, go... go... I tidy this shithole of a farm up, then we go eat.'

'I hate you Alexei... whatever your name is.'

'And we see about how much you hate me later. Now go, go, go!'

He watched as she turned and tottered up the stairs. Then he went to the back of the pickup and pulled back the tarpaulin.

Bishop Osgood was relieved to be out from his appointment with the consultant. It had been hot and stuffy in his office and the oncologist had been sweating profusely. Perhaps, speculated Nigel, he always did when he had bad news to deliver. The cancer had spread to the bones, and, he was informed, time for him was short, as his condition was now terminal. It was this news that prompted Osgood when he got home to pour himself a nice cup of Earl Grey, tap the barometer on his wall, (an annoying habit he'd inherited from his father) and begin to write an account of how he had first betrayed his country and then inadvertently signed the death warrant of the only person who he had ever, truly, loved. If Callum and Chloe from Janus Films were intent on getting his story, they might as well have it straight from the horse's mouth. He would start the account in his favourite decade, the 1960s.

The world, thank the Lord, was changing. The laws regarding same sex relationships were gradually being relaxed. Some things, however, seemed interminable; my job in the Foreign Office was stretching me intellectually but felt oddly, irrelevant. The disgusting war in Vietnam dragged on and on, and dear old GB carried on in its parochial and blinkered way for the most part. Young people, however, had a vision of a different way of being, gentler and not bound by the old certainties of class, position, and wealth. As an official (however unimportant) of HM's government I found myself having to be a little more discreet in my living arrangements. My partner, as we would call it now, was Julian, and he was the world to me. It was as if a venetian old master had summoned Julian to step down from one of his paintings and into my life.

My disenchantment with my country of birth had begun when as a child. I endured that rite of passage of upper, middle class children, in private education. Being what was termed then a sickly child, I had neither the mental fortitude, nor for that matter physical strength, to stand up for myself. My tormentors would vary their torture from the psychological, for example, syphoning urine into my bed as I slept, to more direct physical assaults with ruler and compasses, or anything else that came to hand. My housemaster, a Mr Regent, was pleasant but ineffectual. My school life was one of unending misery, interspersed by episodes of such terror that I still wake from nightmares concerning these events to this very day.

Osgood got up from his computer and went over to his porter's chair in the window and closed his eyes, half in thought, half in prayer.

DCI Stella Kingsley had not done anything like this before. She was shown into the green room to await her slot on *Crimewatch*, by a researcher who looked about eleven years old.

'Can I get you a coffee?'

'Tea, two sugars please.'

'Right you are. I think we can manage that,' smiled the girl superciliously.

'I'm afraid you're a little stripey. You'll get distorted on screen. Would you mind if we gave you a change of clothing?' This was the wardrobe mistress, a motherly lady in a Kaftan who whistled through her teeth when she spoke.

'Oh, I'm sorry. I'm new to all this,' explained Stella.

'Don't worry sweetheart, we had an assistant commissioner in here last week in a herring bone suit. I ask you? Don't you lot get any media training?'

'Excuse me, I'd better take this,' said Stella.

7
Vanishing Acts

Alexei worked quickly, lifting the metal lid, and then the heavy grill to the slurry pit. He'd backed the pickup as close as he could, and now wrestled Drac's heavy corpse from the bed of the truck. Drac's jacket snagged on the tail gate of truck, but he had plenty of time. He was confident that Lizzie would be taking a long, hot bath. He took Drac's watch from his wrist; it was a cheap copy and worthless, but the less there was to identify Drac, the better. He then weighted down the body with various items from Lizzie's late husband's work shed. He secured the weights with snow chains (he'd found in the truck) around the torso of the corpse, and then he rolled the body with his foot into the pit, watching as Drac's remains sank into the green, brown slime. The whole operation had taken about twenty minutes; as a clean-up job it was not one of his best, but it would do for now. Lizzie would be waiting, and it was now him who did not smell so good.

In the *Crimewatch* green room, Stella Kingsley had taken her call. It was from Chief Constable Poulson.

'Hello Stella, sorry to ring you just before your big break on TV, but I've just had New Scotland Yard on the line. Apparently, someone has claimed responsibility for killing that chappy of yours, Hardeep.'

'Hanif, Sir' corrected Stella.

'Quite. Seems it's one of these loony tunes, white supremacist outfits. Very amateurish stuff apparently, you know midsummer murders style; all set out with letters from one of the red tops; any way I'll... er... get it sent down to your boys. See what they make of it.'

'Perhaps you could send it to me first, Sir? said Kingsley pointedly.

'Yes, of course, of course, didn't mean any... well... good luck with tonight... they always say being on telly takes a few pounds off you, but looks like we may have got a breakthrough anyway.'

'Thank you, Sir. We will certainly follow this up and see where it leads us.'

'What a prat that man is!' whispered Stella under her breath as she returned to the make-up chair.'

'It comes with the gender darling, tell me about it,' said the woman in the Kaftan. 'Now, let's tackle those crow's feet, shall we?'

Jason had done as instructed by Alexei. He returned to the caravan at Killpeck Farm, showered and changed his clothes. He found it difficult to stop shaking even with a large mug in his hand and the Calor gas heater full on. Nat, and Sean had walked back from the pub, in various drunken states; even Nat, who didn't seem to be affected by alcohol usually, seemed a little worse for wear. He looked at Jason.

'Are you alright comrade?'

Jason just stared into space reliving the night's events.

Nat retired to the sleeping quarters at the other end of the caravan.

Jason looked at the time on his phone. It was 6.30 am. His shift started at 7.00 am. He had hardly slept, anxiously waiting for news from Alexei. There was a peremptory knock on the door and Grant Lomax walked in. The boss of Killpeck Farm was a short, stout man in his mid-forties. He was wearing cavalry twills and a blue and white striped, expensive looking shirt. He was sporting a corduroy cap on his head and a gold chain round his neck. His sunglasses were a lightly shaded green and allowed a partial view of his narrowly set, blood shot, eyes. By his side was his dog, Ratface, a considerable specimen, with the body of a Bullmastiff and a Dobermann's pointy, muzzle.

'Alright Jason, where are those two clowns? I know they've taken my truck. No bleedin' respect. They're both out of here, when I find them. You people coming over to this country taking the piss.'

Lomax had two modes of speech. One was a kind of flat northern, and the other was reserved for customers and staff meetings and was altogether posher. A spell in the army had taught him how the toffee-nosed officers, who he half hero worshipped, half despised, spoke without prepositions or ending words pronouncing huntin' rather than hunting. But he knew such affectations would be wasted on an oik like Jason.

'I'm from Felixstowe!' said Jason. Fatigue and a sense of unreality were beginning to overcome him. He had more to be scared of than Lomax, for whom none of the pickers had any respect.

'You tell me where those two scumbags are nipper, or I'll...'

'Search me,' said Jason.

'Right, this is how it is!' Lomax was turning a vivid shade of purple and the veins on his neck protruded like ivy tendrils on a dying oak tree. 'You tell me right now and you keep your job. You don't tell me, and you can kiss goodbye to your job, and I just might be forced to let Ratface here give you a little nip. So, there's a good lad. Where are Drac and Alexei? And more's to the point, where are my wheels?'

Jason seemed emboldened by the events of the night. In other circumstances, he would never have dared to do what he did next.

'Oh sod off, Lomax, and you know where you can stick your strawberries, and your job!'

He pushed passed Lomax, who although too stunned to react at first soon called after Jason's receding figure.

'Hoy! Come back you little runt,' Lomax shouted, knowing that he would never catch the lad on foot, as he was twice his age and still hung over from the bottle of vodka, he'd drunk the night before. Besides running made his chest hurt. 'Get him Ratface!' Lomax bawled at his dog.

'Can you keep the noise down! Some of us are trying to get some kip,' called Sean from his bed.

Ratface, although imposing in stature, was not the brightest biscuit in the barrel, and instead of relentlessly pursuing Jason, he ran into Sean's room and started to lick the Irishman all over.

'Mr Lomax can you extricate your dog, please? I need my beauty sleep,' said Sean.

'Piss off Paddy,' bawled Lomax, steadying himself against the door of the caravan. He'd get the little sod and the two Pollacks or whatever they were. Bloody free loaders the lot of them!'

8
Fruits of Love

Nigel Osgood had spent the morning at his solicitors in Lincoln, ensuring his will was much as he would want it. His estate as a single man and a senior cleric with a fine Georgian house, stuffed full of antiques and pictures, some family pieces and others that he had bought on the way would not be inconsiderable. In fact, he had supplemented his income in later years by writing coffee table books on Stanley Spencer and Basil Spence's contributions to religious art, which although not huge sellers, had been well received by the cognoscenti of such things. Most of the money would go to his favourite causes, Amnesty International, Green Peace, The Cat's Protection League and The Disaster's Emergency Committee. There would be several smaller bequests to Art Galleries and particular religious organisations, such as The Society for the Resurrection.

Osgood felt strangely energised by having put his financial affairs in order and now set about continuing where he had left off in writing his life story for Chloe and Callum.

Julian and I had three years of bliss together. The misery of my childhood was left far behind. He was so very different from me: direct, passionate, outspoken, prone to temper tantrums over minor household mishaps, with a vulgar sense of humour. We made plans to leave the UK. He was very mysterious about his early life but said that as a child he had been a displaced person and his family had led an itinerant life. One day, he said how he would love to take me back to where he was actually born, but according to him, they liked to string up queers there for something to do on a wet weekend.

It was Christmas 1970 and I'd had the summons to go down to my parents' place in Sussex. The festivities, if one could call them that, followed the same format: early morning church (which at that point in my life I had no time for) and then sherry and canopies, before a six course. Christmas dinner, over which my father presided, was decidedly unmerry, until he had got himself drunk enough to communicate in more than monosyllabic grunts and snorts. Once the embarrassment of cracker pulling had been got through, the men retired to the library. I'd opened one of the windows, to let the fug of cigar smoke out, when Sir Timothy Galloway, a retired civil servant and confidante of my father, approached me. I can still hear his words all these years later...

'Well, my dear Nigel, another year comes towards its close. I've heard very good reports of your work at the Foreign Office, by the way.'

'Oh, that's kind of you to say.'

'Only one fly in the ointment as far as I can see,' said Galloway.

It was at this point that Sir Timothy dropped the bomb that would destroy my happiness and change my life for ever.

It was difficult to know where Alexei ended and Lizzie began, as they made love on the battered old sofa by the fire in her living room. Lizzie's sheepdog, Tess, seemed to think it was a game, and started prancing around the couple on her hind legs.

'Get away Tess, you stupid dog!' screamed Lizzie.

Tess had been her husband's dog and Lizzie resented the fact that Tess was very much alive, while her husband was very much dead.

'What you being cruel to dog for? He only wants to play,' said Alexei, uncoupling himself from Lizzie.

When they had disentangled themselves from one another, Lizzie almost danced across the room to the kitchen to put the kettle on. The affirmation sex gave her was such that even Alexei's eagerness to make his getaway failed to anger her. She came back with the tea and draped herself around him.

'So, where are you off to in such a hurry?'

'I need to take truck back, explain to Lomax. You know what he's like.'

'Nasty piece of work. I don't know why you don't come over here full time, give me a hand with the farm. We make a good team, I reckons' said Lizzie.

'In bed perhaps, but no farming. Not my kind of work. I'm not cut up for it.'

'Cut out for it, you mean; bloody foreigner!' corrected Lizzie holding her cup of tea close to her slightly bloodied lips.

9
Coming Clean

WE KILLED HIM! NO COLEREDS!
BRITIAN FOR THE BRITESH
NIGHTS OF THE NEW GLORY

DCI Kingsley dropped the note on her desk.

'Well, it's not the best spelt mea culpa I've ever read.'

'No Ma'am,' said DS Bob Coombs. But shouldn't be difficult to pull the silly little toe rags in.'

'Potential murderers, do you mean, Bob?' Stella admonished her DS gently. She'd known Bob Coombs for twenty years and despite disapproving of many of his views of the world, she had a soft spot for him. She had witnessed him fail to get promotion, fail to save his marriage and fail in preventing his children becoming estranged from him. Her life was a bed of roses compared to poor old Bob's.

'Yes, quite Ma'am.'

'Listen Bob, find out all you can about these nut jobs. I'll give them Knights of the New Glory.' You know the form, websites, links to the British National Party, English Defence League. Bring me what you have, by end of play.'

'Absolutely Ma'am, no problem. By the way, saw you on the telly. Very good; you're a natural,' said Coombs, eager to gain some brownie points.

'Thank you, Bob. Oh, and Bob, bring us a cuppa will you? I'm parched.'

'Will do, Ma'am. I'll get Jenny to get you one now.'

'No, Bob. You make it please. I need to have a chat with Jenny, see if she wants a brew too, would you?'

Jenny James was even newer to the team than Nick Mycroft. She was small, with dark hair and a vivacious smile. She had topped out in her exams to become a DS and had shown herself adept as a family liaison officer in a particularly nasty child abduction case. She would walk over hot coals, if Stella Kingsley asked her to.

'Come on in Jenny!'

'Thank you, Ma'am.'

'Jenny, how much do you know about modern day slavery?'

'Well not much, Ma'am, but I wouldn't say having you as a guv'nor was that bad.'

'Careful DS James.'

'Sorry, Ma'am.'

'It is a hidden problem, but there's no doubt at all that it's a growing one.'

Stella looked at Jenny. She was yet to make her mind up about her. She was eager and efficient but a little cocky for Stella's liking. Of course, using one's initiative was to be encouraged in the young but being too Gung Ho, as Stella's father would have put it, can bring problems of its own. However, Stella had few female officers to pick from and with supervision, she felt Jenny was ready for the assignment Stella had in mind.

'What are we talking about here, Ma'am? Sex trafficking?' asked Jenny.

'A big part of it yes, but in our neck of the woods, it's far more prosaic. It's foreign nationals and Brits being paid well below the minimum wage, charged for rat infested, unheated, insanitary, accommodation and expected to work until they drop.'

'So where do I come in Ma'am?'

'Jenny what do feel about covert work?' enquired Kingsley

'Intrigued Ma'am,' said Jenny.

'Well, here's the thing. We believe we have a particular problem at a place called Killpeck Farm,' the DCI explained.

'How do you know, Ma'am?'

'Several former employees have reported verbal bullying and not having been paid their wages.'

Alexei Shalikov was on his way back from Lizzie Rimmer's Farm when his mobile went off. Jason's name came up on the screen as it had several times before; this time Alexei decided to take the call.

'Hello Jason. You, okay?'

'Yes, just about. Listen, have you managed to take care of everything, like you said you would?'

'Of course! If I say I do something, I do it.'

'So, our problem is solved?'

'Yes Jason. I have solved your problem,' said Alexei pointedly 'Now, are you back at the caravan?'

'No, I had a bit of a ruck with Lomax. I'm in the village. Kipped in the bus shelter last night.'

'Have you a place to go?' asked Alexei.

'No. My old man said he'd skin me alive if I ever turned up home again.'

'Not very fatherly thing to say.'

'Well, as I said, I have been in a spot of bother once or twice. Nothing heavy you understand, but you know how it is,' said Jason.

'Yes, Jason. You stay where you are. I shall come and find you, okay?' instructed Alexei.

'Yes, alright thanks. I owe you one,' said Jason.

'Yes, I suppose you do, Jason.'

DS Nick Mycroft was sifting through the responses that had come in after his boss' appeal for information on *Crimewatch*. There were the usual confessions from the mentally ill; one or two supportive emails towards the killing, which he would forward to the Crown Prosecution Service, and a phone message from a Clive Latimer, saying he had something that might interest them, but it was of a very, very, sensitive nature. He left a number to ring.

'Hi Sir. You, okay?' It was Jenny James.

'Morning Jenny. Yes, I'm fine. How are you?'

'Couldn't be better,' said Jenny.

'How's the new flat working out?'

'Good, thanks. It's a bit further for work but handy for choir.

'Choir?' queried Nick.

'Yes, I sing in a church choir.'

'Oh right.'

'In Stamford.'

'Oh.'

'Where my new flat is,' said Jenny speaking very slowly.

'Yes, I see. Very good. Glad it's um, working out well for you.'

'Thank you, Sir. All housewarming presents welcome,' said Jenny with a cheeky grin. She turned and walked over to the photocopier.

A little out of his league, thought Nick, whose heart beat a little faster whenever he was in her presence. His reticence around women who he found attractive had seen him make several unfortunate romantic choices in the past. He had never understood how disorganised his love life had been, given his methodical approach to most other things in his life.

He pulled himself together and rang Clive Latimer's number.

'Is that Clive? It's DS Mycroft, East Midlands Police here. I understand you may have some info for us.'

'Look, it's probably nothing and to be honest... it's a bit awkward.'

'Anything you can tell us could be extremely helpful, Clive, and as they said on the programme, would be treated in the strictest of confidence.'

'Well, I can't tell you over the phone,' said Latimer.

'That's okay. We'll call round your house.'

'No that's no good either... I'll meet you at that Italian coffee place in town.'

'Stefano's?'

'Yes, that's it. I'll be there at 11.30 am and...'

'Okay, we will take it from there,' said Nick reassuringly.

Meanwhile, Stella Kingsley was holed up in her office looking at the note found on Hanif's body and the claim of responsibility for his death from New Glory. It was full of spelling mistakes, with letters roughly hacked from a red top paper and clumsily stuck on old, notepad paper. Was this just New Glory taking credit for something they hadn't done or was it a confession that one could trust?

Back at Stamford, Nigel Osgood had been writing long into the night. Memory was a strange thing. When you became very old, what you did five minutes previously completely escaped you, while the events of sixty years ago came back to you with such extraordinary clarity; he continued typing.

Sir Timothy Galloway was someone I had known all my life. He was a tall, willowy man with bushy eyebrows, who had had one leg blown off at Arnhem, during the Second World War. Sir Tim had a wry sense of humour and a twinkle in his eye, and I'd always thought him a perfect foil to my father's austere and reticent presence. However, what he was now suggesting to me seemed unutterably cruel.

'The thing is my boy, we believe you have been duped by that chum of yours, Julian Markovich.'

'Firstly, Sir Tim,' I said, 'Julian is my boyfriend. We live together and whatever I have, or have not done, be assured, I have not been duped.'

'I am sorry to have to tell you this, dear boy, but Markovich is an experienced operative of the soviet state, and you have been passing classified information to him, which, were it not for your dear papa, could see you imprisoned for the rest of your natural life.' Sir Tim's tone of voice changed completely from avuncular to business like.

'Look I don't care. You know as well as I do that the establishment in this country are a bunch of hypocritical class-bound, amoral snobs and the sooner the whole bunch of them are shown for what they are, the better,' I replied angrily.

'And Soviet Russia is the new Utopia?'

'Give me some credit, Sir Tim. I know it's not perfect... but god knows, it's not a cesspit, in which afternoon tea is served everyday precisely at four, like this country surely is.'

'Nigel, you know that I've always had a soft spot for you. We both know your father can be a sore, old bear and we've both had the sharp end of his tongue.'

Sir Tim put both hands on his walking cane.

'But if you care nothing for your own future, think of the disgrace for him... and then, of course, there's your mother. This news would certainly destroy her.'

Osgood leant back in his baroque, mahogany chair, checked the email address for Chloe Whiting and pressed send.

10
Natural Causes

'Thank you for coming in, Mr Tomms. Now you understand that you are not under caution, and this is just part of our ongoing enquiry. As Detective Sergeant Coombs has explained, we are investigating the recent murder of Hanif Singh, a murder that an organisation of which you are the founder, namely New Glory, is claiming responsibility,' said Stella, ushering Terry Tomms into one of the smaller interview rooms.

'I really have no idea what you are talking about, Inspector, but happy to assist you, of course.'

'Well, I'm obliged to you, Mr Tomms,' said Stella warily. She had met quite a few men like Mr Tomms over the years and starting off softly, softly often bore dividend in any inquiry.

'I have to tell you, Detective Chief Inspector Kingsley, we admire what the police force has to put up with these days,' said Terry Tomms. He was in his late fifties, wearing a zip-up windcheater, over a smart, shirt and stripey tie, dark cords and expensive looking shoes.

'If we can stick to the matter in hand, you claim to have no responsibility for this.'

Stella handed Tomms the sheet of paper, claiming Hanif's murder to be the work of New Glory.

'Give me some credit, Inspector! The spelling here's appalling and I'm a grammar school, educated boy.'

'So, this is not from you or anyone in your organisation?' queried Kingsley.

'Certainly not! We are merely a pressure group, lobbying for the restoration of power to the indigenous or generationally settled, good people of this island. This is some crank, some hanger on. Got no time for them at all. I mean, this makes us look bad, Inspector Kingsley. I shall launch an internal investigation as soon as I get back to the ranch.'

Stella noticed that Tomms' complexion was becoming increasingly florid as he spoke. When people lied, she had found that their physiology usually gave them away. However, in Tomms' case, he might be bigoted, opinionated, and full of a sense of self-importance, but a liar? She wasn't convinced.

'I would prefer it, Mr Tomms, if you would give me names and addresses of all your members before you leave the station.'

'Well, I would love to oblige, but you know as well as me, Detective Inspector, the milksops, who are our political masters, have introduced strict instructions around data protection.'

'Well, in that case, I will be forced to arrest you, and I have to say it will give me a great deal of pleasure. I've come across many versions of people like you, Mr Tomms, inadequate little men looking for a cause,' said Kingsley, deciding to move away from the kid gloves approach.

'Let me tell you mad...' said Tomms, his face now turning lobster pink.

'I'll get our desk sergeant to read you your rights and book you in.'

'Inspector!' said Tomms, who appeared to be getting his emotions under control. 'Let's not get in front of ourselves, shall we?'

Stella watched as Tomms unzipped the case of his laptop.

Alexei had found Jason in the village and taken him to Eddie's, a greasy spoon transport café. They were both tucking into 'Eddie's Belt Busting All Day Breakfast.'

'So, what's happening? Did you manage to... er... you know?' asked Jason in between mouthfuls.

'Yes, but the less you know, the better,' Alexei responded.

'So, does he sleep with the fishes?' said Jason who seemed to have got over the death of his friend and mentor extraordinarily quickly.

'Excuse me?' queried Alexei.

'Have you not seen *The Godfather*?' said Jason stabbing his last sausage as if to emphasise the point.

'May be, but a long time ago... so tell me what your plans now?'

'Well, I haven't got any really, but the world is my lobster, as they say. Especially if you've got rid of the problem.'

'I think it best if I find you safe place to go, till all this dies down.'

'Yes, the heat you mean?'

'You've watched too many of those gangster films, Jason.'

'Yes, mostly with gangsters in the nick,' laughed Jason. 'Are you going to eat the mushrooms, or can I have them?'

It was then that Alexei saw the headline on one of the lorry driver's papers.

NEW GLORY CLAIM RESPONSIBILITY FOR RACE KILLING

'You see that?' asked Alexei.

'Bloody hell, the coppers must have got it, then!'

'What do you mean?'

'Drac and I sent it to the paper. Thought it would be a laugh and a bit of a warning!'

'So, this Hanif Singh, you kill him?'

'No, of course not, but you know what they say, "All publicity is good publicity,"' said Jason wiping the last of the baked bean sauce from his plate.

DI Nick Mycroft's mother died four days after his visit to the hospital, her death hastened by an infection she'd contracted as an inpatient.

'Mr Mycroft, it was very peaceful at the end,' the nurse had said. Nick had raced back to the hospital, only to be told that she had died ten minutes prior to his arrival.

'She was ready to go, Son, honestly she was,' said Nick's father.

Yes, but I wasn't ready, thought Nick, he had been in morgues and Chapels of Rest many times before. They could never quite get rid of that sweet, sickly aroma. It was as instantly recognisable as a fox's scent, or a newly mown lawn. His mother was laid out before him, her curly, dyed yellow locks, a ridiculously colourful add-on, like some gaudy, religious statue.

'So, Dad, are you going to be okay?' Nick asked his father.

'Oh, you know me Nicky boy. If I can survive a quadruple bypass, I can survive this.'

'You know you're welcome to come up and live with me,' said Nick, imagining the hell it would be, cooped up in his tiny house in rural Lincolnshire, with his father uprooted from his natural habitat: two men bound by blood having to keep up the pretence that they cared for one another.

'It might be a bit of a squeeze in that rabbit hutch of a house of yours. Besides, we both know it would never work, you doing what you do.'

'Being a police officer, you mean.'

'Well, you made your choice, Son, a long time ago. I have to say, I sometimes wonders whether you is my son. Now let's get out of here. You can buy us a bit of lunch and we can discuss arrangements, if you like. It'll have to be a full East End send-off; you understand. None of your bleeding willow basket under an 'edgerow somewhere. We'll go halves on the cost, if you like; I've got a bit put away.'

Alexei had taken Jason back to Lizzie Rimmer's Farm, as he had nowhere else. Besides, Alexei had plans for him. The first day or two had been fine, but Lizzie had not taken to Jason at all and by the fourth day she'd had enough.

'I tell you Alexei, he makes my flesh creep. He walks around looking at me all the time with his tongue hanging out.' Liz squirmed with disgust.

'You be nice to him, you understand!' ordered Alexei.

'Look, I don't know what you have in mind but...'

'No, I don't mean like that. All you have to do is smile, make food. He is a greedy pig, so just feed him well. It won't be for long, I promise.'

'It had better not be. He's not right in the head.'

'You tell no one about him being here, you understand?'

'Yeh, yeh, you told me that at the beginning. Who is he then? Lord Lucan?'

Alexei put his hand around Lizzie's throat.

'It is very important that you do this, Lizzie, very important.' His eyes narrowed and Lizzie struggled for breath.

'Okay, okay,' she spluttered.

At Killpeck Farm, Lomax was fuming at having to recruit more pickers, since that little runt, Jason, and the Pollack, Drog or Drac, whatever his name was, had disappeared. He was down two staff and there were loads of fruit still to be picked. He'd had words with Alexei about the night his pickup had gone missing but had kept him on. He was a good worker and he kept the others in line; besides, he'd put a full tank in the pickup and had had the truck cleaned and valeted. Alexei had made some story up about being grief stricken by news of the death of his grandmother back in his motherland. And then he had the nerve to ask for more time off! The thing was, the toe rag had found out one or two things that Lomax would rather have kept under wraps, so it looked like he might be even more short-handed.

The two applicants he was interviewing were both girls. Now normally he wasn't keen on female pickers. Lomax thought them unreliable, always feigning illness: 'Oh Mr Lomax, it's my time of the month.' All that claptrap, but he was desperate. Besides, one of the girls was a neat little brunette. The other was no oil painting, but she carried herself well and she'd done the work before, and even brought references. The brunette called herself Jenny. He might have a crack at her, he thought to himself; she was as ripe for the picking as them strawberries.

'So, Jenny?'

'Jenny Jarvis,' said Jenny.

'Yes, whatever. Have you had any experience?'

'Oh yes, loads. I used to pick fruit on my father's farm, before he kicked me out that is,' Jenny James said, embellishing a little, the cover story DCI Kingsley had come up with for her. Why the DCI couldn't have given her a better alias than Jenny James, Jenny couldn't imagine.

'Oh, so you are persona non grata, at home are you, young lady?' said Lomax, giving her one of his best smiles.

'Something like that,' said Jenny, smiling back.'

'Well, we take all sorts here, as long as you can get the job done and don't mind mucking in with everyone and everything. I have to be honest, the money ain't great, but the more you pick, the more you earn, and your accommodation is for gratis,' said Lomax, overdoing his slender knowledge of Latin somewhat.

'Does that mean, I've got the job, Mr Lomax?' enquired Jenny.

'Yeh go on then, you can start whenever you like. Oh, and Jenny, if any of the lads gives you any cheek, you come straight to me, you hear?'

'Oh, thank you so much. I won't let you down, I promise.'

Lomax hired both girls. Jenny introduced herself to the other girl as they walked down to the bus stop on the main road.

'Hi, I'm Jenny. Looks like we might be working together.'

'Alright love. I'm Wanda. You got any fags? I'm gasping, here.'

'Mr Lomax seemed nice, didn't he?'

'Don't ask me, love. All men are tossers in my eyes.' Wanda shielded the cigarette Jenny had given her with her hand, and then drew in a lungful of tobacco.

'So, what's a nice girl like you doing in a place like this?'

11
The Tender Trap

Nigel Osgood was having a bad night. Whether it was because of his cancer, or the thought of his cancer, he wasn't entirely sure. As the present seemed a little gloomy, he decided to return to writing up his past, as the next instalment for Chloe. Once he'd started, his mood became gloomier still.

Sir Timothy had, as he knew very well, touched on my weak spot. I could never do anything to harm my mother, Martha. She had been a silver, shimmering presence in my life, even though we spent a lot of my childhood apart. Martha was the third daughter of Charles Cattermole Junior, an American oil millionaire. She was tall and striking with ash blonde hair, always tightly controlled in a French pleat except, that is, when she would allow me to come to her bed chamber and brush out her exquisite tresses in front of her jewel encrusted art nouveau mirror. She spoke with a wonderful Texas drawl, referring to me always as 'honey' as opposed to my father who would address me as 'boy' or 'Nigellus,' if he was in a rare, good mood. Martha was everything my father could never be: loving, affirming, comforting and enormous fun. Whenever I smelt her Chanel perfume around the draughty corridors of home, I would feel once again secure and loved. Now it appeared, Sir Timothy was giving me a choice: betray my lover or destroy my mother's happiness.

'Dear boy,' said Sir Tim, the twinkle in his eye dimming, 'I wouldn't ask, but we need to put a stop to all this. I promise that once we have put your friend out of commission, by feeding him a few bits of false information, we will take him into custody and arrange a swop for one of our own operatives.'

For Martha's sake, and hers alone, I agreed. I was told the information to feed to Julian with the term used in those days, 'pillow talk.' At first, things seem to go along as normal; Julian was his usual, high spirited, outrageous self, but gradually he seemed to become more guarded. His mood would change rapidly and he'd sit for hours in our window seat, deep in introspection and gloom.

Eventually, Sir Tim made arrangements whereby Julian would be 'picked up' by the intelligence services, and reluctantly, I agreed. God knows, I still loved Julian, but he was becoming very difficult to live with. Also, in all truth I was terrified of the alternative: me in prison, where no doubt I would be targeted in the way I had been at school, and my darling mother would be in total misery.

The arrangements for the pickup were made. It would take place on Hampstead Heath, where Julian and I would often go walking before Sunday lunch. The operation would be carried out discreetly I was told, and there would be, I was assured, no violence, although knowing Julian as I did, I couldn't see how that could be avoided. He was sure, I felt, to put up a fight. As it turned out, he couldn't. I was just peering into the window of a little antique shop near Hampstead station, when out of nowhere, a car came up the hill at high-speed, pinning Julian to the wall. He died in the ambulance, on the way to hospital.

For a moment, Osgood hesitated, weighing up whether to send the information via email, but then decided he needed to see the two young researchers from Janus Films, to make such a full confession of the soul.

DI Mycroft was on his way to see Clive Latimer, who had not turned up on the first two occasions they'd arranged to meet. Nick was in two minds: part of him wanted to have Clive charged with wasting police time, but there was something in the man's voice that suggested he was offering information that might be of significance in the Hanif Singh case.

DCI Kingsley had taken Nick into her office and suggested he take more time off after his mother's death. She had lost her mother young and had never really recovered. Her subsequent marriage had been a mistake. She knew it was really just a cry for help, not a union of passion, but a way of escaping from her controlling father. Her career had kept her going, so she could empathise with Mycroft when he explained.

'To be honest Ma'am, I'm better off in work, and besides it looks like the funeral is going to be delayed. There's a lot of organising to be done. Apparently, it will require some road closures, with all the people who are coming. My dad wants a bubble machine, the lot, with she and him being West Ham Supporters.'

'I know you come from a big family, Nick.'

'It's only on occasions like this, you realise quite how big, Ma'am.'

'How's your father bearing up?'

'Oh, he'll survive Ma'am.'

'I'm sure your mum was very proud of you Nick, with what you've achieved,' said Kingsley.

'I don't think so, Ma'am. My family, as you know, tend to look on the police as the opposition.'

'Well, if she wasn't, she bloody well should have been. You're going places in the force Nicholas, mark my words.'

'That reminds me. If you'll excuse me, Ma'am? Right now, I've got to be somewhere else.'

'Any luck with that shrinking violet of a witness of yours?' said Kingsley

'That's where I'm off to now.'

Stefano's was an independent coffee shop that Nick had frequented a few times in the past, sometimes with Jemima, his ex-girlfriend. He liked the place, although it reminded him of the way that like many of his 'relationships,' Jemima's and his had fizzled out. The café aped much of the décor of the numerous chains of coffee houses that had sprung up over the country in the last thirty years. A smattering of framed sepia pictures of wistful women and boater hatted men leaning against each other, staring into the middle distance were interspersed with little 'self-help aphorisms like: *Aroma wasn't built in a day* and

Coffee time any time. The place was empty apart from a furtive, middle-aged man, in a tight-fitting t-shirt, wearing shades and reading the menu, or using it to hide behind: Mycroft was not sure which. This, hopefully, was Clive Latimer.

'Clive? Clive Latimer? DS Mycroft. May I join you?'

'Yes, yes, but be quick about it, if you don't mind.'

'Have you ordered?' asked Nick.

'No, can you, do it? I'll have an Americano,' whispered Latimer.

'Right!' said a bemused Nick.

'I'm not asking you to pay. I've got money. It's just... well... it's a bit tricky.'

'Forgive me, Clive. I'm a police officer, so if you are worried that I'll be shocked, don't be. I've seen most things.'

'Well, I've been having matrimonial difficulties and er...'

'Take your time Clive...'

'There's this girl in the office. God alone knows what she sees in me.'

'Takes all sorts, Clive,' said Mycroft.

'Oh, gee thanks!' said Latimer giggling nervously.

'No, I mean cupid's arrow. You never know when it's going to strike.'

'Oh, I'm not in love with her. She's all Kim Kardashian and Instagram.'

'I'm more Coldplay and *The West Wing*, but I tell you what, when someone offers you it on a plate... well anyway we'd popped up that slip road, you know by the tip, and well, she suggested it.'

'What the sex?'

'No, no: that we filmed what we were getting up to.'

Alexei and Jason were sat out in Lizzie's back garden with a six pack of lager each.

'The thing is, I keep seeing his face in the mud. Bloody hell, if I could only undo what happened that night. I mean how unlucky can you be?' pondered Jason. Jason's bravado over Drac's death had now turned to a maudlin preoccupation with it.

'Unlucky for Drac, yes, but you, no,' said Alexei.

'How do you make that out?'

'You. You... stood up for yourself to Lomax of all people. That takes guts.'

'But what am I supposed to do now?'

'You must carry on your work. That's what Drac would've wanted.'

'What do you mean, my work?'

'For New Glory of course, sweeping away the elites and the institutions of this moribund country.'

'How much do you actually know about New Glory?'

'Anyone who is interested in such things knows about New Glory and how they've come to... how you say, 'drain the swamp.'

'But you're a Ruskie or something like that: aren't you all commies?'

'No, I was with my parents when the wall came down, cheering.'

'I thought Trump's wall hadn't been built yet.'

'Not the Mexican, the Berlin Wall.'

'Oh right, bit before my time,' said Wilkes.

'There are people around, Jason, who would like the old ways back: state control, nobody able to do anything without approval. I tell you now the reds are coming out from under the bed. They're all in league with the Muslims. The world is going backwards New Glory is, as far as I can see, a beacon of hope.'

'So, you are with us?'

'I am Jason; I will support you.'

'New Glory is all I have left now.'

'And you have a chance to really do something that would have made Drac proud, Jason. Show the elite you mean, business!' said Alexei, handing Jason another can of lager.

12
Full Disclosure

Nigel Osgood was in the process of preparing Grizelda's fish supper. She was a very particular cat.

'Here we are Grizzy. I hope it meets with your approval.'

The doorbell rang, Chloe and the film crew were running late.

'Thank you so much. Oh, I'm so sorry that I'm late.'

'Grizelda and I built that into our calculation. Come through.'

'Can I introduce the film crew? This is Cosmo on camera, and Gaz is our sound recordist.'

Osgood looked at the stringy young men, who both looked no older than thirteen at the most, to him.

'A bit of an emergency with his chickens, I'm afraid. So, it's me and the film crew,' said Chloe, explaining Callum's absence.

'Oh, I see. Well you'd better come in. If I hadn't a reputation before, I would certainly have one leaving a young lady and her two urchins outside on the doorstep.'

Osgood was dressed in an expensive looking, black turtleneck jumper and black slacks. On his feet were a pair of sage green espadrilles, between which Grizelda curled her sinuous body.

'I have a feeling from what you said in reply to my email that you want this filmed account to be the unexpurgated version,' said Osgood showing the film crew through to his study.

'That would be great. Of course you will have full editorial control over what's broadcast,' said Chloe, who had always found telling fibs surprisingly easy.

'Well! When we are all sitting comfortably, I shall begin.'

'Don't mind us Reverend. Act is if we are not here,' said Gaz, untangling a length of cable. 'Ain't that right,' he added rhetorically.

'Quite so,' said Osgood.

A bit early to be watching porn isn't it, Sir?' said Jenny James.

Sometimes Nick felt she pushed the familiarity a little far, but he found it difficult to pull her back into line. She was like that with everyone, he would tell himself.

Jenny was not the type he usually went for, but there was an attraction on his part. He had a poor record with girls in the past, a few one night stands over the years, and then there had been Jemima, tall, willowy, and very posh. He'd met her at his gym. Coffee after weight training had developed into a drink at the pub and then weekends at her father's country house. He'd found it all rather undignified: separate bedrooms were insisted upon, so he would have instructions to creep to her room in the middle of the night. She, of course, found this incredibly arousing. 'Like having a midnight feast, isn't it?' she would yodel in the middle of their lovemaking. To Nick, it was demeaning and the sex left him feeling a bit used. He really couldn't understand why he had allowed himself to be her 'bit of rough' for three years or so.

Jenny had made them both a coffee, and once she had put Nick's down, she perched herself on the side of his desk, sipping her drink. Nick was watching the video recording Clive Latimer had reluctantly handed over to him. Although a little distracted by the undulating bodies, positioning and repositioning themselves in the back seat of the car, he kept re-running the piece of film, trying to make out the car which had driven up and stopped some distance behind the 'courting couple.'

'Get your head down, you silly cow,' Nick shouted at the screen.

Every now and then Clive's dogging partner would lift her head and grin in a silly, suggestive way.

'I need it enlarged,' Nick continued.

'Is that what she's saying?' giggled Jenny.

'Jenny, if you can't be helpful, haven't you got some place to go? I thought you were going off-piste anyway, on an undercover job.'

'Who told you that?

'Little birdy.'

'Bob?'

'I'm not at liberty to say.'

'Anyway, just come to collect a few bits. I tell you what, when you've finished looking, take it down to logistical support. They'll blow it up for you. The car looks like a BMW to me, but it's difficult to tell with all that steam on the windows.'

'Thank you, DS James. I think I can take it from here,' said Nick.

'Hey, I tell you what, Sir. Once I've finished this assignment, you can take me for a coffee. Not by car, mind, don't want you getting any funny ideas. I'm not that kind of girl.'

'Oh right,' said Nick shyly. 'Anyway, look after yourself out there.'

'You sound like my dad,' said Jenny, taking the key to her locker from her desk and walking out the door. As she did so, she turned and smiled at Nick, who was engrossed in the video once more. Behind the writhing buttocks of Clive and his girlfriend, he could clearly make out three figures dragging a large object from the car: both were wearing hoodies and ski masks.

13
Demonstrations of Loyalty

In Stamford, Nigel Osgood had spent the night, in between bouts of nausea, writing.

The recording session with Chloe had left him completely drained but he was determined to get his thoughts in order. The filming had been a bit of a disaster. Griselda had had one of her funny turns and thrown up all over some of the recording equipment, so they were forced to pause things, while he cleaned up the mess. Then, one of the local parishioners had called round, collecting money to put towards a statue to be erected of Margaret Thatcher, of all people.

Chloe had left an audio tape of their conversation, as he had recounted the events of all those years ago…

In the weeks after Julian's death, my mood swung from utter despair to burning anger. I received a letter from the Foreign Office expressing their sympathy for the domestic difficulties and offering me a generous severance gratuity in view of services rendered to Her Majesty's Government. Hush money in other words. Sir Timothy had rung me two days after the crash. I wanted to slam the phone down on him but couldn't resist listening to the old bastard trying to squirm out of it.

'Oh, my poor boy! I'm most terribly sorry. The other side must have got to him first. I do know how you must be feeling. I had a tremendous school chum of mine killed at Passchendaele.

'You promised he would not be harmed.'

'Nigel, my dear chap, I swear to you this was not HMG's responsibility. By all accounts, he was something of a loose cannon for the Soviets, dipping his wick all over the place, if you get my drift. You really are well rid of him. But of course, we all understand your distress.'

If this was meant to make me feel better, it didn't.

I took my pay out and determined that I would never set foot in my country of birth again.

I kept my pledge for the next six years. I travelled around Europe, sofa surfing, I think they call it. After Paris, Berlin, then some time at a kibbutz in Israel. Then to Italy, to marvel at the great art of the Renaissance. Here, I took on several gardening jobs. It was something I'd always enjoyed as a child with my mother and Frank, our gardener at home. The physical exertion of digging was a new experience for me, but I found it therapeutic, as the image of pure Julian being pinned against that wall continued to haunt me. One of the jobs I got in Italy was in a small Jesuit community in Lombardy, near Cremona; this was a blissful place, apart that is from a grim harridan of a nun, who acted as a kind of housekeeper for the establishment. Her withering remarks about all and sundry earned her the nickname, 'The Sacred Cow.' Partly to escape her, I spent much of my time in the large walled, kitchen garden. The community was made up of very elderly clergy and it was here that I met Father Vivyan, possibly the most remarkable person I've ever known.

Back at the station in Lincoln, DCI Kingsley was not her usual maternal self.

'What is it now, Bob?' she snapped.

'Well, it's probably nothing, Ma'am,' said DS Coombs.

'Good! I could do with a bit of nothing. Have you seen the state of my in- tray?'

'Well Ma'am, it's New Glory. They're planning a series of marches on our patch Ma'am.'

'Oh, that's great news. That's the same New Glory who claimed responsibility for Hanif's death?'

'It won't amount to much, Ma'am; they only get about half a dozen turn up. Besides didn't you have Terry Tomms in and he denied any involvement?'

'Still, this is not what we need now. There's enough tension out there already after Hanif's murder and the Betsy Mulligan case. All these people like New Glory and the English Defence

League etc. are loving it. If you believed them, every sexual crime committed in the country is down to people hailing from the sub-continent.'

'But Ma'am, if those taxi drivers hadn't pimped poor Betsy around to all and sundry, Rex Priday would never have got the opportunity to...'

'Bob, if you don't mind, that evil psycho occupies enough of my mind, thank you. And just to remind you, all but one of those bloody taxi drivers were white Caucasian! Now give me some good news!' said Kingsley, who was getting to the end of her tether.

'Well, Ma'am, apparently after your appeal on *Crimewatch*, they had a hundred calls in support of whoever did it.'

'I want these marches properly policed and filmed,' said Kingsley. 'You never know, we might actually get a match with the goings on in the background of that piece of film from Clive Latimer.'

'Quite a lot of goings on in the foreground too, as I understand it,' said Coombs, smiling sheepishly.

'Thanks, Bob. That'll be all for now, unless you want to help me with the staff rotas for the next three months.'

'I think I'll leave you to it, Ma'am,' said Coombs. 'Paperwork's not really my thing.'

Alexei Shalikov and Jason had finished their six packs of lager and were now moving onto a half bottle of vodka.

'If you ask me, to really shake this country up, you must strike it where it hurts. But most potential targets are so well protected, you would never stand a chance. Even ordinary MPs receive a level of protection, which makes it difficult. The only people left are your priests, bishops, archbishops.'

'What? You think we should pop the Archbishop of Canterbury?' queried Jason, draining his glass.

'No, no. I was using them as an example... but...'

'Go on.'

'Well, who is the man of the cloth the press most like to quote?' said Alexei passing Jason the bottle of vodka.

'The Pope?'

'No! Whenever they want a soundbite on encouraging multiracial Britain, or gay rights or immigration or any other loony left cause, who do they go to?

'Oh, that old geezer, Nigel someone or other.'

'The Red Bishop, exactly. I tell you, it is his sort who are ruining your country.'

Lizzie came across the lawn at the front of the house.

'Having fun boys?' she said sarcastically.

'Yeh, want to join us?' said Jason, emboldened by the vodka.

Lizzie gave him her most withering look.

At Killpeck Farm in the office, Lomax was instructing his two latest recruits.

'Okay, everyone clear? I want the two tunnels completely stripped today and you two girls just follow the lads. They'll show you the ropes. As you know, the more you pick, the more you earn.'

Nat Von Troon, the politics student, whispered to Jenny.

'Makes it sounds like we will all be millionaires before the end of the day.'

'Penny pinching gobshite that he is,' said Sean under his breath.

'What's that you say Paddy?'

'I was just saying we'll have it all done by tonight, Mr Lomax.'

Wanda pulled up her t-shirt to strap a body belt around her now bare midriff.

'Don't gawp at what you can't afford, you dirty Irish git!' She glared at Sean.

'You're alright darling. I'm abstaining from all that now. Given women up for Lent so I have,' explained Sean with a broad grin.

'It's not Lent,' said Nat.

'Is it not, professor? Well, there you are then!' said Sean.

Jenny took her basket from the stack and rolled up her sleeves.

'Oh well; here goes!'

She picked one fruit, held it up to the light and placed it carefully in the plastic bucket.

'You'll be used to this of course,' said Wanda chuckling, as they made their way along the first metal trough of strawberry plants.

The New Glory march day arrived in Grantham. The sun shone and as Terry Tomms and his companions got out and donned their crash helmets and scarves, and unfurled their St George flags, a little rain started to fall. Terry briefed them on the agreed route through the town. They were to hand out literature that he had prepared. Each was to carry a placard. One said *SHARIA LAW –NO THANKS!* Another said *GROOMERS GO HOME* and a third *CRUSADERS FOR OUR COUNTRY.*

Fifty or so of the Anti-Fascist League were gathered in the High Street, dressed in an assortment of old parka's, great coats, and woolly hats. Some of the men wore flappy caps the type of which Bob Coombs remembered Huckleberry Hound wearing in the cartoon of his childhood. Several uniformed officers lined the street. Coombs had parked in a side road, so he could observe proceedings. Terry Tomms had a leather jacket on, and his head was covered in a baseball cap and scarf covering his mouth and nose. His strutting gait, however, gave him away. The five Knights of the New Glory started to march up the High Street in silence, while the anti-fascists blew whistles and shouted 'Shame!' and 'Fascism out!'

As the Knights of New Glory got about halfway down the road, it became obvious that Terry Tomms was in some kind of discomfort, as he was blowing hard and bending over double. A second man also appeared to be unwell. He was grasping his stomach. The group attempted to continue, but it was clear that they all required urgent use of the public lavatories and a disorderly retreat ensued with Terry himself taking the lead in seeking the sanctuary of the amenities. As the bedraggled Knights of the New Glory returned to their minibus, one of the Anti-fascists League started singing 'The Red Flag' to which one of the marchers shouted from the minibus as they drove away:

'We will be back, and no dodgy curry in Leighton Buzzard will stop us next time.'

Bob Coombs looked on from his car. It was the best bit of fun he'd had at work for many a long year. He lit a cigarette and wandered over to the leaders of the Anti-Fascist League.

'Seems they didn't have the stomach for a fight lad... that curry eh? Sweet revenge!' said Coombs.

'I don't know how you can allow them to spout their vicious bile on the streets,' said a young man with an old face in a bright pink duffel coat.

'Our job is to uphold the law and the right to protest,' said Coombs. 'Besides, I don't think they will be going much farther than their bathrooms for the next couple of days.'

'Wouldn't your time be better spent catching which ever white supremacist butchered poor Harood Singh?'

'Hanif, it's Hanif Singh,' said Coombs.

14
Farewells and Reunions

It was the day Nick Mycroft had, for a variety of reasons, been dreading: the glass, horse drawn, hearse stood outside the Mycroft home. Many of the families in the street had collected around their front doors and garden gates. On the face of it, this was an everyday east London suburban street. Most of her neighbours would not have known of Nellie Mycroft's membership of what had been one of the capitol's more notorious crime families. All the headlines now concerned knife crime in the under twenty-fives. The days when gangs like the Krays, the Richardsons, and the Collins ran every racket going north and south of the Old Kent Road had long gone. Most of his mother's family had now gone legit, working in the city, or in call centres, but they all came back for weddings and funerals, rallying to the tattered flag of the old order, the state within a state, that, in reality, only existed for a few fleeting post war years, when fortunes were there to be made, and no one else much worried about how they were made, as long as it was kept out of the shires and the home counties.

'Alright Uncle Jimmy?' said Nick.

'Nicholas,' said Jimmy, acknowledging his nephew. He was dressed in a three-quarter length, frock coat and black bootlace tie; his white hair was brushed into a duck's arse. He was the oldest Teddy boy in town at ninety-two. He still stood ramrod straight, but his eyes were failing him. Hence the shaded glasses and the white cane in his hand.

'Have you seen my dad anywhere?'

'No Son, I haven't seen him yet. Mind you, I don't see a lot of him these days.'

'How are you keeping, Uncle Jimmy? Still got the stick, I see.'

'Different stick,' explained Jimmy. 'Well, you know how it is boy, never expected to get old and then suddenly, flash, bang, wallop, you're fucked.'

'I know you and Mum were very close,' said Nick.

'Thick as thieves, you were about to say, Nicholas, weren't you? Nicked any lately, by the way,' enquired Jimmy.

There was an awkward pause in the conversation. A woman in the crowd started to sob very theatrically. At this, one of the black plumed horses pulling the hearse took momentary fright and reared into the air.

'She thought the world of you, you know,' said Nick.

'That's no good to neither of us now though, boy, is it? You were the apple of her eye, you know, and even after you went off and did what you did. She'd never have a word said against you,' Jimmy said drawing on his cigarette and blowing smoke rings into the dank air.

'I remember we used to pester you to blow smoke rings when we were kids,' said Nick.

'Yes, you'd probably arrest me for it now though, I reckon.'

'Look, Uncle Jimmy.

'I'm kidding you lad. Let an old man have a bit of fun.'

Nick's father waddled out from behind the back of the house. He was wearing a dark brown, crumpled suit and a grey shirt with a button missing, so that a small, hairy triangle of his ample belly was on full display. He greeted the other mourners cheerfully.

'Well, thanks ever so much for coming. I'm sure old Nellie would have really appreciated it.'

One or two of the neighbours had come to their garden gates out of curiosity. But a thin drizzle meant they did not stay outside for long.

'Hello Jimmy. Hello, Son. Well, I suppose we better get this show on the road.' Jake Mycroft turned to the top hatted undertaker.

'Wagons roll! Charlie'

And so, the cortege started to move; all the family filed in behind the hearse for the three-quarter mile walk to the church.

'How's Brodie doing, Uncle Jimmy?' inquired Nick after his cousin and Jimmy's eldest son.

'Just dandy, Nicholas. He got an eight stretch, but I expect you know all about that. Your mates in the Met stitched him up with a GBH charge, and you know as well as I do, Brodie would never hurt a fly.'

'Now Gentlemen, no talking shop today. Nellie never ever liked it as you both know. I hear they're putting on a great spread at The Black Lion for us after the funeral. Mind you what I forked out, so they should!' said Jake.

'We forked out, actually, Dad.' corrected Nick.

'Oh, copper's treat! Can't wait,' said Jimmy caustically.

In the pickers' caravan to the side of Killpeck Farm, the men were assimilating the fact that Alexei had returned.

'Hello, stranger. We thought you'd vanished completely like Drac,' said Nat.

'I had to go home for a few days. My grandfather very, very, sick,' said Alexei.

'Right! So, do you know where Drac's got to?'

'No, but I know he sick and tired of working for Lomax. He tell me.'

'So, how come Lomax agreed to you having time off and didn't tell you to feck off?' queried Sean.

'He knows I'm good worker and who else going to shift his bloody strawberries?'

'Ah, so you haven't met the girls yet,' said Dave Cheung. 'One very pretty.'

'The other one is feisty. Got Sean's measure straight away,' said Nat distractedly searching under the cushioned seats for his book on dialectal materialism.

'Where these girls?' asked Alexei.

'They're over in what Lomax laughably calls the converted stable block, you know, those couple of old barns attached to the house,' Nat explained.

'Don't change the subject now! It's unlike Lomax to give time off for bereavement. I'm not sure he'd give me time off even if I died,' said Sean.

'Look, I'm back! What does it matter? Who's turn is it to cook?'

'Nat's, I think,' said Dave Cheung.

'Yep, it's veggie night peeps!' confirmed Nat with a sardonic grin.

A collective groan went round the caravan.

At The Black Lion, Nellie Mycroft's wake was warming up. A karaoke machine was attracting various of Nick's relatives to sing sixties country and western standards. The men at the bar had taken their suit jackets off and were making full use of the tab, which Nick had arranged. There were several faces which were family to Nick and one or two of them would glance across warily at him. He raised his glass in acknowledgement, while thinking to himself that it wasn't the fact that he was a police officer that unnerved them; it was the fact that they knew he was a straight police officer.

'Just like she would have wanted,' said Nick's father, Jake.

A woman, who Nick only vaguely recognised, began to totter unsteadily towards them.

'Who's that Dad?'

'Oh, my god, it's Kathleen, Nellie's cousin.'

'Better make ourselves scarce.'

'Jake... Jake Mycroft you big fat, ratbag, ruined our Nellie's life, you did, you great lump of shit!' said the woman, who seemed so enraged that she might have a stroke at any moment. Her face was all screwed up and red like the discarded end of a Christmas cracker.

With this, the elderly Kathleen hurled her gin and tonic straight at Nick's father.

'Are you alright, Dad?' Nick enquired.

'Yeh, yeh.'

'Come on, let's go to the gents, get you cleaned up a bit.'

A thin trickle of blood ran from the top of Jake's great bald dome of a head.

Uncle Jimmy (the Stick) was now up at the karaoke machine giving a mauling to Sinatra's 'My Way.' Not bad for a nonagenarian thought Nick, as he dabbed his father's bald pate with toilet paper.

'The thing is, Son, she hates me with a passion, thinks your mum could have done better for herself, vicious old cow.'

'I tell you what, Dad, I'm really glad I don't live down this way anymore.'

'I know what you mean, Son. Families, they can bloody kill you sometimes.'

Jenny and Wanda had both been told they could use the bath and shower in the main house, which Jenny had done. She'd never had back ache like it before and soaked for half an hour before returning to the stable block.

'You not going to go over, Wanda?'

'No, you're alright love. I'm too knackered. Might go and join that Sean for one later,' she giggled. 'Besides, there's something about Lomax gives me the creeps.'

'I thought you'd blown Sean out anyway,' said Jenny.

'I only just met the lad. Don't want him getting any ideas. Treat 'em mean, keep 'em keen; that's my motto,' explained Wanda.

Lomax seems harmless enough, though, doesn't he? said Jenny.

I wouldn't be too sure of that love,' said Wanda, giving her armpits a suspicious sniff.

15
Encounters with the Other Side

'So how did it go?' asked Stella Kingsley.

'Oh, you know, Ma'am: understated and uneventful.' Nick smiled grimly.

'Yes, I think I can imagine.'

'In the end, I managed to get away early. Told them I'd been called in to work.'

'I'm sorry if you missed anything.'

'Oh, believe me, Ma'am. I'm not. It's still going on now. It'll end in violent recrimination and glass throwing as usual.'

'I see. Typical funeral then,' said Kingsley.

'Anyhow, our boys down there will appreciate the overtime. When my Granddad Collins died, my family put six officers in hospital and trashed one of the oldest pubs in Walthamstow.'

'Well, I'd like to say come back to work and have a rest, but things are starting to hot up here a bit as well.'

'How do you mean, Ma'am?' said Nick.

'I had the Chief Constable and the Police Commissioner on the phone wanting to know what progress we are making in the Singh case.'

'Do they know how busy it's been getting round here lately?' said Nick. 'I mean, it has gone mental the last few days.'

'They're not that interested, Nick, but it's never enough. We had that video of Latimer's enhanced, and traced the BMW. It was reported stolen in Leicester, the night before the attack. I wondered whether you would go and interview the owner. Here, I've got the name somewhere, it's a Mr... Chowdry. He owns several curry houses around Leicester, Tory councillor; he can give us a timeline on when the car went missing, from where, etc.'

'How about New Glory, Ma'am?

'I've had their leader in. Odious little chap, called Tomms. Put the frighteners on a bit. He totally denies any involvement but admits it could be a rogue element acting on their own. Anyway, he's given me a list of his membership. Makes quite interesting reading,' said Kingsley.

'What's Tomms like, Ma'am. Do you think he'd be the type to instigate something like this?'

'Pompous. Dislikes women. Full of bluster and blows hot and cold, but I can't see him as a murderer, but who knows what anyone is capable off.'

Lizzie Rimmer slammed Jason's breakfast down onto the table. Jason winced; he had the mother of all hangovers.'

'Thanks.'

'I don't suppose you've had any luck finding alternative accommodation, have you?'

'No, not yet, but I am looking, honest,' lied Jason.

'Well as long as that's all you're looking at,' said Lizzie wrapping her dressing gown more securely around her.

'I'm sure I don't know what you mean,' protested Jason.

'I go now,' said Alexei.

'Have the boys at Killpeck been asking why you're not staying on site?'

'No. You know how it is there. Mostly people mind their own business.

'They still talk about you, though.'

'Oh, what do they say?'

'They say how good it is not to have your snoring keeping them awake!'

'Oh, thanks very much.'

'We need to talk tonight, Jason. Okay?' said Alexei.

'Right, yes, sure thing,' said Jason.

Lizzie went to the door with Alexei and threw her arms around him.

'Are you going to kick him out tonight, Honey?' she pleaded, when she had finished kissing him. She placed her tongue in his ear in an attempt to seal the deal.

'No. He stays but not for long now.' Alexei looked directly into her eyes. 'Everything is good, yes? We do good fuck tonight, Lizzie. He put his hand between her legs.'

'Anymore black pudding?' shouted Jason from the kitchen. 'I need it to mop up my eggs.'

In Stamford, Nigel Osgood was being interviewed by a young journalist from *The Sunday Times* on what Jesus would say about mixing religion and politics.

'But didn't Jesus say "Render unto Caesar?" asked the reporter.

'He was talking of money, not one's humanity, or conscience, if you will,' said Osgood, grasping the pectoral cross that hung around his neck.

'So, you think it is acceptable to call all Conservatives irreligious, do you?' queried the reporter, who couldn't have been more than twenty-four and was wearing a trench coat that was far too big for her, heavy rimmed glasses, and a hat the kind his father used to wear on fly fishing expeditions.

'If the old school cap fits,' replied Osgood.

'Aren't you just kicking against your upbringing? Your father was an ex-cabinet minister, wasn't he?' asked the journalist earnestly.

'A rather minor one, as it happens, but don't you see how that makes what I say more relevant? I was an insider; I know what the establishment is like and what lengths it will go to, to protect itself.'

'But you then went on to become a bishop in the established church,' trilled the young woman, who was beginning to annoy Osgood.

'Which again allowed me to at least try and change things from the inside.'

'So is your first loyalty to socialism or Christianity?'

'My first loyalty is to Jesus, the Socialist,' said Osgood. 'Now, if that's all, I really am rather tired.'

'Will you not have to get clearance from Lambeth Palace for what you've said in this interview?'

'My dear young lady, I am a retired Bishop, i.e., off the staff! No one is going to come along and snap my dog collar or poke my crozier through my mitre.'

At that moment, the doorbell rang. It was Chloe and Callum.

'Oh, I'm sorry! We just called in on the hop... wanted to ask you a couple more questions for the programme,' Chloe explained. 'But if we are interrupting something.'

'Not at all. Camilla is just leaving,' said Osgood.

'It's Perdita, actually,' said the girl as she flounced past them on the doorstep. The cameraman gave Osgood an apologetic smile as he followed in her wake.'

16
Exposing the Truth

'Mr Chowdry?' said DI Mycroft.

'Why, yes, do come in. Please excuse the mess. We are having the house extended. We found that we were all a little cheek by jowl.'

Nick had been ushered into the palatial hall of the Chowdry residence. There was a sweeping central staircase and what appeared to be at least four reception rooms. The extension Chowdry mentioned seemed to involve replacing the conservatory with an enormous, galleried dining room.

'Being in my business, you would think I would have had enough of food at the weekend. But my darling wife loves to entertain. Ah! there you are Indira. I was just saying...'

Mrs Chowdry was exquisitely dressed and very, very beautiful. She glided slowly towards Nick.

'Oh, an Inspector, indeed! How kind of you to concern yourself with this car business. You probably have so many more important cases to investigate,' said Mrs Chowdry.

'Not at all. In fact, I'm rather hoping you can help us. You see, we believe that not only was your car stolen, but it was used in another crime.'

'What? A smash and grab, you mean?' said Chowdry.

'No, Mr Chowdry... a murder,' said Mycroft.

At Lincoln's main police station, the reception area was busy as usual for a Saturday morning: people coming to complain about neighbours, sheepish looking late-night revellers, who after a night in the cells were collecting their personal belongings, visiting briefs, waiting to see their clients, and a harassed and exhausted looking duty doctor, off to the hospital to do the day job.

'I believe you have something of mine, or at least concerning me.'

'And what would that be? said Dick Hedges, the duty desk sergeant.'

'I think I'd like to talk to someone a bit more senior please,' said the young woman. She was in her early twenties wearing a floaty, blue mini dress and substantial wedge heels.

'I'm sixty-two next birthday, Madam, so pretty senior, now. If I could just take a few details?' said Hedges.

'Well, it's concerning a friend, well more of an acquaintance of mine, Clive Latimer.'

'It's okay Dick, I'll take it from here,' said Stella Kingsley, who was just coming in from grabbing a sandwich. 'Do step this way, Miss?'

'Sadie, Sadie Rickard,' said the girl before bursting into tears.

'Come with me Sadie. Let us find somewhere to chat.'

Stella led Sadie down to a room usually assigned to interview those reporting sexual violence. It had a couple of easy chairs, a children's corner and several tranquil seascapes on the walls. There was a small kitchenette with tea and coffee making facilities.

'So how can we help, Sadie?'

'I've just come to reclaim what belongs to me... or... um... us. Well, we are consenting adults you know.'

'We?'

'Me and Clive... Clive Latimer.'

'Your boyfriend?'

'Yeh, yes, if you like, poor lamb. He was having a rotten time. His wife's an embittered old cow, but you know it's complicated, life I mean,' said Sadie.

'Tell me about it?' agreed Stella.

'I have been out with boys my own age, but all they want is to talk about their cars and then a knee trembler round the back of the pub at the end of the evening.'

'Doesn't sound very comfy to me.'

'But Clive it was different, I'd do anything for him. That's how we came to... you know.'

'Make that little film... and I'm so glad you did; it's been extremely helpful to us, you know,' said Kingsley.

'Well, I'd like it back now please,' said Sadie defiantly.

Nigel Osgood was pleased to see the back of the girl *from The Sunday Times* and her photographer, although he was certainly easier on the eye and the ear for that matter than the girl. She really was a fright with what his mother used to call 'pick up stick's' hair and a whiny, wheedling voice. Although, it had perhaps been a little injudicious to mention that he believed the British government had involved itself in state sponsored murder long before Northern Ireland and the killings on Gibraltar. His parting shot as she tottered down the road was, 'I tell you my dear, HM's government make the CIA's activities in South America look like a Sunday school outing.'

Osgood made coffee for Chloe and Callum, after which Callum dropped his bombshell.

'Actually Bishop, I want to ask your advice. I have been considering studying for the ministry myself.'

At this, Chloe's mouth fell open. She had known Callum and his partner Oliver had become regular members of the church in the village, where they had moved to a year or so ago, but Callum as a vicar, the idea seemed faintly ridiculous to her. She also felt betrayed by Callum not having mentioned this to her. They were, after all, supposed to be best mates.

'Well, all I can say is god help you,' said Osgood, giving Grizelda a contemplative stroke.

That seemed to be all the advice Callum was going to get.

The conversation went on to Osgood's love of art and his authorship of books on the subject. He waxed lyrical about Stanley Spencer's 'The Resurrection Cookham.'

'Yes, you see at the end of all things, everyone who has ever lived returns and Spencer imagined this might take place in the little village in which he lived,' said Osgood, turning to the page in the reference book he had compiled.

'Must have got a bit crowded,' said Chloe flippantly.

There was a long, awkward pause before Osgood pulled out from under a rosewood sideboard (in the French style) what he called his Pandora's Box, full of cuttings, orders of service, photographs and of course correspondence. He knew what he was looking for and would recognise the writing once he saw it. It was written on air mail paper rendered even more translucent with age.

'If you are serious about ministry Callum, I will do what I can do to help but if you are not, you will incur a bishop's curse,' said Osgood staring sternly at Callum. 'I can only say that I was considering what I should do and whether I had a vocation, when I received this letter from the most spiritually enlightened person I ever knew.'

4th April 1978

My Dear Nigel,

I was so pleased and excited to get your letter this morning and decided to respond immediately as my memory is not what it should be these days. What news! What news! That you are considering ordination into the priesthood. No matter that it is not that of the Holy Mother Church, the great thing is that you've had the calling, the same calling that Paul had on the Damascus Road. For me to have lived all this time after we met (I was practically on my last legs then), to hear that you, my dear friend, have truly come to Christ, means I will go to my maker with a real skip in my step.

God bless you, Nigel.

In Christ and with love.

Fr Vivyan

Osgood escorted Chloe and Callum to the front door telling them he had had enough now and they would have to excuse him. He then tottered back into the hall and almost tripped over Grizelda. He collapsed into his porter's chair, his mind full of memories, both good and bad.

Dear Father Vivyan, may he rest in peace, and now in a few months' time it would be him, thought Nigel. He hoped they could manage the pain. Lord, he felt he'd probably had enough pain in his life.

17
A Murder is Arranged

'So' said Alexei. 'We learn from the Islamic State.'

'How do you mean?' said Jason.

'The bloodier the event, the more terror we strike into their hearts.'

'So, axes, knives, hammers and you, Jason Wilkes, New Glory's own, lone Wolf.'

'Hooooowl,' screeched Jason 'Didn't they kill a priest in France like that a while back?'

'Yes, but nobody had heard of him. Everyone in Britain has heard of The Red Bishop.'

'Don't you think we need get approval from you know that Terry Tomms bloke, the one what Drac used to call the Generalissimo.'

'No, no. We do not want to incriminate them before the event, in case the operation is compromised, you know. British Intelligence has a sniff of this and they will disrupt us. But once you have killed Osgood, you can wrap yourself in St George's flag and shout out "England and New Glory." That'll get them noticed, put them in the premier league of terror: you see if I'm not right.'

'Yes, okay, but you know the thing is, I have been a bad lad in the past, but killing someone?'

'Don't forget Jason, you and I know that you already have killed someone, your best friend in fact. How much simpler to kill someone whose views you despise?'

Stella Kingsley had asked Nick to be Jenny James' point of contact during her covert work at Killpeck Farm.'

Mycroft and Jenny had arranged to meet at a multiplex cinema to discuss any progress Jenny may have made in the first few days she had been there. The cinema screen was filled with a woman's mouth as she devoured some tasteless, fast food or other. Nick had brought Jenny a tube of embrocation for her back.

'That's exceedingly kind of you, Sir, but not very romantic on our first proper date.' She gave him a cheeky smile.

'Hey! Have a bit of a respect but I think we can drop the "Sir" when we are in a public place. Makes it sound like I'm your teacher and as if we are up to something. Now are you going to update me on this Killpeck Farm operation?'

'Only if you buy me some popcorn.' She smiled at him mischievously. Like most women, she had a shrewd idea when men were attracted to her. She'd swapped her grubby t-shirt, the one she wore for picking at the farm and now was wearing a short black dress, with her hair swept back in a ponytail.

Nick had that familiar feeling of sweaty, awkwardness, when confronted by a woman he fancied. 'Get on with its DS James!' He managed to sound almost professional.

'Sorry, Sir. Well, I haven't really got much to report. There's no doubt the pay isn't great and the accommodation's basic, but I've got nothing to compare it with. Is it worse than packing shelves in a supermarket?'

'What is your shift like?'

'Well, you either work splits, four hours morning and evening or ten-hour straights.'

'Have you had a chance to talk with any of the other workers?'

'Well, I'm billeted with this girl called Wanda, who's been round the block I fancy, although she's still young. She has been a picker before, so probably just takes it as it comes.'

'What about the boss?'

'Lomax, well he's a chauvinistic sod. I can tell you that. But he doesn't have much to do with us, thank god.'

'And the male pickers?'

'Well, those I've met so far seem okay, Sir.'

'That's helpful DS James,' said Mycroft sarcastically.

'I haven't had a chance for much of a chat with them yet. There's one rather good looking one... I think he is probably Russian.'

'Oh right,' said Nick, trying to hide his schoolboy jealousy.

'There is one thing, Sir.'

'Go on.'

'Well, there aren't many strawberries being grown, as far as I can see.'

'How come?'

'There are about thirty poly tunnels on the site, but only six have any strawberry plants in them.'

'A bit strange. Anyway look after yourself. I'll pass this on to the DCI. See what you can get out of this Lomax character. Any probs, you know the procedure. Your safety comes first. At present, this is a low-level enquiry. We may need to call you back in anyway as there's a lot going on.'

'Okay boss. Now how about that popcorn?'

'Now Ma'am, I don't want to be labelled racist, but does that face look white to you?' said Coombs as they both poured over pictures of the other occupants of the BMW.

Stella could have given Sadie her film back. She wanted to keep both her and Clive Latimer sweet but also keep a little leverage on them. She hadn't mentioned that she'd had a copy made and some magnified stills enlarged from the original anyway.

'How can you tell, Bob?' queried Stella Kingsley.

'Well, look at the skin tone of the bum in the foreground. Now compare it to this still, where we can see a little of the face of one of the figures lifting the body out of the car.'

'I suppose you've got a point, Bob.'

'Thank you, Ma'am. The other thing, Ma'am, one of them's wearing a t-shirt with a face on it.'

'Well, it could be anyone from Bob Marley to Che Guevara.'

'No, there is something familiar about it.'

'Nick, I'd like you to go back to Mr Chowdry. See if there's anything we are missing.'

'Will do, Ma'am?

'Bob, I've got a job for you. I want you to cross reference all the members of New Glory. See who's got form etc. You will need to liaise with antiterrorism on this. I don't want us treading on any toes.'

'I have a meeting with the Chief Constable tomorrow and I would like it if I were to be the bearer of good news.'

18
Dangerous Liaisons

Lizzie Rimmer had never felt like this about anyone before. Her husband had been a good man, hardworking, generous with a good sense of humour, but she'd never been in love with him. Alexei, on the other hand occupied her thoughts nearly every single minute of the day. Apart from his dark, brooding good looks, lithe and muscular physique, there was something more profound that attracted her. It was a sense that Alexei was somehow laughing at a world that he saw as ridiculous, that chimed with her. She had lost both her parents in her early twenties and while still grieving for them, miscarried a child in late pregnancy. After this, intimacy with her husband had been at best business like and often had left her dreadfully frustrated. He grieved for the baby in his own way by working every hour God gave him and it was probably this, that in part brought on the undiagnosed heart condition, which was eventually to kill him. Lizzie had been told after the miscarriage that she could no longer have children and so the fact that Alexei appeared to treat life as one sick joke resonated with her. Sex with him was a way she could blot it all out and just allow her body to be pleasured and come alive in a way that the rest of her never would and for this, if nothing else, she was totally in thrall to the man.

Jason came in complaining.

'I tell you what, your place don't half stink.'

'It's a farm, what do you expect?'

'No, I mean it's really beginning to honk.'

'Look, I've had a gut full of you. You eat like a pig, you ogle me like a thirteen-year-old school boy would, and worst of all, you don't lift a finger to help. My farm doesn't run itself you know.'

'Well, I'm sorry love, but I don't know the front end of a cow from its arse, so I'd be no good to you. Now horses, that's a different matter. Besides, I've got stuff to attend to.'

'What kind of stuff for Christ's sake,' snapped Lizzie.

'You just wait and see darling. Now what time's dinner?'

The young man at Bishop Osgood's door was very presentable, so Nigel presumed he could not have come from the press.

'Good morning, Your Grace. May I beg a few moments of your time?'

'You've come from Lambeth Palace to tell me to put a sock in it, haven't you?' said Osgood.

'No, Your Grace. I'm not here on church business.'

'Oh right. You can drop the Your Grace business. Nigel will suffice. 'Now what is it that you want?'

'Well, it's a security matter, Sir, a bit delicate, so I wonder if I may come in for a moment or two?'

'I'm sorry but it really isn't very convenient.'

'It's concerning the late Julian Markovich.'

'Well, that makes it even more inconvenient,' said Osgood. 'Now if you'll forgive me.'

Osgood attempted to close his front door, but the young man was too quick for him and wedged his expensively shod foot in the jamb to prevent the door from closing.

Stella Kingsley knocked on the Chief Constable's door.

'Come on in Stella; take a seat! I thought we better have a bit of a tête-à-tête about this Singh business, see where we are up to.'

'Well Sir, I'm pleased to say I think we are making some progress.'

'Oh goodo; so can we expect some arrests. Get these neo-Nazis locked up.'

'Well, we are not quite at that stage, Sir.'

The Chief Constable was a man of ample girth these days. He did not – like many of his rank – have the lean and hungry look of a hedge fund manager but rather more that of a country

GP. He went across to the wall of his office and straightened the photograph of him holding a large, freshly caught carp across his midriff. Stella couldn't help but notice a strange similarity between angler and fish.

'What stage are you at exactly, Stella?' said the Chief Constable, changing the tone of the conversation somewhat.

'Well Sir, we have two different lines of enquiry. One looking at what exactly the capabilities are of New Glory to carry out such an attack,' explained Kingsley.

'And the other?'

'Early days, Sir, but I have one of my best officers on it.'

'Oh, who would that be, Stella?'

'DI Nicholas Mycroft.'

'Ah, yes, I remember now. Isn't he the chap with interesting connections in the East End?'

'Yes Sir.'

'The Collins outfit wasn't it? Yes, that's right. I remember from my days in the Met. In fact, I think I was the arresting officer when we nabbed the uncle, Jimmy Collins. I think it was for a smash and grab job in Hatton Garden. Small world, wouldn't you say?'

'Yes Sir,' said Stella Kingsley. 'Will that be all Sir?'

'Yes, Stella, for now. We need you to come up with the goods. People who matter will have their eye on this one. So, I wish you tight lines.'

'I beg your pardon, Sir?'

It's an expression we in the fishing community use, Stella.'

'Oh, you learn something new every day in this job, Sir,' said Kingsley, mentally working out when it was precisely that she would get her pension.

'Inspector, how delightful to see you again. What can I do for you this time?' Mr Chowdry showed Nick Mycroft into his study. 'Please call me Colin.'

'I'm not sure that's appropriate.'

'A little joke! All my friends loved cricket, so they gave me the nickname Colin after the best batsmen in Kent, and for my money England ever produced. So, you are here on a more official footing, Inspector. Have you by any chance apprehended the miscreants who stole my car?'

'No Sir. I'm afraid we've yet to locate the car.'

'But I thought,' said Chowdry.

'That we had the car?'

'No Sir. We just know it was used in a crime, Sir. That's all.'

'How very distressing. Oh, you haven't met my daughter, Inspector,' said Chowdry, motioning for a waif like young woman to step forward.

'Shani, this is the police officer who is helping locate our car.'

'How do you do,' said Nick.

'Pleased to meet you,' said Shani in a barely audible whisper.

Nick looked at the girl, she was very beautiful like her mother, but there was something about her expression, something familiar, not visually perhaps. What exactly it was, Nick couldn't put his finger on.

'The thing is, Sir; we were wondering whether the criminals involved might by any chance be known to you,' said Nick. 'I have a photograph, I wonder if you'd take a look at for me. It's a little indistinct and you may find it offensive, as there is sexual activity on show, that has not, as far as we know, any relevance to the crime.'

'Oh, don't worry, Inspector. I am very broadminded.'

At this, Shani ran up the grand staircase without a backward glance.

'Daughters! I ask you! Have you any children yourself, Inspector?'

'No Sir.'

'Well, let's take a look at this photo.'

Chowdry took the glasses, which had been resting on the top of his head and placed them on his nose.'

'It's the men at the car in the background, Sir.'

Chowdry took a long look and then paused before saying, 'Detective Inspector Mycroft, I hope that you are not insinuating that I should know them, purely on the basis of my sharing the same skin tone as these criminals. I thought those sad days when the police were, as the papers liked to put it, "institutionally" racist were well behind us!'

'I'm sorry, Sir. It's just a routine question I am obliged to ask. A young man has been murdered and we need to get to the truth.

'Well, this particular truth, Detective Inspector Mycroft, is I have no idea who these people are.'

Well, that could have gone better, thought Nick to himself as he drove back to Lincolnshire.

'I'm sorry about that bishop, but we are concerned about your personal safety. We believe certain parties intend to do you harm and we wish to offer you some protection.'

Osgood looked at his visitor, who could be any age between twenty-five and forty, and was quite good looking in a rather obvious way. He was smartly dressed in a force's haircut and one of those stubbly excuses for beards that seem to be *de rigueur* for some men these days.

'May I ask exactly where you are from?'

'I was born on St Lucia and come from a long line of slaves, Your Grace.'

'You know that's not what I meant. Which department.'

'Does that really matter, Sir? We are on the same side.'

Nigel Osgood clutched the crucifix that hung around his neck.

'Excuse me but you would be far too young to know that many years ago, the safety of someone very dear to me was assured by Her Majesty's security forces, what you so glibly call "our side." They either failed miserably or, as I rather suspect, were complicit in his death.

'I am familiar with some of the circumstances of the case, Sir,' said the young man, who Nigel presumed was an entry grade MI5 operative or some such.

'Then possibly you will understand why I do not have a great deal of faith in anything you people have to say. Now if you will excuse me.'

'Were you aware, Bishop, that Julian had a younger brother?'

I knew very little about Julian's personal circumstances, only that I...'

'Loved him,' said the young man. 'Forgive me, Sir. Perhaps if I explain more of what we know. Dimitri Markovich is fifteen years Julian's junior. He is now what the press like to refer to as a Russian oligarch and has grown unimaginably wealthy with the fall of the Soviet Union and the insatiable requirement in western Europe, in particular Germany, for oil and gas.

'And how is this relevant to me here and now?'

'It is relevant, Sir, because rightly or wrongly, he holds you personally responsible for his older brother's death.'

'Oh and no one has seen fit to disavow him of such an idea.'

'Sergei has links to the top echelons in the Kremlin.'

'Friends in high places ay, a bit like us bishops are supposed to have.'

'It seems he has had the green light to, as he sees it, avenge his brother's death.'

'How do you know all this?'

'Markovich's financial affairs are of interest to us. He is one of Putin's associates whose assets in the UK we have been trying to freeze as part of sanctions agreed by the West.'

'All of course very interesting on a geopolitical level, but as I say, thank you for your concern, but I put my faith in higher powers these days. Now I must insist that you leave me in peace.'

'Please think about it Bishop; you may be in real danger.'

'To be frank with you, I would think some of your political masters would not be broken hearted if something did happen to me, and they were rid of "one troublesome priest."'

'Here's by mobile, Sir,' said the man. 'Please ring me night or day if you change your mind.' He handed Osgood a card with a number on it.

'I won't change my mind. Oh, and I'm sorry I didn't catch your name.'

'That's probably because I didn't give it to you, Sir. My name is Riddell. Sorry about my intrusion. It sure is a mad old world these days. I'll close the door on my way out, shall I Bishop?'

'I accept your apology Mr Riddell. Manners maketh the man, or so they say.'

19
Restricted Vision

The fog hung over the flatlands of Lincolnshire obscuring everything from view apart from the church spires in the scattered villages. It was an unusually, cool summer's day, and traffic was moving slowly as Nick Mycroft made his way home. He could see trouble ahead. Chowdry was just the kind of person to put an official complaint in about him, for racial harassment. This seemed ironic as the enquiry had started out based on investigating a possible race hate crime. As he drove into the drive of his little cottage in Shappington, his mobile rang. It was his father.

'Alright, Dad?'

'Yes, Son. I'm going along okay. We are just sorting out your mother's clothes and things and I was wondering whether there was. any of, what do they call 'em now, her personal effects... and we thought you might like to have first dibs, before it all goes down the charity shop.'

'The thing is, Dad, I'm really busy at work at the minute, and also, I still think it's all a bit soon.'

'I understand lad; it's just that she would want us to move on with our lives.'

'Yes, you may have a point. Look can we just leave it for now. I'll pop down home as soon as I can.'

'Right, you are, Son.'

'Are you really okay, Dad?' asked Nick.

'Oh, you know me, Son, I'm a coper,' said his father.

Nick opened his emails, fed Bodkin Adams, his ginger tom, and put a ready meal in the microwave. He was shivering for some reason, so decided to light his wood fire; soon the room became smoky. He couldn't find a reason why the fire had this blowback feature. He'd probably die from carbon monoxide poisoning and Shappington being so remote, they wouldn't find his body for weeks. He settled down to read but found it difficult to switch off from work. He couldn't help thinking that the Singh case was not all it seemed. Eventually sleep overcame him and he found himself in a very pleasant place with Jenny James, while his ginger tom took the opportunity to finish off the microwave meal.

Killpeck Farm was under the same shroud of unseasonable fog as Shappington. Jenny and Wanda had finished their shift and had just had a brew. There was a tap on the door. It was Sean from the men's caravan.

'Ladies, how are we?'

'Fine, thank you,' said Jenny.

'What are you after?'

'The lads and I were just wondering whether we might tempt you two lovely ladies to accompany us to the local hostelry for a wee glass or two?'

'Well, ye...'

'You're alright. I've got things to do,' said Wanda 'You go, if you like, Jenny, but watch him; horny, little bugger, if you ask me.'

'Oh, come on Wanda. If you say you'll come, Jenny will. Let's go and drink to Lomax getting his head caught up his own arse,' said Sean.

Wanda started giggling.

'Well alright; we're not walking, are we?'

'No, no; you certainly are not. I shall be honoured to give you a piggyback all the way.'

Sean turned his back and did a pig impression. 'Oink, oink, oink, oink.'

'Silly Sod,' chuckled Wanda.

'Okay, give us an hour and we will come over to the van and give you a knock,' said Jenny.

'Until then, ladies,' said Sean, turning to give one of his best smiles.

'So where are you off to in my bloody Land Rover?' Lizzie Rimmer was not happy

'To meet boys; lads' night out,' explained Alexei.

'Can I come?' asked Jason. I'm getting bloody cabin fever. It's worse than being in the nick.'

'I don't think so, Jason. The boys ask too many questions. Besides, you must get rest. Prepare for your big day.'

'Oh, what big day would that be?' asked Lizzie. 'The day he gets a personality.'

'You nasty woman, Lizzie. I see to you when I get back.'

'Promises, promises. Anyway, who's going to do the milking tonight?'

'You be fine. You managed before I came along.'

'Oh, come on Alexei? You know I bloody hate it.'

'One night, Lizzie, that's all. Get Jason to help you.'

'No, it's alright. I expect I'll manage. Just tell your idiot friend to stay out of my way and he can make his own bloody meal tonight.'

'There you go, Jason. The queen has spoken,' said Alexei in mock deference. 'Now come out in the yard. I need to have a word.'

Jason followed him out.

'Phew; it really does stink out here you know.'

'Okay, never mind about all that. You listen... all is good... I have the Bishop's address. Tomorrow we will go and do, how you say, reccy. See what he gets up to. Then next week, we do it. You will go down in history: defender of Great British way of life and commie bastard priest gets what's coming to him.'

'Yes right,' said Jason. 'Here, I reckon you better have a drink for me down that boozer.'

In the farmhouse at Killpeck, to Lomax it was just like watching one of those adult channels: harmless fun. After all, they were all going down the pub without him, apparently. Why they never thought to invite him, god only knew. The thought had occurred to him when he was putting a wall light into the dividing wall between his study and the bathroom. It was an easy enough job to put one of them flash little cameras into what had once been a smoke detector. What that little Jenny didn't know wouldn't harm her. Lomax watched as Jenny sponged the grime of the day's pickings from her body. This taking on girl pickers might not be such a bad idea after all, he thought to himself.

20
Work and Play

The night down The Shiring was warming up nicely. Sean and Wanda were duetting on the karaoke machine to, 'Love lifts us up where we belong.'

Nat, who had been playing darts very badly against one of the locals, came over to the table where Jenny was sat.

'You having a good time?' said Nat.

'Yes thanks, Nat. Now, you're the brainy one, they tell me,' said Jenny

'Oh, I wouldn't say that.'

'So, what makes you come to work in a place like this, where the money is dreadful and the accommodation appalling?'

'Oh, it's no worse or better than other fruit picking I've done. If your parents bring you to live in a country where the bottom line is everything, that's market forces for you,' said Nat.

'You reckon,' said Jenny.

'Yes. I gave up trying to save the world a long time ago.'

'Do you miss Holland?' said Jenny.

'I was very young when I left.'

'So what... so what do you get up to other than fruit picking, if you don't mind me asking?' said Jenny, who by that stage of the evening was a little tipsy. 'What floats your boat?' she giggled.

'Books, I suppose,' mused Nat.

'Oh yes. Nat here likes it between the sheets, don't you my lad.' It was Sean now hand in hand with Wanda.

Alexei arrived back from the bar with another round of drinks. 'Everyone having good time, yes?'

'Yes, thank you,' said Jenny, realising she was blushing slightly.

'Good, good,' said Alexei. '*Na zdorovie.*'

'Same to you, you Russian bastard,' said Sean, who was now fighting drunk and eager to impress his new girlfriend.

'Hey, come on, Sean. Cool it,' said Nat.

'Oh, the professor wants a chance to chat up little Jenny wren there does he? You gobshite.'

Perhaps it's time we all got back to Killpeck. Early start and all that,' said Nat.

Alexei looked at Sean and thought of all the ways in other circumstances he might have killed him. He'd met his type before: all mouth and emboldened with drink. Drunk or drugged men were always the easiest to dispose of but in the end, they all died the same way, crying for their mothers.

'Oh yes; come on, Sean. It has been a good night, yes? You have beautiful woman,' said Alexei. 'I have nothing. I not even drink tonight so I can be taxi for you.'

'Oh well, we wouldn't want to spoil the party would we now,' Sean said loudly.

'Come on Dutchie, come on China man! Alexei here is going to whisk us back to darling old Killpeck Farm.' He continued, while being held up by Wanda, as he weaved his way to the door, which Alexei and Nat were holding open.

Alexei gave a mock bow as Sean staggered past them, while Nat shook his head.

'You never been drunk, Nat? enquired Alexei.

'Never seen the point,' said Nat.

'Does everything have to have a point?'

'It does for me,' said Nat.

The day slowly awoke, and Lincoln came to life once again. Clusters of people waited around the banks and bigger shops. A postman jogged on his rounds; he was in training for a charity marathon. Cleaners and office workers trudged their way up the vertiginous streets that led towards the cathedral. The school run was in its death throws; anxiety ridden mums and dads were attempting to get unhurriable children to educational establishments of various kinds, on time. Nick Mycroft came out of the baker's as he did most days, with a bacon butty in one hand and a large expresso in the other. His first meeting of the day was with DCI Kingsley and he was not particularly looking forward to it.

On the other hand, DS Bob Coombs had a bit of a spring in his step. It looked like he might be proved right: this was not a hate crime after all, but he had prepared a list of any members of New Glory who had form anyway, just in case.

'Morning Nick. Hope you've brought your hard hat.' Stella Kingsley had her headmistress face on. 'I do like my officers to show initiative but there are limits and ways of going about things. This guy Chowdry is not someone I would choose to tangle with. I received this email from his solicitors this morning, threatening legal action for "discriminatory practice from the police force that appears still to be endemic within the East Midland Force."'

'Ma'am, I don't know why I took those stills with me, but something is ringing a bell for me.'

'Well, that's good, because quite frankly DI Mycroft, I feel like wringing your neck.

'I could go and personally apologise, Ma'am.'

'No, I think possibly the best thing you could do is take some gardening leave.'

'Sorry boss...' it was Kingsley's admin assistant. 'There's someone called Chowdry downstairs in a bit of a state... insists on seeing DI Mycroft.'

Lizzie Rimmer was in the kitchen when Alexei got up, after the night at The Shirings.

'You okay?' Alexei inquired.

She did not answer him, just pulled the blanket she'd brought down from the bedroom tightly around her. Her eyes were red and blotchy. It was obvious she had been crying.

'Cat ate your tongue?'

'It's "Cat got your tongue,"' said Lizzie sternly.

'No breakfast this morning?'

'No!'

'It doesn't matter. Jason and I have trip to make. We get food on the way.'

Lizzie stared out vacantly into the farmyard.

'Lizzie, I say we get food on the way.'

She didn't reply just wrapped the blanket even more tightly around her.

'What's up with her?' said Jason.

'Time of the month, maybe?' Alexei replied.

Jenny and Wanda were an hour into their shift of strawberry picking. Wanda was going into graphic detail of her first night of passion with Sean. Jenny who was already somewhat hungover and queasy from the evening down the pub was feeling nauseous.

'Well, it sounds like you had a really good time.'

'I tell you, he's good,' confirmed Wanda.

'Sounds like it,' said Jenny, still feeling she might vomit at any moment.

'Morning troops! How are we?' It was Lomax striding up the strawberry rows. 'Now, I know this is payday, but there's a slight problem, a fly in the ointment, if you will.' The pickers all got up from where they had been crouching or kneeling to harvest the fruit. The ground was stained red with strawberry juice.

'One of my customers, and a big one at that, has failed to come up with the money what they owes me and as you will know, margins in this business are tight. So, I'm sure it'll be only a matter of a few days and then it'll be sorted. Anyway, I suppose we are all in it together. So, I'll let you get back to work. Time is money as they say.'

'Yes, just not our money,' said Nat.

'Look my friend; if you don't like it, you can have your cards today.'

'What cards would they be?' asked Sean.

'You're too chopsy for your own good. One day that mouth of yours will get you in big trouble,' said Lomax.

'It'll be okay, you see,' said Dave Cheung.

'How do you make that out?' said Wanda.

'He pay soon, honest,' said Cheung.

'How do you know?' asked Jenny.

'He doesn't; he's just hoping like the rest of us,' said Sean.

'A bit of a man of mystery our David,' said Nat.

'Well as I say, if you don't like it, you can collect your belongings and get off Killpeck land.' With that, Lomax strode out of the building, leaving nothing but the whiff of his cigar behind him.

'Please take your time Miss Chowdry. Anything at all that you think might help in the investigation, I'd be very grateful for.'

The young woman looked up but would not look directly at Mycroft.

'This is very difficult for me, you understand?' said Shani.

'Yes, I can see. Has your father come with you? Perhaps you would like me to ring him?'

'No please. He would kill me, if he knew,' said Shani Chowdry.

Nick sensed this might not be an exaggeration.

'Can I get you a cup of tea or a drink of water?' asked Nick.

'May I have a glass of water?'

'Off course; would it be okay if my boss came in too?'

'No! Please! I can only speak to you. You have a kind face.'

'It's been called many other things, but thank you,' said Nick softly. He could see the girl was terrified. 'Can I get you tea, coffee?'

'May I have a glass of water please?'

Nick went out of the room and down to the water cooler.

Stella Kingsley came out of her office.

'Have you found out what this is all about?

'No, she's very anxious, though, Ma'am.'

'Shall I come in with you?'

'No thanks, Ma'am. She says she'll only talk with me.'

'Nick, the thing is, her father is going to kick up such a stink, if we put one more foot out of place. I think it best if I come in with you.'

'I think she'll clam up, Ma'am, but it's your decision.'

They went down to the interview room but there was no sign of Shani.

21
Under Observation

The Right Reverend Nigel Osgood had felt strangely liberated after his visit from the young intelligence officer. Whatever the truth of the matter, the fact was, he was dying.

There were no two ways about it and if this Markovich or his associates wanted to harm him, what of it? Who could blame them? Markovich had, after all, lost his brother, a victim of a cold war feud between two nuclear superpowers. Well, all and sundry had the damn things now. If Markovich came for him, Nigel hoped he'd have the courage to tell him how much he'd loved his brother, and that he never would have wished for the way things had turned out. He took his favourite walking stick from the umbrella stand in the hall and went out to take a stroll around Stamford. The little town had afforded him a great deal of solace, with its fine architecture and two rather beautiful churches although he got the feeling that he was not universally popular. He was aware that there were some likeminded people, one such was Keith, a local roofer, whose heart was in the right place, even if his turn of phrase wasn't. He was to political correctness what Lucretia Borgia was to catering. It was Keith who greeted him now from among the chimney pots of one of his neighbour's roofs.

'Morning, Right Reverend, Comrade!'

'Morning Keith!'

'Looks like we've both got our mind on higher things today. These old stacks are crumbling into nothing.'

'I know the feeling, Keith,' replied Osgood.

'Are you coming to the quiz night?'

'When is it?

'Next Wednesday.'

'What's it in aid of?'

'Relief for Gaza. It's in the church hall.'

'I'll be there.'

'Good man.'

Across the street in Lizzie's Land Rover, Alexei and Jason were listening in on the conversation.

'Looks a harmless enough old geezer to me.'

'Harmless? Let me tell you a bit more about our friend, The Red Bishop, and how he betrayed queen and country,' said Alexei, taking a long draw on his cigarette. We do it then, quiz night? More people see it, more people know we mean business. What you say Jason?'

'I was never any good at quizzes,' said Jason absently.

'So, no one thought to try and stop her?' Stella Kingsley was getting to the end of her tether.

'I beg your pardon, Ma'am, but we had no reason to. She wasn't anywhere near the arrest suite. Quiet, little, thing wasn't causing any aggro,' said Sergeant Hedges

'You will be,' said Kingsley, glaring at him over the top of her glasses.

'I'll go to the train station, Ma'am,' said Nick. 'I don't think she came by car.'

'No! Chowdry would probably add an extra complaint to the charge sheet and make out it was some kind of harassment!' said Kingsley, who at that moment was longing for retirement, but suspected she would be losing her pension at this rate. The world and his wife seemed to hold her personally responsible for practically everything.

'On a brighter note, Ma'am,' said Coombs, 'I've cross referenced membership of New Glory with anyone who has a criminal record; in fact Ma'am, the membership is only one hundred strong, of whom eight have at some time or other been naughty boys and girls, three now live abroad, which is slightly ironic don't you think, three are still inside and then that leaves two, one of whom is none other than their great leader, Terry Tomms.'

'What's was he done for?'

'Tax fraud, I believe. He was declared bankrupt at one point but then was left money by an aunt, so the story goes.'

'Who's the other one with a record?'

'A chap called Jason Wilkes. Nothing much... a couple of driving and taking away, and one charge of bank fraud. You know, using someone else card to buy stuff.'

'Yes, thank you Bob. I think we are all aware of the nature of such offences.'

'Well, we have an address for Mr Tomms. How about Wilkes?'

Nothing current Ma'am. Last known address he apparently moved from three years ago.

'Well, he can't just have fallen off the planet. More checks please, Bob, National Insurance, no next of kin, you know the form.' Stella Kingsley prowled up and down the briefing room, peering over a pair of gold rimmed spectacles she kept on a chain round her neck.

'Nick, I need you to re interview Tomms. Lean on him a bit.'

'But Ma'am, I thought I was on gardening leave?'

'Oh, sod gardening leave. I also need Jenny James from that wild goose chase up at that fruit farm. We've got bigger fish to fry.'

Nick stifled a giggle at his boss' clumsy phraseology. 'I'll make contact and try to pause the whole operation, in case when things calm down, we want to have a look.'

'Thanks Nick, but I think I'll be the one taking future decisions about operational matters,' Stella said icily.

'Yes Ma'am. Absolutely Ma'am,' said a chastened Mycroft.

22
What lies Beneath

Lizzie had managed to get dressed while Alexei and Jason were out, but her day had been in flashbacks to what she'd seen the night before, floating at the top of the cow slurry pit. When the two men returned, she was in combative mood.

'Look Lizzie. Have I done something wrong? If so, what?' enquired Alexei.

'I don't know, Alexei, if that's your real name,' said Lizzie. 'You tell me, have you?'

'You talk in riddles, woman.'

'You know what I am talking about. It was you wasn't it? I knew you were trouble that first night. I said to myself, Lizzie, watch it my girl, he's got trouble written all over his face, but then I let my affectionate nature get the better of me.'

'What is she going on about?' queried Jason.

'There's a body in my bloody slurry pit... Don't tell me someone must have topped themselves by jumping into a tank of shit,' said Lizzie angrily.

'It could have been an accident.'

'You have to open a heavy inspection lid, then unlock a heavy gauge metal cover. It would have to be someone even stupider than you to fall in.'

'Why you look in pit, stupid woman?' said Alexei angrily.

'To check the levels. I have a farm to run. You seem to forget,' countered Lizzie.

'Oh god Alexei, you didn't?' said Jason, beginning to put two and two together.

'It was temporary measure.'

'Too bloody right, poor bugger. Whoever he was didn't deserve that,' said Lizzie. Her life had taken so many nightmarish turns, the body in the pit seemed just one more vision from hell.

'Now is someone going to tell me what happened, or shall I just not bother asking and get straight onto the police.'

'Alright... look it's my fault... it was an accident though,' stuttered Jason. He was my best mate for Christ's sake. Alexei was just trying to help. The thing is, I've been inside before and no one's going to believe what happened. It was just a bit of bad luck.'

'Worse luck for whoever it is in my slurry pit, I should say,' said Lizzie, stubbing her cigarette out on the draining board in her kitchen and reaching into one of the cupboards for the vodka bottle she had squirrelled away.

'Thank you for coming in, Mr Tomms.'

'Only too happy to assist the boys in blue where we can.'

'As you know, we are investigating a murder, which may have been racially aggravated, and which New Glory apparently have claimed responsibility.'

'As I told your boss, DI Mycroft, we are a legitimate, political interest group, who have never been involved in any kind of violent direct action.'

'Not strictly true, is it Mr Tomms, though. Your marches have ended in violent melees on several occasions,' countered Mycroft.

'The only trouble was caused by Trots and anarchists. New Glory was merely exercising its right to peacefully protest against the destruction of our British way of life.'

'I must ask you for your movements on the night of the 15th June and whether you have anyone who can corroborate that information.'

'I live alone, Inspector; do you think anyone else could share the kind of life I lead?'

'Well, as I say, I will need as much evidence as you can find to confirm your movements on that night.'

'I will supply you with the information you require as far as I can. Will that be all Inspector?'

'There is one other matter you can assist us with. We would like to trace the whereabouts of a certain Jason Wilkes,' said Mycroft.

'Can't say I know the fellow.'

'Well, he's on your membership list.'

'I can't be expected to know all the ins and outs of all our members.'

'You only have one hundred members, Mr Tomms. You're not exactly the National Trust now are you?'

'I have given you our membership list. Now you really must excuse me. New Glory has a busy month ahead. Oh, and we are always looking for new members with a law-and-order background.'

'Just send me the information I require Mr Tomms. Otherwise, you will need legal representation, as our next meeting will be under caution,' said Nick.

23
Modus Operandi

'Does anyone know whether there was ever a Mrs Lomax?' asked Jenny, as the pickers sat round the table outside the men's caravan.'

'I pity her, if there was,' said Wanda.

'Who'd marry a gobshite like that,' observed Sean.

'He's just symptomatic of what's wrong with this country,' said Nat.

'By the way, where's Alexei? I haven't seen him all day,' said Jenny.

'God only knows. He was seeing that farmer's widow, Izzy or Libby, or some such.'

'He doesn't seem to do much work.'

'He must have something on Lomax, the way he works when he wants to,' said Nat. 'I'm getting out of here tomorrow; I'm not working for no money anymore. Who does he think he's kidding?'

'Oh, don't go, Dutchie. I love the way you bump your head every time you get in the van and seeing those great big plates of meat sticking out of the bunk opposite me,' chuckled Sean.

'How about you, Jenny. Have you had enough of this place yet?' asked Wanda.

'Oh, it's not all bad. I've heard of worse.'

'Yes, Jenny right, Mr Lomax not bad,' said Dave Cheung.

'Ah Jesus, why do you make excuses for him? He's a feckin' miserly bastard.'

At that moment, Alexei drove up in Lizzie Rimmer's Land Rover.

'Hi folks, just dropped by to say I'm leaving, going back home in couple of days. It's been good to know you... yes, even you, Sean. I collect my stuff from van, then go see Lomax.'

'Ask him when he's going to pay us, while you're there, will you?' said Sean.

Once Alexei had gone into Lomax's office the disconsolate group of pickers huddled around the embers of last night's campfire.

'Where'd he get those wheels from?' queried Nat.

'Oh, probably that fancy woman of his,' said Sean. 'I think he's a bit of a dark horse that one.'

At the station in Lincoln, DCI Kingsley had now received a full post-mortem report on Hanif Singh.

'Okay, the lab has confirmed cause of death: ligature around the neck. There was severe bruising to the chest, abdomen and arms, which all points to the poor chap having been given a good kicking before being killed. Fibres in his hair and clothes suggest that the attack took place somewhere other than where the body was found. No fingerprints that didn't belong to members of the Chowdry family were detected in the car, which suggests gloves were used throughout.'

'Professional job then,' said Coombs.

'Not necessarily. All and sundry watch crime dramas on the TV these days. Everybody knows the deal where gloves are concerned.'

'Now Bob, I would like you to call on Hanif's mum and dad again. Bring them up to date with the investigation as far as you can. See if we've missed anything, but go very gently, Bob. Hanif was their only son.'

'Yes, Ma'am.'

'I'm particularly interested to ensure we have not missed a line of enquiry. So, find out as much as you can about Hanif's interests and any romantic involvements we have not been made aware of. He seems to have been a quiet lad, but you never really know.'

'No, Ma'am. I bet half the mums and dads of those jihadi fighters thought they were little angels and look at those shooters in America always the quiet ones, Ma'am, are the ones you have to watch,' interjected Coombs.

'Bob, we are talking about a murder victim here, not the perpetrators of mass killings.'

'No, Ma'am, quite so. But I was just thinking out loud, Ma'am. None of us really know our kids, do we Ma'am,' mused Coombs.

'Having never had children, Bob, I wouldn't know. Now run along, there's a good boy and remember, softly softly!'

'Watched every episode, Ma'am.'

'Are you still here?' Stella stared at Coombs in mock annoyance. She knew that his children were estranged from him, and it was a genuine mystery to him why they no longer wanted to keep in contact. He was a man stranded in the middle of his own life, thought Stella, who was both fond of him and irritated by him, in almost equal measure.

'I have booked us two rooms in the nearest travel lodge to Stamford for the night before the operation. I have couple of jobs to do before I join you. You take Land Rover,' said Alexei, aware that it would be convenient all round.

'Yes, but how are you going to get over to Stamford,' asked Jason.

'I hire car for now. Don't worry; I get there.'

'What are you going to do about Drac's body?'

'That's one of the jobs I have to do.'

'Now you go and book in hotel. Here money. I join you for meal tonight yes? We go over final details. That commie bastard gets what he deserves.'

'Yes sure. There's just one thing: is you sure we ought not get the go ahead from that Tomms fellow at New Glory?'

'Listen my friend, it will be good. No contact before, but they will be happy to take the credit and you, you're biggest hero for the right, since Oswald Moseley.'

'Who the hell was he?' asked Jason.

'Or Enoch Powell.'

'Oh yes, "Good old Enoch!" That's what one of my stepdads used to say,' said Jason.

'Anyway, I have something for you,' said Alexei pulling a large, partially serrated hunting knife from under his coat.

Bob Coombs knocked on the door of Mr and Mrs Singh. After several minutes, Hanif's father opened the door.

'Mr Singh? DS Coomb. I wonder if I may have a word?'

'May I see your ID. It's just that we've had several press people here masquerading as the police.'

'Of course, and listen, if you can give me a description, I'll follow it up. It's a criminal offence you know, although my boss has been known at times to accuse me of it,' said Coombs in an effort to lighten the atmosphere.

'Thank you, but we don't want any more trouble.'

'I'm calling just to see if you can give us anymore background around Hanif's friends and family.'

'I think we've told Detective Inspector Mycroft all the details that we know.'

'Anything at all might be useful.'

'I'm afraid my wife is not very well at the moment, so it is not convenient.'

'I'll leave you my number and anything at all... and if you like I can put a uniformed officer on your door.

'Would that be round the clock, Sergeant Coombs.'

'Well, I don't know if I can swing that with my boss...'

'Well anyway, if you don't mind, this has hit my wife very badly. Please keep me informed of any developments, but by telephone only please, if possible.'

'Okay, I'll leave you in peace now.'

'Peace is something I fear my family will never have, Sergeant Coombs. Goodbye.'

Nick Mycroft had decided he couldn't put it off any longer and so drove straight down to his father's house after work. It seemed so odd calling it his father's house. He'd always used to call it Mum's place, because in reality, until a couple of years ago, his father was never there. He was either at one of his shops, or at the local conservative club, or The Black Lion. Even when Nick was little, his father was only ever a transitory presence, either eating huge meals his mother had prepared or asleep. Nick remembered often being intrigued by a copy of the *Racing Times*, rising and falling in line with his father's snoring.

'Anyone home?' called Nick, when he could get no reply at the front door.

'We are round the back,' he heard his father's voice in response.

The deck chair Nick's father was sitting on seemed unequal to the task of supporting his weight, like an overstuffed fishermen's net which at any moment might deposit his father onto the decking outside his conservatory. He was wearing shades and a violently mauve shirt and khaki shorts, but it was the remnants of his father's hair that attracted Nick's attention. He seemed to have gone for the comb over, two long dark lank strands straddled the dome of his head, like the liquorice laces he used to buy coming home from school. Not a good look, thought Nick.

'You remember Carly, Son, don't you?' said Jake Mycroft.

Carly Raymond had managed one of Nick's father's betting shops. She was a woman in her fifties, who dressed as if she was in her twenties, with dyed auburn hair, hooped earrings, and her cleavage cluttered up by gold jewellery. She had her hand on his father's knee but what was ten times worse was that she was drinking out of his mother's Poole pottery mug.

'I'll pick you up from the farm in the morning. The boss wants all hands on deck at the minute, so you're being taken off this slavery thing, okay?' said Mycroft. He had called her from the car on his return from his father's.

'But Sir, I think there's a lot going on here. It may not be slavery as such, but we haven't been paid this week. This Lomax character, he's up to something.'

'Look Jenny, we'll worry about that later. If you're really concerned, we can send a squad car down, let them have a sniff around. See you tomorrow. Keep your head down till then, is that understood?'

'Yes, I've got you, Sir,' said Jenny looking down from the upslope where she'd taken Mycroft's call. In the moonlight, the poly tunnels spread out from the farm below like tentacles of some creature in a sci-fi movie. Jenny thought she might have a little bit more of an explore later on; it couldn't do any harm. She just had a feeling there was more going on here than met the eye and felt frustrated that her first juicy undercover job was about to be cut short. She had also started to feel something for Nick and would love to do something to make him sit up and take notice.

24
Uncovered

The visit to his father had been something of a disaster in the end. Nick brought very little of his mother's things back to Shappington. There were a couple of photos of them together when Nick was about five and a few bits of China, mostly fairings and seaside souvenirs, one with 'Marvellous Margate,' underneath a girl in a bikini, prancing about in very unMargate-like waves with a palm tree of all things fluttering in the background. The mealtime at his father's had been excruciating. He knew Carly wasn't a bad woman; they'd actually had a date or two some years back; her life hadn't been easy, he knew. But it was the fact that his father had no understanding or respect for Nick's feelings about his getting another pair of – however shapely – female legs under his mother's kitchen table.

Bodkin Adams gave Nick a quizzical look, as if to say, 'What time do you call this?' Then he returned to licking all the jelly from the meat in his cat bowl. The animal knew his cohabitee, (master would be entirely the wrong word), kept regular habits and late nights and more importantly, mealtimes had been a rarity, until recently. Nick settled down to a new Saul Bellow book. He had decided to work through the twentieth century cannon of American literature, when his mobile rang: it was Stella Kingsley.

'Hi Nick. I'm sorry to disturb you, but uniform have been called to a farm not far from Sleaford. Multiple bodies found.'

'Sorry Ma'am, did you say multiple bodies found?' said Mycroft.

'Well yes; it's two actually, but two too many given our workload at the moment. I need you to go over and have a chat with the SOCO boys. I've been called back in tomorrow to give evidence again in that bastard Priday's case.'

'Right Ma'am. I'll get up to that farm. You try and get some beauty sleep. I'll call you if I think you're needed. Let's hope it's just two old dears died in their beds.'

Stella's attempt at sleeping was in vain. She'd always had difficulty processing what occurred at work when she got home. Since Marcus left her twelve years ago, there had been no one who she could use to jettison some of the frustrations of the day. All Marcus had done was listen. but then one day he wasn't there.

She went downstairs in her smart, new, town house and put the kettle on. The image of that first interview with Rex Priday kept playing in her head. He looked nothing like the public perception of a psychopath. If anything, he had quite a kindly face: soft blue eyes, a ruddy complexion, greying wavy hair, horn rimmed spectacles. He could have been that uncle you invited around at Christmas. It was only when he smiled, that something of the man's character was betrayed. It's often said that the tiny minority of doctors who go rogue, carrying out unnecessary procedures on their victims, have a god complex. Rex Priday's criminal activities were on another level, however.

Nick arrived at the Rimmer's Farm in the middle of a violent thunderstorm in Lincolnshire's huge skies. This meant everything was lit up like one enormous firework display. Lightning was forking and arcing everywhere one looked. There were about half a dozen squad cars parked in the farmyard: he could also see Perks' (the pathologist's), battered old Rover near the milking parlour. Dr Idris Perks was a dapper little Welshman. Nick showed the uniformed officer, who he didn't recognise, his ID card and then ducked under the blue and white police incident tape.

'Oh, hello Nicholas. You could have brought better weather with you,' said Dr Perks.

'Idris, how are you?'

'Wet, and somewhat peeved to be called out at this time of night, but probably worth it, as it's a bit of a curious one to be honest. Could be double murder or possibly suicide after a murder. It could even, at a pinch, be two accidental deaths.'

'Keeping your options open then are you, Dr Perks?'

'Yes, too right boy. Now where do you want to start? In the kitchen or in the – pardon my French – shitpit?'

'Doesn't sound like any game of Cluedo I've ever played,' quipped Mycroft. 'I suppose we might as well start out here as we are all wet already.'

'Very well; you're the boss, but I hope you're not feeling queasy. Oh no, I was forgetting, you were on that poor girl Betsy's case weren't you? This'll be a piece of cake then.'

Jenny James had waited until she saw Wanda creep out of their shared room in the stable block at Killpeck Farm, presumably for a lover's tryst with Sean. She took a small torch from her kit bag and stepped resolutely out into the thunder and lightning affecting most of Lincolnshire. That night she made her way around the back of the main house, checking in the other outhouses. She wasn't even sure what she was looking for; then she shone her torch into each polytunnel. Each of them was empty apart from rows of strawberry plants, a few boxes and tools, and one had an old tractor in it. The last one she checked by shining her torch through the plastic sheeting, which was some three hundred metres from the other tunnels beyond the old farmhouse orchard. It was padlocked, but also appeared from the outside on first inspection to be largely empty, but something wasn't quite right. The tunnel had been partitioned by a piece of opaque plastic stapled to the main frame of the structure. She loosened a piece of the sheeting, which came away relatively easily. The light from her torch revealed a large separate area which was anything but empty.

'Well Jenny! What brings a nice girl like you out on a night like this?'

It was Lomax with Ratface and just behind him Dave Cheung.

Nick and Dr Perks were sharing a cup of tea from Dr Perks' thermos. Drac's body had been retrieved from the slurry pit with considerable difficulty. It was quite well preserved; the tyre marks from the pickup truck were still clearly visible on his torso. The corpse was now safely zipped into a body bag.

The young police constable approached Mycroft: 'Where do we go from here, Sir?'

'Well, I think what's required, Constable, is a fingertip search of the slurry pit. You did bring your wellies, didn't you?' said Mycroft cheerily.

The young officer for a moment looked non plussed.

'Just kidding you, Constable. If required, we will get police divers in tomorrow. Tell you what: you come up to the house and keep away any undesirables, the press and the like, while Dr Perks does his stuff. You say the other body's a woman's, is that right?'

'Yes Sir. Looks like Lizzie Rimmer to me. She was the owner. We all knew her in the village. Used to get rat arsed every weekend after her husband died, that is. A couple of times, we were called out because there was a scrap breaking out in The Shirings, at closing time, which usually involved Lizzie and some man or other. My wife thought she were a real old slapper.'

'Well thank you, officer. Perhaps we'd better make sure it is the lady of whom your wife speaks so highly,' said Mycroft.

Chloe and Callum were sat in Callum and his partner, Oliver's kitchen.

'Well from what we've got so far, you could make a miniseries. It's like something out of a John le Carré novel,' said Callum.

'Poor guy! What a tragic story. No wonder he's a bit prickly,' observed Chloe.

'I tell you, I wouldn't like to get on his wrong side. It was a bit dodgy to begin with, but I think he's warming to me a bit. We've got enough material here to make about three programmes. Should keep Goldwyn quiet. Although, I wonder how much of the tale certain people in the establishment want being made public.'

'Good point,' said Chloe. 'So, come on then, Callum, spill the beans. What's all this finding God malarkey? There'll be hell to pay when the Bish finds out you're a godless swine like the rest of us,' said Chloe, sipping at an enormous cup of camomile tea.

'Well young lady, not that it's really any of your business, but Ollie and I are thinking of trying for a baby.'

Chloe spluttered over her drink, spraying tea all over the kitchen table.'

'Right, and how is that going to work exactly.'

'Oh, come on Chlo, don't be so naïve. It doesn't suit you.'

'So, what adoption?'

'No, that could take for ever, surrogacy.'

'Well, I know we are mates and all that, but if you invited me over...'

'Oh, wash your mouth out young lady, no. Besides, you're not a good genetic match.'

'Oh, thanks very much,' said Chloe in mock indignation.

'As a matter a fact, we've found someone, who could be ideal, but...'

'But what?' said Chloe, 'she's refused to countenance the idea?'

'Oh no, she agrees in principle, says surrogacy as the ultimate example of God's love.'

'So, what's the problem?'

'There are conditions attached to her having Oliver's and my baby,' said Callum, wiping the mess off the table that Chloe had made.

25
Hostage to Fortune

'The thing is, Jenny, I'm really not sure what's to be done with you,' explained Lomax. 'You see you had nothing on you that would identify you. Now my friend here, Mr Yui, or as you know him, Cheung, thinks there is a possibility that you are a police officer. Mr Yui is virulently opposed to law enforcement and wants rid of you altogether.'

'So, Mr Lomax, you'd risk what, a two-year sentence for farming marijuana plants, with a whole life tariff sentence for murder?'

'Oh, so you're a member of Her Majesty's Constabulary?'

'Might be or might just be a curious strawberry picker.'

Jenny started to yell for help. The two men grappled with her before winding an electrical tape around her mouth so tightly she had difficulty breathing.

Jenny looked at Lomax defiantly. She had been tied to one of the water tanks used to irrigate the five hundred or so cannabis plants.

'Mr Yui has agreed to go away and sleep on it. So, I've agreed to keep you company, along with Ratface here, and see if in the morning, we are all not getting on a little better and can find a way out of this.' Lomax put his hand on Jenny's knee, but she kicked it away with all the force she could muster.

Ratface bared his impressive set of teeth. The dog's lenient approach to humans didn't appear to extend to policewomen.

Idris Perks made an initial examination of Lizzie Rimmer's body. Her head had been lolling over the arm of the sofa. Bottles of anti-depressants and paracetamol were spread out on the carpet and a nearly empty bottle of vodka lay by her side. She appeared to be clutching a framed photograph of her late husband to her breast.

'Well, it could be suicide, but I'm not sure. Need to take a closer look when I get her back to my place... sorry, that sounds a bit yucky... you know... I mean the path lab. There are a couple of things I'm not entirely happy with. But I tell you one thing buddy; she smells a hell of lot better than that boy in the yard. Not a good place to end up... not a good place at all. I'll get a report to you... well... as soon as poss.'

'Thank you Idris. I'd appreciate that very much. I'll hang on for a bit and see what the SOCO team turn up, if anything.'

Stella Kingsley was at her desk by eight in the morning after the grisly discovery at the Rimmer's Farm. She was anxious to make an early start. She was due in court at 11.00 am to give evidence in the Priday case but hoped to get some emails responded to by then. She also wanted to hear exactly what had taken place at the strawberry growing outfit farm that Nick Mycroft had been called to.

Kingsley couldn't understand the number of spam and unwanted, electronic posts she was getting and was just about to ring up IT support, and give them a flea in their ear, when Bob Coombs knocked on her door.

'Come in Bob,' she said.

'Need to update you, Ma'am,' said Coombs.

'What about the unexplained deaths, out in the sticks?'

'No Ma'am. DI Mycroft was dealing with that. It was meant to be my day off,' said Coombs pointedly.

'I'm sorry Bob, but it's all hands to the pump at the minute, so what news do you have for me?'

'Well Ma'am, there's been a suspicious fire at the Singh's house.'

'Oh my God! Are they okay?'

'Yes Ma'am. Fortunately they both got out and the house was not seriously damaged according to the brigade. It was a pretty, half-hearted attempt; a bit of rag soaked in petrol posted through the letterbox.'

'Still, someone's got it in for that family.'

'Will you go over and find out what you can, you know, reassure them?'

'I don't think he cared much for me, Ma'am.'

'Well just muster up a bit of charm, Bob. You remember how to do that don't you?'

'Just about, Ma'am.'

'Now, where's Nick?'

'He were up at the farm half the night, Ma'am.'

'Call him, please. I need a report on that before I go into court this morning.'

'Okay, Ma'am.'

Nick Mycroft was woken as usual by Bodkin Adams, coming into his bedroom and seating himself directly on Nick's chest. Sometimes, having been roused from a deep sleep, Nick would wonder if he was about to have a heart attack before realising it was merely his overweight cat pressing on his rib cage. His mobile was ringing.

'Wakey, Wakey! Boss wants you in Pronto.' It was Bob Coombs.

'Does she know I didn't get to bed until 4.30 am?'

I tried to tell her, but you know what she's like when she's got to give evidence.'

'Oh god, it's the Betsy Mulligan case today, isn't it,' exclaimed Nick.'

'Yep. Let's hope they nail the bastard,' eh Nick.

'Okay listen; tell the DCI I will be in as soon as I can. Also Bob, and this is important, it's possible we've got a double murder investigation on our hands.'

'Oh, that'll cheer her up no end,' said Bob.

The rain was still falling as Nick began to make his way into Lincoln. Last night's events were playing in his head. It all appeared pretty bizarre: who was the man literally in the shit?

Had he been the victim of some kind of crime of passion, involving this Lizzie Rimmer character? If so, could she have weighed the body down and then had the strength to drag it and dump it in the slurry pit? She would have to have been something of an amazon. It was then he remembered Jenny. It would mean a twenty-minute detour, but he had promised to pick her up and it was pouring with rain. He was beginning to realise he really did quite like her a lot.

26
In Peril

In Stamford, it was the day before the charity quiz night, an occasion The Right Reverend Osgood was looking forward to. It was a bit of good-natured competition and as he was to be on Keith's team, he knew he would be among friends. On a whim, he had invited Chloe and Callum from the television company to come along. They had apparently wanted to see more of what his life was like now and as the quiz was the most exciting thing he would get up to that week, he'd called Callum and suggested they be part of his team. He had also agreed to give them a further few titbits about his life, his years at theological college, a curacy in a very deprived east end parish, getting to be a vicar in Buckinghamshire, a minor canon at Lincoln Cathedral and then a post as a Suffragan Bishop in Carlisle: fairly humdrum stuff really. As for his emotional life, that was slightly different. All through this period, Father Vyvian and Osgood had corresponded. Nigel had told Father Vivyan all about his love affair with Julian, but not exactly the circumstances in which Julian had died. Father Vyvian had provided steadfast spiritual guidance to Nigel over the years. He had told him that the Kingdom of Heaven was the only place to bring the kind of unshareable suffering that Nigel had experienced to an end. He wrote too of the need to open one's heart fully to whatever God's purpose should be. This, Nigel had done in most respects. He had never ever, however, been fully able to forgive the establishment for what they had done. Now that his beloved mother was long gone, he was determined that the world would know that Julian was the victim of Judicial Murder by the British State.

At Killpeck Farm, Wanda awoke to find Jenny's bunk empty. Either she'd got lucky with one of the male pickers or something was up. She grabbed her clothes and thought she'd go for a look round. There was nowhere really for her to have gone. Perhaps she was poorly. Whatever it was, she was concerned she'd grown fond of Jenny, despite her initial misgivings. She'd proved a good worker and could give as good as she got when bantering with the men. Wanda pulled on a pair of boots and went outside. The rain had diminished now to a kind of wet, steamy mist that hung around Killpeck. There was a light on at the farmhouse, but the last thing she wanted to do was enlist the help of slimy Lomax. Anyway, Jenny couldn't have gone far. She'd just have a little shifty, see if she could find out what she was up to. She quite liked Jenny but there was something not quite kosher about her.

Just outside Stamford, Jason Wilkes was tucking into breakfast. He'd gone to the café next to the hotel and had ordered the full works. He wasn't quite sure why Alexei was looking after him so well, including helping out moneywise, but he wasn't one to look a gift horse in the mouth. He had had to rethink his opinion of Alexei. He was alright and this bishop he wanted taken out seemed a right ponce. Anyway, there was still a day to go. He had done as Alexei had suggested and purchased from a local hardware store a hammer, a small axe (as used for firewood) and a leather sheaf for the hunting knife Alexei had given him. The bloke in the hardware shop had given him a funny look, but he'd just stared back at him. He was excited and nervous... this was going to be big... Jason Wilkes, headline news. Who'd have thought it? He wondered whether it would feel any different to shooting rabbits.

When DS Coombs arrived in Leicester at the Singh's family home, there were still several appliances and brigade vehicles parked outside the house. The white plastic on the front door, which was open, showed signs of heat damage. A brown triangular stain covered the lower half and there was an acrid smell in the air. The Chief fire officer, a man called Lockesley, filled Bob in.

'Well, it's not pleasant, of course, but doesn't look like a serious attempt to torch the building. Probably kids messing about.'

'You sound pretty relaxed about it.'

'Sorry, but this is our second big shout this shift.'

'Busy night then,' said Coombs sarcastically.

'Yes, I suppose so. The other call was cutting multiple fatalities out of vehicles on the A17.'

'Touché,' said Coombs.

'Where are the occupants?'

'Next door with the neighbours.'

'How do they seem?'

'Almost catatonic. I mean I know it must have been a shock, but it affected them really badly.'

'Well, it's a bit of a tale really, but I'm not surprised, poor beggars, with what they've been through.'

'How do you mean?'

'Their son was murdered recently.'

'Oh God! Do you think this is connected?'

'I really don't know but I'll pop over and have a word.'

'What's the neighbour's name?'

'Lynette and Norbert Coleman. They seem like a lovely people. Couldn't do enough to help the Singhs.'

'Just to warn you, the Coleman's are not very impressed with the police by all accounts,' said Lockesley.

In the polytunnel at Killpeck Farm, Jenny had just dropped off to sleep and Lomax saw his opportunity. He waddled towards her, undoing his trouser belt.'

'Get away from her you great slab of shit!' It was Wanda standing in the opening of the plastic sheeting.'

'How did you get here?' said Lomax.

'Unlike scum like you, I look out for people. Now I won't tell you again, piss off and leave her alone!'

'Okay, young lady. It seems I might have to teach you some good manners,' said Lomax, moving towards her. The look of surprise when Wanda kicked one of his legs hard was followed by a yell of pain as she threw him across her shoulder and onto the ground. She followed this up with several kicks to Lomax's midriff.

'Now, you stay there like a good boy, while I attend to Jenny.'

'Who the hell?'

Nick had heard the commotion as he'd pulled up the drive of the farmhouse. He ran towards where the shouting was coming from.

'It's okay, Wanda, he's on our side.'

'Can you cuff him, Sir?' said Jenny, as Wanda untied her.

At that moment, Dave Cheung arrived with a rifle in his hand.

'Okay, everyone keeps nice and calm. All on floor please.'

'It's okay, Dave. This is DI Mycroft.'

'That makes things a little unfortunate. Now as I say, everyone on floor now.'

Cheung made it clear he was in no mood for a discussion by bringing the rifle up to his eyeline.

'What are you going to do Dave, or Mr Yui? Or whoever you are... kill us all?'

'If necessary, yes.'

'Look mate, that's no way to treat me,' said Lomax getting up on his knees.

'I have a mind to kill you first, Lomax. You are the reason for this mess,' said Cheung, smashing the butt of the rifle into Lomax's head and kicking him to the ground for good measure.

At this, Lomax's dog, Ratface, took exception and leaped at Cheung, knocking him of balance. Nick seized the opportunity and grabbed the gun out of his hand, and with Wanda's and Jenny's help, Lomax was overpowered.

Bob Coombs knocked on the Colemans' door.

'Good morning. I understand Mr and Mrs Singh are with you.'

He was ushered into the house but then met with a tirade of disapprobation.

'What you are doing, leaving these people with no protection? You got no brain? They lost their son: a beautiful, young man, he was. Now you leave them defenceless. What we pay our taxes for? You tell me that Mr Policeman!' Lynette Coleman filled the front door frame of her house, but Bob Coombs could just see the Singhs in the Colemans' front room, perched on a sofa.

'You let the police officer in, Lynette; you hear me now?'

'It was Norbert, Lynette's husband. You can't blame one man for a broken system.'

Lynette stood to one side and Coombs was just about able to slide his way through from the hall into the living room.

'I am so sorry. When I heard what happened, I thought I'd come out, make sure you're okay.'

'Bit late in the day for that,' said Lynette.

'Come on woman, give the man a break, eh, why don't you?' said Norbert Coleman.

'We are alive, which is something to be grateful for,' said Mr Singh.

'What can you tell me about what happened?' asked Coombs.

'Very little, Detective Sergeant,' said Vasander.

'We were both asleep at the time,' said Som Singh.

'May I ask what alerted you to the fire?'

'We have smoke detectors now sergeant,' said Vasander.

'Now?' queried Coombs. 'Have you had a problem before?'

'Oh well, not really... we can't be...' said Som, her voice almost a whisper.

'I'm sure I smelt petrol in the hall some months ago and there it was over my doormat, stinking the place out.'

'So, when was this? Was it before Hanif's ...

'Murder? Yes Sergeant Coombs. It was several months ago.'

'May I ask why you haven't mentioned this before?'

'Because we are not the only family in this area to be targeted by racists, Sergeant,' said Vasander.

'If only that were true,' said Mrs Singh looking her husband straight in the eye.'

27
The Aftermath

'That Wanda is quite some woman,' said Jenny James as the backup squad car drove off with Lomax and Yui in the back.

'Oh god! I'm really sorry, Jenny. I got tied up with a new case,' explained Nick. 'If anything had happened to you, I would never have forgiven myself.' He moved his arm towards her shoulder and then realised that perhaps he shouldn't.

Jenny smiled at him and rubbed his arm, as he retracted it.

'Look Sir, you weren't to know it would turn nasty the way it did,' said Jenny.

'I know but anything could've...'

'Sir, it was my own fault. I don't know what made me go snooping around in the first place.'

'A copper's instinct, I reckon. Anyway, looks like we've caught us a couple of villains,' said Mycroft.

'Lomax is just a slime ball, Sir, but Yui or Cheung or whoever he is, I think he represents quite a serious player.'

'Well, we'll get an idea after we've interviewed them. We'll need to interview all the pickers as well.'

'Shall I organise that, Sir?' asked Jenny.

'Yes please, but not until you've had some sleep. You're going to need it. That other case I mentioned, well could be we've got a double murder on our hands.'

DCI Kingsley had given her evidence in the Betsy Mulligan murder case. She was aware that she would be needed back at the station to get an update from Nick re what had happened at Rimmer Farm. But she couldn't resist going back into the public gallery to hear some of the evidence of the next witness, a young man called Mick Mason. The prosecution barrister was questioning Mick, who was standing in the witness box holding his hands across his chest in an attempt to stop shaking with nerves.

'Now can you tell us please, Mr Mason, when it was you first met the accused?'

'Well... he started using our firm... when he wanted taxi.'

'So how long ago was this?'

'I don't know... maybe two... years ago?'

'And can you confirm this is the man you see, in the dock?'

Rex Priday seemed completely oblivious to the court proceedings. Instead he appeared to be reading; what Stella wasn't quite sure.

'Yes, that's him. That's the Prof. That's what we knew him as. Didn't know what a twat he was like then.'

At this point, the judge intervened.

'Mr Mason, I must ask you to curtail your language. This is, after all, a court of law. So, when you are asked a question, just keep to the facts, please, when giving your answer.'

The young man looked at the judge as if he was speaking in some incomprehensible, foreign language.

'Sorry your honour.'

The prosecuting counsel continued their cross examination.

'Mr Mason, can you confirm you were acquainted with a Miss Betsy Mulligan.'

'Yes, I knew her. She used to hang round the booking office.'

'I have to ask you, Mr Mason, were you intimate with Miss Mulligan?'

'Yes, I suppose you could say we hooked up for a while.'

'And you've said previously that you were unaware of her age. I have here your police statement at the time.'

'I had no idea man, honest.'

'You had no idea that she was fourteen years old?'

'No.'

'Mr Mason, I need you to tell the court on what occasion it was that you introduced Miss Mulligan to the accused, Rex Priday?'

'Well, the thing was, he seemed a nice old geezer, a bit lonely like.'

'So, you organised for Professor Priday to have some company. Is that right?'

'Now look, I never asked her to do anything that she wasn't happy with.'

'Can I suggest you introduced Betsy to the accused, Rex?'

'No, it was nothing like that... I had nothing to do with it... I mean how was I to know he was a sicko,' said Mason.

Stella Kingsley could afford no more time in court. All she could hope for was that the evidence mounted up to enough to see Priday put behind bars for the rest of his days.

28
An Evil Endeavour

At a low-end hotel just outside Stamford, Jason Wilkes was getting a bit twitchy. Alexei was not responding to his calls. Jason had rung ten times and ten times it had gone to voicemail. He began to wonder if Alexei had got cold feet or perhaps the cops had got him in connection with Drac's death, or that Lizzie was keeping him so busy he'd lost track of time. Jason wasn't sure he could go through with the whole thing on his own. He'd done as Alexei had instructed, gone to a local hardware store and purchased a few bits and bobs. He laid them out on his bed. There was a claw hammer, a small axe, the type you use for chopping kindling wood, and of course the hunting knife, which Alexei had given him. He wasn't one for quiz nights himself, but it takes all sorts. It looked like he might be flying solo, so he was glad of the bottle of vodka he'd bought with some of the money Alexei had given him. He might need just a bit of Dutch courage.

In Leicester, Mrs Singh was sitting on her neighbour's settee sobbing softly.

'Well, I suppose it had all better come out now,' said Vasander Singh.

'It is not quite true what we have told you about Hanif not having had a girlfriend.'

'We know he was seeing someone,' said Som.

'But he would clam up whenever we tried to discuss it with him.'

'He must have thought we would not have approved of whoever she was.'

'Why would you not approve?'

'It is a big deal in our culture, Sergeant Coombs.'

'What is? I'm sorry. Am I being a bit thick here?'

'To go with someone outside your faith.'

'What makes you think that was the case?' asked Coombs.

'We found this photograph,' said Vasander.

The picture was of Hanif and a veiled young woman hand in hand.

'Do you mind if I take this with me?' asked Coombs. 'I don't suppose you have any idea who she might be?'

'No, Sergeant, only that the young lady appears to be Muslim,' said Vasander Singh.

'So, are you saying that the motive for your son's murder may be a religious one rather than a racial one?'

'That is not for us to say, Sergeant Coombs. We were deeply concerned when we found this picture, but in time, if the relationship continued, we would have found a way to accept it. Another family may not have been able to do this.'

'But if that's the case, why go on targeting you after your son's death?'

'This I cannot answer, but perhaps it was a way to draw you off the scent.'

'I do apologise but this is all conjecture at this stage.'

'Yes, it may be so. All I ask of the police, Detective Sergeant, is all I've ever asked: that you catch who ever killed my son,' said Vasander.

'You heard the man,' said Lynette Coleman, who had been listening to the conversation from her kitchen.

Dr Idris Perks moved around his place of work with considerable speed, propelled as he was by a high stool on wheels. Being short in stature, this meant that at times he was pushing himself over the floor by the very tips of his toes. There were four examination tables in the path lab. Only two of them, however, were occupied: one by the corpse of Lizzie Rimmer and the other by a man, as yet to be identified.

'Come in both. Welcome again to our little home from home,' said Perks.

'Let's have a look at the female first,' he continued, wheeling himself over to one of the cadavers. 'Toxicology confirms that she ingested considerable amounts of pain killers and anti-depressants, plus a quantity of alcohol, certainly in combination, enough to cause her vital organs to begin to shut down. It does appear she might have had a little help though; these are definitely pressure marks around the throat and the mouth, consistent with those of a possible assailant's fingers. The bruising, certainly suggests considerable force being used.'

Nick and his boss were only half listening, as they were both finishing tying up their surgical gowns.

'So, she was throttled?' said a distracted Kingsley.

'Well, let's put it this way. It wouldn't have helped. More likely her mouth was being held open while the drugs and alcohol were being forced down.'

Perks now wheeled his way to the other slab.

'Now, for our other guest, there is a large contusion to the head, but undoubtedly what killed this unfortunate fellow was the fact that he was driven over by a vehicle of considerable size. Perhaps a small tractor or off-road vehicle. We are matching tyre treads at the moment, which may give us a better idea.'

'Are we able to get any closer to an identification?' asked Kingsley.

'No, not at this stage. A bit of a mystery man by all accounts. Nothing back from dental records, no distinguishing features.'

'Well, thank you Dr Perks. Do keep us up to speed with any further thoughts won't you,' said Stella Kingsley.

'Oh yes of course. To be honest, it's quite nice to have the place filling up a bit. We'd been pretty quiet recently.'

As they left the path lab, Nick Mycroft whispered to his boss: 'He's quite bonkers, don't you think, Ma'am.'

'Yes, I suppose he is, but I've known Idris for thirty years and he's nothing if not methodical. If there's anything to uncover, he will.'

'Talking of pathologists, Ma'am, how did it go in court today?'

'Okay, thank you Nick, but just being in the same room as Priday makes my flesh crawl.'

'I know the feeling, Ma'am.'

'You did very well there, Nick. Can't have been easy going into that house, seeing what you saw.'

'No, I still have nightmares, Ma'am. What kind of a case can his defence team have?'

'What they're saying is that it was one of a number of let properties he owned and there was no proof he had been near the place in years, and you'll remember none of his prints were found there.'

'Ma'am, if that man walks free, I swear...'

'Enough of that, DS Mycroft. All we can do is catch 'em. Speaking of which how are you getting on with those two cannabis farmers. Have they been charged yet?'

'No, Ma'am, but it'll not be just the dope growing. There'll be false imprisonment, possibly sexual assault and attempted murder somewhere on the charge sheet.'

'Oh, and how's Jenny?'

'She seems fine, Ma'am, considering,' said Nick blushing with embarrassment.

'Tough little thing, isn't she?'

'Yes, Ma'am, tough as old boots, I reckon,' said Nick.

'Lovely eyes though, Nick,' said Stella, chuckling to herself as they headed for the car.

Very unusually for the Reverend Osgood, he had forgotten to lock up when taking his morning walk down to the paper shop. He was feeling childishly excited about the forthcoming quiz. He'd even done a little swotting up on areas where he knew he was, shall we say, light. The old names for the grounds of premier football clubs was one topic, along with past winners of the X factor. He would be starting a further course of radiotherapy next week, which might prolong his life by the odd month or two. He had opted for this, purely as a means of seeing what reaction there would be to his article concerning Julian's murder all those years ago. The news being what it was these days, he suspected very few people would respond, but you never knew and besides he felt he owed as much to the love of his life. With this on his mind, it was not until a few moments after entering his office that he realised he'd been robbed, the room trashed and that his laptop with all his pen drives plus the video recording he'd made with Chloe for *Family Matters* were all missing.

29
Suicide Watch

'The thing is, Son, you and my Brodie used to be close.' It was Nick's Uncle Jimmy. 'And now with your mother gone, to lose him, you know, were he to do something stupid, while he's on the home stretch... Well, you know, I thought you might be able to talk some sense into him.'

'Which prison is he in, Uncle Jimmy?'

'Well, it's that open one in your neck of the woods.'

'And you say he's been on suicide watch?'

'Night and day, Son.'

'Okay, I'll go down and see him.'

'That's good of you lad.'

'I can't promise it'll help. He never forgave me for going into the force.'

'I know you'll do your best; he's been in nearly every nick in the country but this time it's different.'

'Try not to worry, Uncle Jimmy.'

'I know you'll do your best for him lad. Perhaps a word to the parole board?'

'Now that is above my pay grade.'

'Okay, just a thought.'

'Have you seen Dad, by the way?'

'Yes, he's got a new fancy woman with her feet under his table.'

'So, it would seem. I'll give you a call when I've seen Brodie.'

'I don't think you better do the interviewing of these two, Jenny, but you can get busy collecting the witness statements,' said Stella Kingsley as she gave her section briefing. 'Bob you can come and give me a hand.'

'But I've still got my notes from meeting the Singhs to type up.'

'You can do those tonight, Bob.'

'Tonight, Ma'am but I...'

'Think of all that extra overtime you can piss against the wall in the pub once things quieten down a bit,' said Kingsley.

'Come on, we'll do Mr Yui or Cheung or whatever name he's using today.'

'But Ma'am.'

'Yes Bob.'

'I do have a life you know.'

'That's overstating it a bit Bob, isn't it. Now be a good boy and get me a coffee and meet me outside interview room three.'

Nigel Osgood was on the phone to the police.

'So, you say there's been a break in at your property?'

'That's right, well not exactly a break in. I'd left the front door unlocked.'

'I see, Sir, and is anything actually missing?'

'Well yes of course it is: my laptop and various items from my desk.'

'I see Sir, and you wouldn't have put these items elsewhere, Sir, and forgotten perhaps, like you did to lock the front door?'

'Look I don't appreciate your tone.'

'I'm sorry, Sir, we just have to be sure these days, Sir. Every call has resource implications, you know. I'll give you a crime number for insurance purposes and there'll be someone round to see you as soon as practicably possible.'

'Well, if it's not too much trouble, that would be nice,' said Osgood waspishly.

Jason having worked his way through half the bottle of vodka had fallen asleep on his hotel bed. When he awoke, there was still no sign of Alexei. He felt a bit woozy and switched on the TV. He flicked through the channels to see if he could get onto a non-subscription porn site. With no joy, instead he flicked to see if there were any good films on and settled for Clint Eastwood in *Dirty Harry*. It was one of his favourites; he and his real dad had known practically every line in the film. Harry Callaghan, now there was someone you didn't mess with. He took the hunting knife Alexei had given him and started to polish it vigorously.

Meanwhile a couple of miles down the road, Nigel Osgood was quietly fuming. There was a knock on the door. It was Keith, the local roofer.

'Hello, any chance of more tea, vicar,' said Keith cheekily.

'Oh, come on in Keith. I do apologise for the state of things in here, but I've just been burgled.'

'Oh, bloody hell. Oh sorry, excuse my French. Are you okay? Have they taken anything?'

'Yes, my bloody laptop!' said Osgood.

'Oh, sorry Nigel. It's funny: it doesn't sound quite right when you swear, unnatural like a fish giving birth to a camel. Look, I tell you what, why don't I put some music on and make a nice cup of tea? Have you phoned the police?'

'Yes, and they were about as helpful as a fart in a crowded choir stall!'

'My, this has upset you,' said Keith.

'Here there's a strange geezer just went by in a car,' said Keith peering through the bay window of Osgood's drawing room.

'How do you mean strange?'

'Well, he looked foreign to me.'

'That doesn't make him strange, now does it Keith?'

'Oh yes, sorry, but you know what I mean.'

'We must love all men as our brothers.'

'Oh yes quite right, but he looked like he might be my 'adopted brother.'

'That's quite enough of that now. Where's that tea you were talking about?'

In interview room three, Stella Kingsley wasn't having much luck with the enigmatic Mr Yui. With each question she posed, he would stare straight ahead and respond 'No comment.' When Bob Coombs came in with a question, the same response was given.

'I must ask that my client be given a break from answering your questions,' said Yui's brief, a young woman so perfectly groomed, Stella Kingsley became fascinated by an area of rough and reddened skin on her earlobe. Had some errant lover sucked a little too hard on it last night? She imagined he would be toast by the evening.

'Correct me if I'm wrong, but your client hasn't answered any questions yet,' said an exasperated Kingsley.

'I think we best just charge, Ma'am; he makes Jacques Tati look talkative.

'You will be aware that your time is limited,' said Yui's brief.

'My time is, as you say, limited, so I am going to suspend this interview at 11.53 am. And for the tape, Detective Chief Inspector Kingsley and Detective Sergeant Coombs are leaving the room.'

'Right. My turn to make the coffee,' said Kingsley.

Chloe Whiting sat on a bench a little way out of the town centre and was on the phone to Barry Goldwing.'

'Well, I guess that's another episode of *Family Matters* we will have to shelf, Boss,' she said philosophically.

'No way! I think the story is even bigger now and needs telling,' said Barry.

'But after all that's happened, Sir. Surely the Bishop won't want us, as well as the world's press at his doorstep?'

'Listen Chloe, we've got the inside track here.'

'But...'

'And you've been getting on alright with Osgood, isn't that right?'

'Well, some of the time,' admitted Chloe.

'I want you to stay up there for a couple of nights, till the hoo haa dies down.'

'Okay, but I don't kno...'

'Besides, Osgood could probably do with someone to help him deal with the aftermath of this awful business, poor bugger.'

'But I thought you couldn't stand the guy,' queried Chloe.

'Chloe,' I'm surprised at you! There is something called Christian charity, you know.'

From the outside, most modern, open prisons appear quite similar; to all intents and purposes they could be mistaken for small military bases or in some cases even Further Education colleges. Once inside, however, the atmosphere takes on an altogether different feel. Many of the inmates of the prison Brodie Collins was incarcerated in were coming to the end of their sentences, and although this should have given the place some sense of hope, here it didn't.

The prisoners, mostly bearded, trudged between buildings. There appeared to be few guards, but a great deal of discreet and not so discreet surveillance hardware around. The visitor's suite in the prison was spartan and reminded Nick a bit of a police canteen. Although they were first cousins, there was absolutely no physical resemblance between Nick and Brodie, apart from their being the same gender. Nick was slim and wiry, dark haired with blue eyes and of average height. Brodie was an immense, six foot eight inches tall, with receding lank ginger hair. He had spent a lot of his time in the prison gym and his triangular upper body was on such a scale that he encountered no problems from the other prisoners as a result. All Brodie's demons were in his own head.

'Well, hello, stranger.'

'Long time no see, Brodie.'

'Yes, well you will know where to have found me over the years, won't you.'

'On the home stretch now, though. You'll be out in six months.'

'I can't see me making that to be honest, Nick.'

'What do you mean?'

'I mean I've had it up to here, Nick. Twenty-five years of good, honest thieving and what have I got to show for it?'

'Brodie, tell me something. Have you ever considered going straight?'

'No Nick, it would kill me. Your old dad had it right. He said it was in the blood of us Collins.'

'But the truth is, as you just practically admitted,you're not very good at it.'

'Yes, well that's as may be, but if it weren't for people like me, people like you would be out of a job, lad.' Brodie began to chuckle, but his laughter subsided into quiet sobbing, causing the table between the two men to vibrate. Nick looked at his cousin: his life could have taken a similar course, although he might not have got caught quite so often. He placed his finely chiselled hand on the great, calloused paw-like mitt of his cousin, and they sat in silence for some time.

Chloe Whiting had found herself a nice little B & B in Stamford. The Nookery's proprietors, the Trubshawes, were a retired couple. Norman Trubshawe, mused Chloe, with his handlebar moustache and ramrod straight posture, was possibly ex RAF.

His wife, Barbara, struck Chloe as a pleasant enough woman, in sensible shoes, but perhaps a bit defeated by life. Chloe decided to start with her for trying to find out a little more about how Nigel Osgood was viewed in that part of Lincolnshire.

Chloe started with a little disclosure herself as they cleared away the breakfast things.

'I'm after a bit of advice. I'm up here working and I wonder if you can tell me somewhere interesting to visit in my down time. I work in television and I need some distractions,' said Chloe, amused at her own turn of phrase. At the word 'television' she could see she had the woman's full attention.

'Oh, that must be a fascinating world,' said Mrs Trubshawe wistfully.

'Can be,' said Chloe,' but there's a lot of waiting around.'

'I bet you've a few interesting stories to tell, though, people you've met and so forth.'

Chloe went on to tell Barbara Trubshawe of some of the people they'd had on the *Family Matters* show. She was betting on her host asking who the subject was of the show she was presently working on. She wasn't disappointed.

'Well, I shouldn't really tell you. It's all very hush hush at the moment.'

'I promise it won't go any further,' said Mrs Trubshawe.

'Well, it's Bishop Osgood,' said Chloe smiling sweetly.

It was quite an odd experience for Jenny James to return to Killpeck Farm. She half expected everyone to have upped sticks and left, but most of the pickers were still there. A uniformed officer was standing guard over the polytunnel that housed the cannabis plants. Jenny went over and flashed her accreditation at the young sergeant. Then she made her way over to the van, where Sean and Nat and Wanda were drinking cups of tea and having a smoke.

'Don't worry, Officer, we haven't broken into that tunnel and started on the wacky baccy yet,' said Sean.

'What's it like to be out of deep state policing?' said Nat, lifting his head out of his book on ex-President Chávez of Venezuela.'

'You're not back at work, are you?' said Wanda.

'Yes, yes: no rest for the wicked.'

'So, what can we do for you, Officer?' said Sean.

'Oh, give over, Sean, she's still Jenny, even if she is the filth.'

'Thank you, Wanda, I think,' said Jenny.

'I do need to ask you all some questions though.'

'Will we need our lawyers?' said Nat.

'No, I just need to have a chat about Lomax and the guy we knew as Dave Cheung.'

'Who turned out to be a bit of a twat,' said Wanda, handing Jenny a mug of tea.

'Yes, a few people turned out to be not what we thought,' said Sean pointedly.

'Did any of you have an inkling of what they were up to?'

'If we had, do you think it would have been our moral responsibility to tell you?'

'Oh, take your head from out of your arse, Nat. Lomax was about to rape the lass, if it hadn't been for him being disturbed,' said Wanda, 'and no, WPC whatever your name is, we didn't have a bleedin' scooby! Knew he was a mean old sod, but not that he was in charge of growing enough dope to make the whole country float away in a purple haze.'

'You know I can never thank you enough, Wanda,' said Jenny.

'I knew there was something funny about you and even though you turned out a copper, I reckon us girls must stick together.'

'At this point Ratface, Lomax's enormous dog, came lolloping around the side of the van.

'What will happen to the dog?' said Jenny.

'Well, Lomax won't have him back, whether he gets sent down or not and once you've finished your interrogation, we are all off on the road.'

'Poor old mutt. If it hadn't been for him, we could all have been shot.'

'Okay, look. I'll have him for few days, find out what Lomax wants done with him,' said Jenny, stroking the enormous beast's head.

'I wouldn't think that's in your copper's handbook,' said Wanda.

'Well, we will call it protective custody. I wouldn't think he'd kick up a fuss. Too busy trying to avoid a long prison sentence.'

At this, the great dog slumped to the floor contentedly, put its head down on its paws and broke wind loudly.

'A marriage made in heaven,' said Sean, 'that's for sure.'

The Trubshawes' B & B was cosy and reminded Chloe of her grandparents bungalow in Littlehampton: antimacassars on all the soft seating; various wildlife paintings on the walls, some better than others; one of those novelty fish on a plinth, that wriggled as you went past it, while emitting a rather tinny hornpipe at the same time.

The Trubshawes had both made their opinion of Bishop Osgood clear from the start and it was a pretty low one.

'We've stopped going to his church. Well, you know we get enough of that kind of thing from the BBC,' said Mrs Trubshawe.

'I can't stick the fella. If that's the best the Church of England can come up with, it's dead. I tell you, dead,' her husband said, doling out a glass of his rhubarb wine.'

'Thought you might like to try this, on the house of course,' said Trubshawe.

Chloe didn't have the heart to refuse. The taste made her take a sharp intake of breath.

'Some people have compared it to a French Sauterne,' said Trubshawe.

Chloe wasn't sure she could bear to swallow the remainder of the wine in her mouth. So she just nodded her approval and waited for Trubshawe to leave the room, before spitting the offending liquid into a bowl of potpourri on the sideboard.

'I'm afraid there's not much for young people round here to do,' said Mrs Trubshawe. It all must seem so provincial to you.'

'Oh, Barbara, you don't know what you're talking about. The Battle of Britain were won from bases not ten miles from here.'

'I know dear, but I was talking about night life. You know, pubs and clubs and such like.'

'Well, I'm afraid Stamford isn't as safe as it once was.'

'How do you mean, Mr Trubshawe?'

'Well, I have nothing against them. We had them in the RAF during the war, but there's a limit do you see, the country can't take many more.'

Chloe felt a little queasy at the turn the conversation was taking.'

'Oh, I expect I'll be too busy to go gadding about at night.'

'I don't suppose you're a scrabbler by any chance, are you Miss Whiting?' said Trubshawe, taking an appreciative sip of his home made wine.

It should have been Nick Mycroft's morning off, as he was due in court in the afternoon as a witness in the Rex Priday case, but on returning from his visit to see Brodey in prison, he couldn't resist calling into the station in Lincoln first

'What are you doing here?' said Stella Kingsley.

'I don't know really, Ma'am, just wondering how we were doing with the Hanif case, I suppose.'

'Well, Bob's your man on that one.'

Coombs lent back in his chair. He enjoyed holding forth particularly when he had a bit of a story to tell.

'I went to see them after that fire at their place. They're really quite shook up, but they did open up a bit. Apparently young Hanif was a bit of a dark horse, had a girl on the go and she was not of their faith. They gave me this photo of them together.'

Nick glanced at the picture.

'I know that girl!' he said, stealing Coombs' thunder somewhat.

30
Trials and Tribulations

In Stamford, Bishop Osgood had gently shooed Keith out of the house. He was still fuming about the police's response to his laptop being stolen. He resolved to write an incendiary piece and send it to *The Guardian*; he had an old PC up in one of the attic rooms that he'd once used as an office. So, he decamped up there with a cup of tea. He was about to start up the computer when he came across a letter from his mother. It was one of the last ones she had ever written to him, and it was to congratulate him on his installation as Bishop.

My Darling Nigel,

No mother could be prouder of their son. Your elevation within the church is so richly deserved. Your calling has brought this heathen American gal to appreciate a faith she has never had, when that faith is lived the way that you have lived it. Your father was proud of you but was too tongue tied by his good old British stiff upper lip upbringing ever to tell you so. Now that he has gone, I only hope that you will find happiness with some nice chap. You deserve it my darling. Your sacrifices in this area over the years have not gone unnoticed by me, who will always sing the praises of her darling son.

With very much love,

Ma

For a moment, Nigel had to pull himself together. For the most part, he had accepted his mother's passing far more easily than his father's. It was as if relationships troubled in life, remained troubled in death.

He opened the skylight in the eves of the roof. Perhaps that article for *The Guardian* could wait until tomorrow. He read up on the horses that won the Derby, just in case that came up at the quiz that night.

Dr Perks had taken the stand in the trial of Professor Rex Priday and was being cross examined by the defence counsel.

'So, whereabouts were the body parts you were asked to examine in the house in question?'

'Well, they were kept in various places around the house, but the majority were in a chest freezer in the garage.'

'And were you able to determine whether these... er... items came from one or several individuals?'

'It is my belief that the organs and extremities found were from several individuals.'

'Dr Perks you are an eminent pathologist?'

'Oh, you think so, do you? Thank you very much. Not bad for a boy from Abersoch, then.'

'As I was saying, you are greatly respected in you field. Can you be sure that these tissues, body parts etc., were taken from a living individual or taken from a cadaver, as say a pathologist might do in the line of duty?'

'They were taken from the poor souls, whilst they were still alive.'

'And how, may I ask, do you know that?'

'Flesh and tissue, when dead, take on the qualities almost of wood in places; hence any disconnecting by means of a scalpel or small surgical saw leaves a totally different impression than working on a living, breathing, human being.'

'Thank you, Dr Perks.'

'Oh, you're very welcome.'

On another subject, is it true that you once shared a house with the accused?'

'Yes, that's correct. But it was centuries ago, when we were together at medical school.'

'And have you seen or been in contact with Professor Priday since?'

'No, thank God,' said Idris Perks.

'No further questions, My Lord.'

At Lincoln police station, Coombs had been left to interview Lomax regarding the cannabis farm and false imprisonment of Jenny Jones.

'Right Mr... er... Lomax, where shall we begin with this sorry tale? Perhaps you'd like to tell me how there came to be a cannabis plantation, which when harvested would have an estimated street value of 3 million quid, on land that was supposedly designated for strawberry growing?'

A nervous young man acting as Lomax's brief reminded Lomax that he had a right to remain silent.

'I have no comment,' said Lomax, who appeared to be sweating profusely.

'Okay, moving on, would you like to explain how a young lady known to you as Jenny... came to be tied up on your property against her will?'

'No comment,' said Lomax.

'Okay, Mr Lomax. Shall we just run through the options for you now. It's not looking good, apart from the production on an industrial scale of a prohibited substance, we also have false imprisonment and attempted rape. So, if I were you, I would start giving us your side of the story, starting with your exact relationship with Mr Yui, also known as David Cheung, who apparently was one of your employees.'

'No comment from me. Oh, apart from, could I have some more water?' said Lomax, whose face was turning the colour of dry cured bacon.

31
Witness for the Prosecution

Stella Kingsley arrived at the Chowdry's mansion at just after two.

'Detective Chief Inspector,' said Chowdry looking at her ID card. 'Do come into my humble abode dear lady? I am truly honoured to have someone of your rank, come with regard to such a trifling matter as my car. I'll be the talk of the Close no doubt of it.'

'Thank you, Mr Chowdry, but it's not you I've come to see, but your daughter. Could you call her for me please?'

'Well, I'm afraid...' said Chowdry.

'Mr Chowdry, I need to talk to your daughter about the murder of her boyfriend, Mr Hanif Singh.'

'The girl has no boyfriend, Chief Inspector! Now as you will be aware, I have already made one complaint in regard of police harassment and racial profiling.'

'Mr Chowdry, spare me the histrionics; I've been dealing with bullies like you in and out of the police service for thirty years,' said Kingsley, staring over the top of her glasses. 'I either get to speak to your daughter or I have you taken down to our smelly old, police station, which I promise you, you will not enjoy, in a very noisy squad car, which might cause a bit of a stir in the Close don't you think? Now, where is your daughter?'

'Okay, okay, the truth is I don't know. She has left the family home and we have not seen her for several days,' said a seemingly chastened Chowdry.

'And your wife can confirm this?'

'My wife is in India Inspector, visiting relatives. I am having to fend for myself at the moment.'

'Well, as I was saying, or was I, we are still pursuing a murder enquiry in connection with this young man, holding the hand of your daughter, I believe. This is Hanif Singh. His body was seen being thrown from your car, the one you apparently reported missing. So, Mr Chowdry, I will need a complete breakdown of your movements that night, an address where your wife may be contacted in India and any photographs of your daughter you may have, as I would like to locate her as soon as possible. Meanwhile, I have to inform you, Mr Chowdry, that I consider you a person of interest in this case.'

'I have absolutely no idea who this young person is, Inspector, and it seems to me you are concocting a lot of circumstantial evidence to suit some half-baked theory of yours,' said Chowdry.

'Well, we will see, won't we? I shall be checking out the information and coming back if I am dissatisfied with any of the story you have given.'

'And I, Detective Chief Inspector, will be in contact with your Chief Constable. I have his mobile on my contact list.'

'Do give him my regards, Mr Chowdry,' said Stella, 'and don't forget to email me with all your movements on the night you say your car was stolen.'

It was Nick Mycroft's turn to take the stand in the Betsy Mulligan case.

'You are Detective Inspector Mycroft, of The East Midland Constabulary based in Lincoln?' said the barrister acting for Rex Priday.

'That is correct.'

'And you were one of the investigating officers in the case of the disappearance of Miss Betsy Mulligan in the early part of last year.'

'Yes, that's the correct.'

'Now we understand this was a hugely complex and difficult case.'

'Yes, it was the biggest investigation I've ever been involved in.'

'And part of the investigation involved the discovery of a ring of middle-aged men grooming young girls for sexual purposes.'

'That is partially correct; initially there was an investigation into sexual abuse and Betsy Mulligan's enquiry was quite separate.'

'But is it not true that there came a crossover point?' queried the defence barrister.

'Yes, I suppose so.'

'Now, I know we have to be careful here due to other legal proceedings but perhaps you could give us some background?'

'Well, we became aware that young girls in various small towns were absconding either from foster homes or children's residential services and when they were found, they were reporting their experiences to us.'

'Experiences? Detective Inspector, can you be little more precise?'

'Those older men were luring the girls into inappropriate liaisons and holding parties where girls were being passed around.'

'And?'

'Well, we picked up on it straight away, trying to learn the lessons from previous similar scenarios.'

'So, you were taking the girls' stories seriously?'

'Very seriously indeed,' Nick replied.

'And did you think that Betsy Mulligan was one such girl?'

'Not at the time.'

'So, you didn't have any evidence to link the missing girl to the grooming gang.'

'Not at the beginning, but then we had a breakthrough with the statement of one of the gang.'

'The evidence of one of the paedophiles,' said the defence barrister.

The judge intervened.

'I think counsel has considerably overstepped the mark there, so you, the jury, should ignore that line of questioning. And I think at this point we all need a break in this very distressing case.'

Back in Lincoln, Stella had called a section meeting to discuss the Rimmer Farm deaths.

'Right folks, we now are pretty sure that both deaths are suspicious and probably murder. We also know that Lizzie was murdered in situ. Now, has anybody any information about the identity of the other body found in the slurry pit? What have missing people turned up?'

'Not a lot, Ma'am,' said Jenny. There's no one on the current list that really matches the description in this area.

'Well, we will need to liaise nationally, and possibly internationally. It strikes me that if we can find out who this chappie was, other things may slip into place. One thing is for sure from the path lab reports, he cannot be Lizzie's murderer as he predeceased her.'

'Ma'am, regarding Lizzie Rimmer, and her, um, gentlemen friends, well I popped into The Shirings at lunchtime and the talk was she'd taken up with some foreign bloke quite recently.'

'Right so let's get busy following up on those leads.'

'Oh, and Jenny can you do something with your canine friend. I've had some complaints from the staff canteen about the smell?'

'Well, that's rich,' said Bob. 'I think old rat face smells better than the canteen.'

'I'm sorry, Ma'am, I am desperately trying to rehome him, Ma'am.'

'Good,' said Kingsley. 'Now just an update on the Hanif Singh case. Due to the photograph and the car involved, Chowdry is now very much a person of interest. I need someone to check out this email, detailing his movements on the night Hanif disappeared. I have asked for customs and port authorities to check for anyone in the name of Chowdry travelling to the sub -continent. I think mother and daughter may be travelling together. Meanwhile, I want all Chowdry's employees checked. He has four restaurants and about fifty staff working for him. I want to see if we can find a match for the men that night, who dumped Hanif's body, and I want to talk to our amorous couple about what they did or did not see.'

'Sorry Ma'am, there's a call for you,' said Stella Kingsley's admin assistant. 'It's the Chief Constable.'

Dr Perks was glad to be back in his path lab. He was not a great enthusiast of the courtroom. He'd been working on the injuries on Drac's body, specifically on the tyre tread patterns to his abdomen and he was pleased to have narrowed it down a bit. Unfortunately, there was still no means to identify the man. For now, he was simply known by the number inscribed in indelible marker on the plastic tag tied around his left ankle: C19456.

Jenny James arrived outside Nick Mycroft's little cottage in Shappington that evening with Ratface taking up the whole of the back seat of the car.

'I am sorry to bother you, Sir, but I've got a problem, and I just wondered if you could help?'

'Yes, I think I can see the problem... it's in your car isn't it?'

'Well, the thing is, Sir, there's a "no dogs" clause in my tenancy agreement at the new flat.'

'How about the RSPCA?' Nick suggested.

'Miles away, Sir, and Ratface did save our lives in a way, didn't he?'

'The thing is, Jenny, I've got a cat, Bodkin Adams, and well... he's a bit particular. Likes his own space.'

'Just for a week or two, Sir, please.'

'I suppose you'd better bring him in, but I'm warning you, there may be fireworks.'

'Thanks! I can't tell you how much appreciate it.'

'Do you want a cup of tea, while your here?' asked Nick.

'That sounds good,' said Jenny, manoeuvring Ratface out of her car, in such a way that Nick became mesmerised. He hated himself for it: men ogling women was just demeaning for the woman in his mind.

'Do you want a hand?'

'No, you're alright, Sir. He's just a big soft lump,' said Sally backing out of the car, followed by a somewhat bemused looking Ratface.

32
Picking Teams

The church hall in Stamford had been set out already for the quiz, with four tables on either side of the room. Two tables were at the top of the hall, one for the quizmaster, the other for the raffle prizes. There would be five rounds plus a pictures round and there was a £5.00 per team entrance fee. A couple of people had already arrived eager to spy out the opposition. It was usually mostly the same faces who came to these occasions. There would be a table full of teachers, a group from the local bowls club, two or three family teams and then usually a group of single men, who did the circuits of the country and took the whole thing extremely seriously.

Keith had agreed to pick Nigel up on his way through with Penny, his wife, and their daughter, Melanie. This plus Chloe and Callum would be their team for the night. They were quietly determined, having come so close to winning last year's quiz. Chloe and Callum were yet to arrive.

'Any news about your laptop, Nigel?'

'No, no. I'm afraid that's it. I won't see that again and I'm certainly not staying in, just on the off chance that our boys in blue bother to pay a visit.'

'I'm so sorry. If there's any way we can help, please let us know,' said Penny.

'Oh, Keith has been marvellous. I'm fine really. Worse things happen at sea and all that.'

Callum had agreed to pick Chloe up from the Trubshawes' B & B.

'Oh, hello! You look like the cat that got the cream. Looks like you were getting more bed than breakfast, if I'm not mistaken,' Callum observed as she got in his car.

'Oh, don't be disgusting, Callum. Remember your vocation!'

'Oh that, well... it's all kaput!'

'How come?'

'Well, it turns out Dorcas' conditions...'

'Dorcas?'

That was the surrogate's name, Dorcas Pole.'

'Chloe suppressed a giggle.'

'Didn't just involve me going to theological college...'

'Oh, what else?' said Chloe.

'Oliver and I would then have to come and live in her religious community, 'The Wondrous Company,' where I would be enthroned as their spiritual adviser, The Gerontian Prelate.'

'I was up for it,' but Oliver said he didn't like the mistletoe green of the robes they wore in the community.'

Chloe started to giggle. She was about to tell him of the tall, dark stranger with impeccable manners, who she had found so irresistible the previous night. Why, the lord only knew her track record with one-night stands was not a good one, as Callum would no doubt remind her, but then she noticed the tears rolling down Callum's cheek.

When they arrived, the hall was filling up: people were at the bar buying drinks, while others were putting their hands up as if they were still at school, trying to attract the attention of the quiz master to request pens and paper. In one corner was a large, rather portly character with mutton chop whiskers, a broad striped red and white shirt and a pair of gold half-rimmed spectacles dangling from a cord around his neck.

'Right, you horrible lot, the quiz will start in ten minutes' time, whereupon I will be moving amongst you with the picture round.'

'Oh, I'm useless at pictures; hardly recognise my own face when I get up in the morning,' said Nigel.

'Don't worry, our Melanie is shit hot. She'll get them all. Oh, sorry about the language there. I sometimes forget you're a man of the cloth.'

'Oh, please don't give it another thought. Remember, I'm retired now and between you and me, I've seen a lot of shit in my time,' Osgood giggled. 'Now, let me buy you a drink for giving me a lift.'

In Shappington, Nick had just gone to put the kettle on for a refill of Jenny's tea, when he found himself back in that terrible cellar, in the house that Priday claimed he hadn't been in for ten years or more, that cellar, with its sickly-sweet smell, its bars on the skylight and... the bags everywhere... bags and small glass specimen jars. The panic attacks Nick had had ever since were gradually getting worse, and this one was particularly bad.

'Sir, are you okay?' said Jenny alarmed to see the colour drain from Mycroft's face.

He began to shake and sweat. He attempted to breath out and nothing happened when he breathed in. He started coughing.

Sir... Nick... can I do anything? Get you some help?'

'No, I'll be fine. Would you just stay a little while longer? It will pass.'

33
Answering the Call

Jason Wilkes strapped the small axe and the hunting knife to his belt and put on his parka coat, the one with the fur lined collar. He always felt safer when he was wearing this. There had still been no news from Alexei. Still, if he had been taken, it was up to him now. There was no going back; there was really nothing to go back for, he thought to himself, as he checked out of the hotel and set off to walk into the town centre.

Chloe and Callum had got to Stamford early, mostly out of nerves. They both remained a little scared of Osgood. So, they had popped into a local and had a couple of drinks before arriving at the village hall.

'So, what gives?' said Chloe, anxious to find out why Callum had been so upset over the whole Dorcas and surrogacy affair.

'Oh, take no notice of me. Tell me more about your night of passion,' said Callum.

'Not until you tell me what's wrong.'

'Oh... I think Oliver wants to call it a day with me.'

'What? Why?' queried Chloe.

'This baby business. He says he's beginning to feel we want different things out of life.'

'And what do you think?' Chloe replied.

'I don't know, Chlo. God alone knows: speak of the devil,' said Callum.

'Oh, here are my two friends from the telly world,' said Osgood as the two walked into the village hall, 'Callum, Chloe, this is Keith.'

'Right, round one, history. Question one: which two wives of Henry the eighth were beheaded?'

Nigel and his team were busy conferring, so Osgood didn't see the elegant young man, dressed expensively (for the country) ask a group at the back of the hall if he could join their team. At first, they didn't seem eager. But when he said, 'It was Ann Boleyn and Catherine Howard, they changed their tune and introductions were made.'

'Question two, on history: who was the only English pope?' asked the quizmaster.

Chloe whispered, 'I know, Nicholas Shakespeare.'

Nigel corrected her, 'I think you'll find that it's Brakespeare.'

In Shappington, Jenny had found a bottle of vodka and poured Nick a large drink.

'Drink this. It might help.'

'Thank you. Sometimes it does.'

'How long have you been having these attacks, Sir?'

'Over a year now, and it's Nick please. We are not at work remember.'

'Have you asked for counselling?'

'No.'

'Do you mind me asking why not?'

'Jenny, you don't know much about me, do you?'

'I know you're very good at your job; that's what I know.'

'Well, between you and me, I'm a bit of a cause célèbre in the force, you see.'

'I don't get it. In what way?'

'Well, I have family connections.'

'So what if you got a leg up? You're a bloody good cop.'

'No, not those kinds of connections.'

'How do you mean?'

'A lot of my family were, or are career crims, with records as long as your arm.'

'And what's that got to do with anything?'

'Don't you see Jenny, it means I always feel like I have to prove myself.'

'Well, that's crazy.'

'It might be crazy to you, but I live with it every day.'

'You need some time off. After all, you only lost your mother a few weeks ago and that pervert Priday's case, it's really enough to drive anyone do- lally.'

'Look, I will be fine. I've kept you long enough. You need to get home, get some rest. It's only going to get busier at work.'

'Okay, but don't hesitate... if you want to talk, I'm here, and if you don't think it's appropriate with me being a junior rank, that's fine too.'

'Thanks Jenny. You've been great and anyway I've got Ratface to talk to now,' said Mycroft, feeling he had unburdened his soul a little too freely with Jenny, while knowing his feelings towards her were deepening. What had he to offer her, he wondered. The whole Priday affair was gradually turning him into a basket case. A beautiful young woman like Jenny deserved better.

The quiz at Stamford had reached the halfway stage and The Right Reverend Osgood's team were leading the teacher's table by a point. Keith had just gone to the bar, when Nigel thought he recognised the young man on the table at the back as the 'spook' from the security forces, who had barged into his house a few days earlier. He was just about to go over and challenge him, when there was a commotion at the door of the village hall.

Jason took a moment to identify Osgood, but once he had, the rest of the vodka which he'd been sipping on the way in kicked in. He unzipped his parka and pulled the knife from his belt.

'For the New Glory and death to commies!' Jason cried out. He got to within a couple of yards of Osgood before the first bullet hit him. Riddell jumped over his team's table and fired again. Jason seemed for a second to register surprise and then collapsed in a pool of his own blood. Many of the team members, including Chloe and Callum, were cowering under tables or had thrown themselves to the floor.

Osgood got up from his chair and knelt, cradling Jason's head in his arms. He made the sign of the cross on what was left of Wilkes' forehead.

34
Higher Powers

'You are to offer support, Stella, if requested of course, but this is now a security matter, for the anti-terrorist boys,' said the Chief Constable.'

'But Sir?'

'But Sir, nothing DCI Kingsley. The intelligence services were acting on information received, suggesting that Bishop Osgood was a target.'

'Sir, this is an extremely serious incident on my patch. A man has been killed, and a town traumatised.'

'That's precisely why it is not in our hands now. It appears the man making the attack was doing so for these lunatics, Old Glory.'

'I think you mean, New Glory, Sir,' corrected Kingsley.

'Quite. Anyway, as I say, it's over to our friends in the security forces now.'

'But surely the Independent Police Complaint's Commission...'

'No, it appears not, as the man who shot the assailant was not a serving officer.'

'Then it is a police matter? Discharging a firearm in a public place! What about gold command and all that?'

'Stella, you're not listening. The police service was not directly involved. You just need to concentrate on what you have on your plate. By the way, I had that chap Chowdry on the phone again last night. You've really rattled his cage. I hope you had a good reason. And that double murder, if that's what it was, we need progress on that Stella.'

'Yes Sir.'

'It never rains but it pours eh. Got to go now. Need to brief the Home Secretary.'

'Very good, Sir. Have a nice rest of your day.'

'Remember, Stella, keep out of this. It's going to be in all the papers tomorrow and I don't want East Midland Force drawn into the political mire.'

Jenny had received a call from Wanda, asking her to meet, saying she needed to talk to her away from the others, so Jenny had agreed to meet her at The Shirings for a drink.

'Hi! I thought you'd be long gone by now,' said Jenny walking into the back bar of the pub.

'Well, you said I might be needed as a witness, so I wanted to give you a forwarding address. I'm going back to County Cork to be with Sean.'

'Well, you could've just messaged me.'

'I know, but I wanted to talk to you. I read about the lass being murdered up at that farm not far from here.'

'And?'

'Well, you see when you're picking, you come across all sorts, and you learn not to ask too many questions.'

'Yes, I get you,' said Jenny.

'You, for instance. I knew you were a wrong un from the start.'

'Oh, thanks very much.'

'No, what I mean is, I'd sussed you weren't quite what you made out you were,' explained Wanda.

'So, is Lizzie Rimmer's murder relevant to what you are saying?' asked Jenny.

'Well, it was her that Alexei or whatever his name was, was seeing a while back.'

'The dishy Russian looking one?' queried Jenny.

'There were a couple of east Europeans. One picker left a couple of days before you came... you know the one Lomax referred to as "the bloody foreigner."'

'Lomax seemed to think everyone was a bloody foreigner,' said Jenny.

'Except for you, that is. He had a soft spot for you, you know, as we were to find out.'

'So, what happened?'

'Several people all got out the same time, but it's that Alexei you should try and find, I reckon.'

'Well, do you think he could be the other body?'

'Oh god, I couldn't say love. All I know was he were shacked up there for a while, giving her a right good seeing to by all accounts. Well, that's what Sean says.'

'Well look, I need to talk to Sean.'

'Bit late love: he's already in Ireland preparing the family for my arrival.'

'Shit,' said Jenny.

'Well, I know I'm a bit of a handful but...'

'No, not you, it's just... listen I need to go, but can you say to Nat I need to talk to him.'

'Oh, he's buggered off as well. Gone to save the world, I expect,' said Wanda.

Stella Kingsley was bent over the printer in her office tugging at a piece of paper jammed tightly in the machine and swearing under her breath.

'Well, Bob, it better be good news you're bringing me.'

'Sorry Ma'am. Two women with the surname Chowdry booked on a flight to Mumbai yesterday.'

'Oh great! Right, I've got this list now. I want you to go and lean on these. One of Chowdry's lackies must know something.'

'What am I supposed to lean on them with, Ma'am?'

'Oh, I don't know, tax evasion, illegal entry into this country, just get me something.'

'Are you sure that's acceptable procedure, Ma'am?' said Coombs.

'No Bob, I'm not sure of anything anymore. All I know is that one way or not, Chowdry is up to his neck in that poor lad's murder,' said Kingsley.

'Where the hell's Nick?' she queried.

'He's gone over to the path lab to see Dr Perks. Perks thinks he might have something for us on the Rimmer Farm case.'

'Thank god for that,' said Kingsley, closing the window of her office to keep the world and torrential rain at bay.

Idris Perks greeted Mycroft as he arrived at the path lab.

'Ah, Nicholas, come on: it's my break. You can take me over to one of those coffee shops in town, preferably one that doesn't make an infernal noise every time you make an order. It's like being in a shipyard not a café,' said Perks, taking his lab coat off. They walked out and down towards a row of shops and an old-fashioned café, with Formica tables, squeezy ketchup bottles, and the smell of frying onions.

'You wouldn't remember Lyon's Corner Houses, would you?'

'No, I'm afraid not.'

'Well, I can only just remember them. They were nothing like this, but at least it's quiet enough to chat. It was all Milk bars and juke boxes in my day, of course.'

'If you don't mind me saying, it must be odd for you all this Priday business, you having known him all those years ago.'

'He was an odd chap, even then, but we had no idea we were sharing kebabs with a raving psychopath.'

'Sorry I didn't mean to pry,' said Nick. 'So how are things with the present enquiry.'

'Well, I think we are making a bit of progress on your unknown male and those tyre marks decorating his chest and abdomen. They're consistent with tyres of a small truck or multi-purpose vehicle, you know a pickup truck. Also, we've found traces which suggest he or A N other was handling a firearm, namely a shotgun.'

'Oh, that's certainly of interest.'

'We'll keep going and if you can find us a weapon, we might be able to say if it was a match.'

'Yes, but the question is, what match? Neither our unidentified friend, nor Lizzie were killed with a shotgun.'

35
Currying Favour

It was Jenny, who'd suggested they got together to discuss further what to do about Ratface in the future. They'd opted for a pub, one of those chains that goes out of its way to look different, but actually looks exactly the same as all the others with cartwheels, malt shovels and books no one thought of reading, even when they were first published, bought in bulk from a house clearance sale. The Chief Constable was on the television, standing outside the police headquarters in the rain.

'Due to events in Stamford, specialist counsellors and police liaison officers will be available for all those affected. An independent investigation into the use of lethal force is ongoing. We would like to reassure members of the general public that there is minimal risk to them, as this appears to have been a targeted attack.'

'He speaks well, doesn't he?' said Jenny.

'Yes, I suppose he does, but they all get media training these days, you know, residential courses with old hacks from the BBC. Nice little earner for them,' observed Nick.

'That'll be you in twenty years' time,' said Jenny.

'More likely to be you, I think. You're a good cop, Jenny. You are good on detail and you're fearless.'

One drink had turned into several. Nick's awkwardness while in Jenny's company, began to dissipate, and the conversation flowed. In Jenny, he found someone totally non-judgemental. He was tired of having to defend himself at every turn and here at last was someone who accepted him for who he was.

They shared a taxi back to Nick's cottage in Shappington, both aware of where the evening was leading. Nick, though, was still feeling uncomfortable. This situation could affect both of their careers but Jenny seemed to be so certain and he for once was happy to go with the flow.

'So, how's Ratface getting on with Bodkin Adams?'

'Well, they're ignoring each other studiously.'

'So can you keep him a bit longer?'

'Well, I suppose, but he needs someone to exercise him.'

'I don't mind sharing that with you, walking him I mean.'

'Well, I don't kn...'

'That's settled then. We will co-parent Ratface.' Jenny leant forward and kissed Nick gently on the lips. 'And this is to seal the deal, Sir,' she said, gently unbuttoning Mycroft's shirt.

In Leicester, at The Blue Maharajah, Bob Coombs was treating himself to an Indian. He'd spent most of the day interviewing Chowdry's staff, but seemed to be getting nowhere fast, so he was consoling himself with a Chicken Biryani and a couple of bottles of Tiger. He'd even started some banter with a group of women on a hen night. His self-esteem was so low these days that he believed he only had a chance with a woman when she was absolutely sloshed, and it so happened that one of the group was completely trolleyed.

'Why don't you come and join us? You're better looking than this load of old bags,' said the woman, who was not unattractive and in her low-cut shiny top was leaving little to the imagination as she leant forward tipsily on her chair.

Bob was in the process of considering her offer, when a young man came into start his shift. He was wearing a football shirt with a picture of Riyad Mahrez on it.

Bob knew he'd seen it before on the dogging couple's tape. In his excitement, he got up and tipped his Biryani all over himself.

'Hey young man I'd like...' At this, the man took flight.

Bob was carrying quite a few more pounds than when he first joined the force and his pursuit seemed doomed for failure, until his quarry landed badly, having climbed over the wall of a property adjoining The Blue Maharajah. Bob found a dilapidated door which, when he put his shoulder to it, gave way and there was his fugitive in a crumpled heap at his feet.

'Shit, shit,' screeched the man.

'I'll call for an ambulance,' said Bob. 'But first, perhaps we could have a little chat.'

In Stamford, the whole town was full of film crews from many different parts of the world. The local hotels were doing a roaring trade, putting up all the journalists from the media circus. Armed officers patrolled outside Nigel Osgood's house. Osgood himself was not there. He'd been taken to hospital as a precaution, having had some breathing difficulties after the events of the previous day. Riddell was at his bedside.

'I suppose I should thank you,' said Osgood.

'That's not necessary. I was doing my job, Sir, that's all.'

'You people probably think this business makes us quits, but I'm telling you…' said Osgood, who appeared to be only semi-conscious

'It would be best if you rested, Your Grace.'

'Shouldn't you be on gardening leave or something. After all, you did kill that poor young man,' said Osgood, much more with it, and giving Riddell a hard stare.

'You mean the chap who wanted to saw your head off,' responded Riddell.

'Well, aren't there any procedures to be gone through, when people die like that?'

'Yes Sir. There will be an inquiry, but for now I am still assigned to keep you safe and that is what I aim to do.'

'But they're hardly likely to strike again, surely,' said Osgood.

'Until we can establish what's really gone on here, you will be receiving twenty-four-hour security from us.'

'So, you're saying that young man is not the only person trying to bump me off?'

'What I'm saying, Sir, is that you need to rest and leave everything else to us.'

36
A Question of Identity

DCI Kingsley, frustrated by being excluded from what had gone on elsewhere on her patch in the last day or so, was continuing to interview Clive Lomax about his involvement with the cannabis factory and the false imprisonment of Jenny James, but was making very little headway. She was taking a break vaping for all she was worth at the back of the station, when she saw Nick and Jenny arrive for their shift, deep in conversation.

'Well you two, what time do you call this? What have you been up to? You look as thick as thieves! Sorry Nick, that was a bit clumsily put.'

'Sorry Ma'am; we were dog...' said Nick. his face colouring with embarrassment. Stella Kingsley could have this effect on him, and he couldn't explain why. It wasn't as if he'd led a particularly sheltered life, but she could make him feel like the junior chorister in some provincial cathedral choir.

'I don't really think I wish to know,' said Kingsley, in mock horror. Just get up to the briefing room and get ready to impress me with the progress being made.'

'Absolutely! Will do, Ma'am,' said Nick and Jenny almost in unison.

The section was assembled around the white board in the briefing room.

'Okay, let's deal with the deaths at the Rimmer Farm first,' said Stella Kingsley. 'Where are we with this, Nick?'

'Well, there are a couple of things, Ma'am. Firstly, Dr Perks has found gun powder traces in the fingernails of the body found in the slurry pit,' said Mycroft.

'So, he had been handling a gun, but no gun was found on the premises.'

'That's correct, Ma'am.'

'What else have we got?'

'Dr Perks has also narrowed down the tyres to the type used by off-road vehicles pickup trucks, that kind of thing, so we know he wasn't hit by a saloon car,' Nick explained.

'And we know the guy in the pit predeceased Lizzie Rimmer,' said Kingsley.

'The other thing, Ma'am, is after I had a little chat with Wanda, we now know that there is a link between Killpeck Farm and Lizzie Rimmer. She was having a fling with some bloke called Alexei, who had been a picker at Killpeck,' said Jenny.

'Who you met?' queried Kingsley.

'Yes Ma'am, briefly,' said Jenny.

'So, why aren't you down the path lab to see if you can ID him?'

'I'm going there this morning, Ma'am.'

'Look, I'm sorry, but we need to be out there being – as the Chief Constable would say – proactive.'

'Ma'am, it's the first opportunity they've had for me to have a viewing.'

'Okay, point taken.'

'So, apart from Wanda, what about the other pickers?'

'They've all hopped it, Ma'am.'

'Great! So where does that leave us?'

'Both people killed at Lizzie Rimmer's by a jealous suitor from Killpeck Farm, Ma'am?' said Bob, trying to earn some brownie points.

'Brilliant! So he comes across them 'at it,' drags the bloke out into the yard, runs over him, dumps him in the shit, then comes back several days later and bumps her off as well. A somewhat prolonged and unlikely crime of passion, I think Bob.'

'Well, we haven't got anything else at the minute, Ma'am, have we?'

'Yes Bob. I think I've got a migraine coming on. Jenny, report directly after you've met with Dr Perks. Now Bob, you have a person of interest in the Hanif Singh case, I hear?'

'Well hopefully Ma'am. His name is Shafiq. He's in hospital at the minute having his broken ankle set.'

'But he matches a description of the man in the background of our couple's romcom; is that right?'

'Well, it's his t-shirt, Ma'am, more than anything. I recognised him when I saw him in the restaurant, me being a Leicester City fan.'

'So, he's now singing like a canary?' said Stella, referencing her own support for Norwich City.

'Not exactly, Ma'am. All he's said at the minute is mumbling about being no killer, but he's clearly very frightened of Chowdry, more afraid of him than the law Ma'am, by all accounts. He's said that if he didn't help, he was told he'd be the next.'

'Right, I want Chowdry brought in and put under caution.'

'But Ma'am, Mr Chowdry's alibi for that night is watertight. He was at the Midland's Curry House of the Year Awards in Birmingham. He's got over a hundred people vouching for him.'

'I don't care. I'll do him for conspiracy, if we can't get him for anything else.'

'What are we going to do about the farm manager bloke from Killpeck Farm, Ma'am?' asked Nick.

'Charge them with the cannabis and charge Yui or whatever his name is with attempted murder. The sexual assault charge against Lomax: hang fire on that. I want him to sweat a bit more. Mr Yui wouldn't know how to sweat in a Turkish bath... Now listen up, I'm sorry if I was a bit brusque this morning, but all this business in Stamford has got to me a bit. I don't like it when these fly boys from intelligence come like flipping Curt Eastwood, riding rough shod over my inquiry.'

'I think you mean Clint, Ma'am,' said Nick.

'Yes well, whatever,' said Kingsley.

The papers were full of events at Stamford:

Right wing terror cell attempts to assassinate Red Bishop. Man shot dead at the scene purported to have links with Knights of the New Glory, named as Jason Wilkes. Manhunt underway for other members of the cell.

Terry Tomms had arrived at the front desk of Lincoln police station.

'My name is Tomms. I thought you'd be coming to arrest me, so I thought I'd save you the trouble.'

Dick Hedges, the desk sergeant, who had seen most things, replied.

'And what would we be charging you with, Sir?'

'You'll no doubt think of something,' Tomms replied.

'If you just bear with me, Sir,' said Hedges. 'I'll ring upstairs and get someone to come and see you.'

'Tell them, Tomms, Knight Commander of the New Glory has voluntarily handed himself in.'

'Right, you are, Sir, if you'll just take a seat,' said an unfazed Hedges.

At that moment, Clive Latimer and his girlfriend walked in.

'Look, we need to see somebody in charge,' said Latimer. 'It's about our property.'

'Have you had a break in, Sir?'

'No, it's a piece of our property that you police have, and it's imperative we have it back,' said the girl.

'Well, I will have to check. Was it a piece of property in connection with an enquiry?'

'Apparently so. The officer dealing with it was a DI Mycroft.'

'Right you are.'

'And you are?'

'Clive Latimer.'

'And you Madam?'

'A friend,' said the young woman.

Jenny James arrived at the path lab for her viewing appointment.

'Ah yes, come in. Jenny isn't it?' said Dr Perks. 'Well, you'll be glad to know our friend is a little bit more presentable than he was when we pulled him out of the shit. I understand you think you might know who he is?'

'Well, that is a possibility,' said Jenny.

'What I would say is, after a few days in the fridge, people do look different, so take your time.'

'Thank you, Dr Perks, I will.'

'I remember my first corpse. It was my mother's mother. Picture of health she was. Always a very sickly woman in life, mind you.'

Perks removed the sheet from the face of the cadaver.

'Oh well there goes that theory,' said Jenny.

'Didn't recognise him then?'

'No 'fraid not.'

'Well, back you go, boy. You've had your outing for the day,' said Perks, pushing the trolley on which Drac's body lay back into the cold storage facility.

The phone call came around lunchtime.

'Hello, Nick. It's me, Brodie.'

'Hi Brodie.'

'Well, I'm ringing about what happened in Stamford, it being your neck of the woods. I thought you might be interested.'

'Well Brodie, the security forces are leading on that, so we've been tiptoeing around the whole thing a bit.'

'Well, the thing is, I knew that bloke Jason. He did a stretch with me way back.'

'Oh?'

'The thing is, I don't want to talk about it over the phone, and I certainly don't want to talk to any of your lot, apart from you that is.'

'Okay. If I can clear it with my boss, I'll be down,' said Nick.

Sergeant Hedges popped his head round the office door.

'Sorry Sir, but I've got his Lordship, Terry Tomms, downstairs wanting someone to arrest him.'

'What for?' said Nick.

'Lord knows what. And also... er... I've also got a stroppy couple complaining that we've got their property. The girl has been in, I think, if memory serves me right. They were the ones filming themselves "at it" in the car. I suggested that to my missus once, but she wasn't having any of it as she didn't know where we'd put the film crew. We've got a Skoda you see, Sir.'

'Yes, thank you, Sergeant Hedges, that will be all.' Stella Kingsley's mood had not markedly improved; in fact, she'd just had news that had left her flabbergasted. The judge had ordered a retrial of the Rex Priday case. Would poor Betsy Mulligan ever get justice, she wondered. Some newspaper had leaked information that might prejudice the jury's verdict. It was a slap in the face for all her section.

'I've just heard the news about Priday, Ma'am,' said Nick. 'What the hell is going on?'

'God knows, Nick. The whole thing was in the balance anyway over Priday maintaining he didn't have a key to the property.'

'But he owned it, for Christ's sake!' said Nick, for once letting his emotions get the better of him.

'He had properties all over the place: London, South of France, Scotland, Jamaica. Remember, he was rolling in money.'

'So, what did the judge honestly think? That it was possible somebody broke into his house in Leicester and used it as a human abattoir?'

'You're not listening, Nick, it's a retrial on the basis of the bloody press. Apparently they'd written a piece on Priday's previous unhealthy interest in taxidermy.'

'Well, is there anything we could've missed, Ma'am. If it comes to a retrial... I mean... those poor girls. If he somehow gets off, I'll never get a decent night's sleep again.

'Nick, we all worked for a whole year to get the thing to court. Everything was gone over with a fine-tooth comb. Anyway, we've got to concentrate on what's going on now.'

Jenny James walked into the briefing room.

'How did you get on, Jenny?'

'I'm sorry, Ma'am, the chap on the slab isn't the guy from Killpeck, that I remember.'

'Well, so that means we are no further forward.'

'I wouldn't say so, Ma'am. I've come up with something,' said Coombs.

'Okay, let's have it then, Bob.'

'Well Ma'am, this chap up in Stamford what tried to kill the priest?'

'Yes, and who was on the register of New Glory?' said Kingsley.

'Well Ma'am, he was on probation.'

'Yes, well we knew he'd been inside.'

'Well, being on probation, he had to give a present address.'

'And?'

'Guess where it was, Ma'am?'

'I'm not in the business of twenty questions, Bob.'

'Killpeck Farm, Ma'am,' said Coombs.

37
Unfinished Business

For Alexei Shalikov, returning to Moscow not having accomplished what he'd been very well paid to do was an unpalatable prospect. He had made the mistake of underestimating British Intelligence and had overestimated the ability of the Wilkes boy to carry out the task. He had to take responsibility a little himself, of course. For some reason, having to kill the Rimmer woman had affected him more than any of the other lives he had taken, and for two nights he had drunk himself unconscious on vodka, bedding down in a ruined barn behind Nipton Wood for two days.

Once he had sobered up, he considered his options, which were now limited. He had intended to catch a flight home as soon as he'd heard the old clergyman was dead, but he knew what he would be going home to, Markovich, who was known for his ruthless approach both in business and family matters. So, the question Alexei faced was how he might finish the job that Wilkes had botched. He had decided while he considered the matter to go upmarket. He'd hired a top of the range saloon car, booked into an exclusive spa hotel just near Rutland water and had swopped his strawberry pickers t-shirt for an expensive Armani suit. He would need a few days for the fuss to die down, if he were to proceed, so he had decided to enjoy himself. The woman at the table opposite him was not his usual type. She was blonde and petite, with a retrousse nose, but she had an electric smile. She was working on her laptop while waiting for her meal. She glanced up occasionally from her screen, her gaze resting on Alexei in such a way as to make him think he might not be lonely, at least for that night.

'Ma'am, can I have a word?' said Nick, gently tapping and opening the door to Stella Kingsley's office.

'Yes, Nick.'

'Well, the thing is, Ma'am,' I may be able to get a bit more info on this Jason Wilkes character.'

'How come?'

'Well, I have a cousin, who reckons he knew him, Ma'am.'

'Well, we'd better have a word with the intelligence boys. Can he come and have a chat, give 'em some background, that kind of thing?'

'The thing is, Ma'am, he can't exactly come and see anyone and he won't talk to the security forces.'

'Oh, right you are. So let me take a wild guess; he's in one of Her Majesty's hotels?'

'Yes, Ma'am, and he will only really talk with me.'

'Okay, here's what we will do. You go down, see what he's got, but keep it under your hat. Don't tell anyone even in the station where you are going.'

'But we are pursuing are own enquiries, Ma'am, into what went on at Killpeck?'

'It won't be viewed like that, Nick, and we both know it. Meanwhile, Bob can lean on that farm manager, Lomax, while I go and talk to my favourite person, Mr Chowdry, and see what he has to say for himself.'

'Right Ma'am.'

'Oh and Nick, get Jenny to talk to the doggy couple.'

'I think you mean "dogging" Ma'am,' said Nick.

'Whatever,' Stella Kingsley replied.

Nigel Osgood had been released from hospital and was glad to be back at home in Stamford. Penny and Keith were fussing around in the kitchen downstairs, while Riddell sent emails on his phone. A uniformed, armed response officer stood outside the property, with a small machine gun slung round his neck, as a musical instrument might be.

Osgood had been out in the garden, as it was the only quiet place he could find to pray.

'You must tell us when you leave the house, Your Grace,' said Riddell.

'Have you become my brother's keeper, young man?' said Osgood.

'If you want to put it that way.'

'You don't think they'll try again, do you?' said Keith.

'We don't know, but we think he might have been under instructions.'

'Bloody fascists!' said Keith.

'Well, I tell you one thing, I'm not living like this for long.'

'You might not live for long without me here,' said Riddell.

'What about the young man at the door with that tommy gun? Couldn't we at least do away with him?'

'It's standard procedure. The local community needs re-assurance.'

'Are you a church goer Mr Riddell?'

'I was but I lapsed, Bishop, and now I never go in no church.'

'Well, you might have to unlapse. I'm taking a service on Sunday, so if you insist on following me, you better brush up on your hymn singing.'

Stella Kingsley went into the interview room, coffee in hand.

'Mr Chowdry, you know why you are here. You have been arrested on suspicion of conspiracy to murder.'

'Yes Madam, I do, and while I'm in here, the real culprits are still running around the East Midlands. I understand you've had two further murders and a Reverend gentleman almost hacked to death. Surely you should be paying attention to real criminals killing innocent people. Why, I've not only had my car recently stolen, but also I found out this morning my smart phone is missing. And all you do is come up with some cock and bull story, making me out to be some curry house godfather. It's preposterous, I tell you.'

The more wound up Chowdry became the better, as far as Stella was concerned, although she was aware this was mostly an act.

'No, Mr Chowdry. To my eye, I'm afraid Marvin Brando is much better looking than you. Now, I have a man in custody, who we can prove was in your car and helped dispose of Hanif Singh's body – Stella used an old tactic of massaging the truth just a little – who seems absolutely terrified of you. Can you tell me why that might be?'

'I have no idea, Detective Chief Inspector;. My staff are everything to me. Without them, I have no business.'

'I put it to you that you found out your daughter was in a relationship with a Sikh boy from a humble background and that he would not break it off, even when you threatened him, so you decided to kill him.'

'And all you have is some photograph? I tell you, Inspector, it sounds like this may be some disgruntled ex-employee of mine trying to exact some kind of revenge.'

'The photograph was given to us by Hanif's parents.'

'You will be aware that on that night, my car was stolen. I was at a prestige event in Birmingham.'

'Yes, I am aware of that.'

'And at that occasion, we were honoured by the presence of your Chief Constable.'

Nick arrived at the prison where Brodie Collins had been held just as the ambulance left. He was shown straight to the governor's office. Was it him or were prison governors getting younger every day? This one looked about twenty-five; he was a sparsely built man with a fashionable beard and expensive looking glasses.

'I'm so sorry you have arrived to such awful news. Brodie Collins was really, I like to think, one of our model prisoners. He had begun to turn his life around, but one really never knows what goes on in people's heads. Can we get you a cup of tea?'

'No, thank you,' said Nick. The droning, faux politeness of the young man was giving him a headache.

'May I ask, if it's not too intrusive, how you and Mr Collins were connected.'

'We were cousins. May I ask how the hell this could have been allowed to happen?' said Nick. He could feel the anger boiling up inside of him.

'Well, of course we will mount a full inquiry.'

'I should bloody well hope so,' said Mycroft.

'I'm sorry, but by its very nature, this prison offers containment but not twenty-four hour a day supervision, Mr...?'

'Detective Inspector Mycroft of the East Midland's police,' said Nick, barely containing his rage.

'You wouldn't be Nick, by any chance would you?'

'That's what Brodie would have known me as, yes.'

'Well, we think this letter he left in his room must be for you.'

'May I have it, then?'

'Well, I'm afraid that breaks every kind of protocol. This death will, of course, have to be referred to the coroner.'

'Look, I'm not here on family business, but we are supporting the security forces in events that occurred in Stamford, which may threaten national security. I believe my cousin had information in regard to an assailant and would ask strongly for your co-operation in this matter.'

'Well, if that's the case, I suppose I could let you have a copy, but I will need to keep the original here. Sorry if that sounds a bit jobsworthy.'

Nick looked at the young man and wondered how long he'd been in his post. He gave him a year before burn-out set in.'

'Have you spoken to Brodie's father yet?' he asked.

The man made a photocopy of the letter and handed it to Nick.

'Well, no. That, of course, was going to be our next task.'

'I'll save you a job then,' said Nick walking out of the governor's office.

38
Final Affairs

'So, if we can go over events that night in detail and see whether you are able to recall exactly what you witnessed?' said Jenny James.

Clive Latimer and his girlfriend, Sadie, looked horrified at this.

'We only came in for the tape,' said Clive.

'In particular, the man in the t-shirt with the image of a face on it,' Jenny continued. Would you be able to confirm his identity? If I were to show you photograph, could you match them as being the same individual?'

'You've caught them, then.'

'Well, let's just say he's one of a number of persons of interest to us,' said Jenny, keeping things vague.

She showed them a picture of the man Bob Coombs had apprehended at The Blue Maharajah.

'Yes, well, I really couldn't say,' said Clive. 'It's possible.'

'How about you, Sadie?'

'I wouldn't like to say. It was dark you know.'

'Well, I'm afraid we will have to hold on to the tape while we make further enquiries.'

'Oh, Clive, I could kill you! I really could,' screeched Sadie. Then, having calmed down, added: 'I suppose it could be him.'

'Now! How about the other two men in the vehicle behind yours, the ones taking the body out of the back.'

'Well, it was pitch black and we were rather busy at the time,' said Clive.

'If there's anything else you can remember, it would be most helpful.'

'Oh god, I've had enough of this bloody waste of time,' said Sadie.

'I must remind you both, it's not out of the question that we might still be looking at a charge of gross indecency in a public place,' said Jenny, knowing that such a thing would be laughed out of court by the Crown Prosecution Service, but having run out of patience with the couple some time ago.

Nick Mycroft pulled into a layby, took several deep breaths and then read the letter. Brodie had written it shortly before taking a small blade (which he had probably had delivered by drone) from a packet, along with a bottle of Temazepam, slitting his wrists and watching quietly as his life ebbed away with the blood dripping onto the lino around his shower cubicle.

Dear Nick

Hope this gets to you. Sorry about what's gone on, but I've had a bellyful. I am sick and tired of starting again and with me coming up for parole, I just didn't fancy it, Nick. Will you look out for Dad? You may not think it, but he is proud of you, though of course he keeps it well hid. Sorry not to see you in person about that lad Wilkes. I don't want to speak ill of the dead and hope you'll feel the same about me, but Jason Wilkes was a prize plonker, as thick as two short planks. He wasn't bright enough to have tried a stunt like this without someone giving him simple instructions. He called himself a neo-Nazi with pride but had no idea what either word meant. Anyway, apologies again, but if there's anyone will understand, you will.

Well, all best from me, Nick, and make sure you look after yourself.

Brodie.

Nick felt the tears well up. He hadn't really cried when his mother Nellie died but this released something, and he found himself weeping with such intensity he could hardly catch his breath. These were angry tears; angry at the waste, angry at how the system had failed to care for Brodie, angry at Brodie for his crimes, and for the fact that he kept getting caught. In fact, there wasn't much he wasn't angry at. As a result, he didn't feel in the right frame of mind for a second date with Jenny, which they'd arranged the day before. He desperately wanted to see her though. She had made love to him so gently, in ways that no other woman had ever done, and he felt about her in a way he had never thought about anyone else. It would be frowned upon if it got out that they were seeing each other. Being of different ranks made it awkward but not impossible, if one was discreet. He'd put her off tonight and try to get his head straight by getting an early night. Besides, more immediately, he now had the job of telling his Uncle Jimmy that his only son had killed himself.

'Well, I suppose it could be him, but you must remember it was dark and well, we were otherwise occupied,' said Latimer.

'We just need an indication at this stage. Remember, you're not on oath here.'

Jenny and he were looking through the peep hole in the door of the cell, which now housed Shafiq, the young man Bob Coombs had apprehended outside The Blue Maharajah. He had been charged with helping to conceal a crime and preventing the lawful burial of a body. But now that his ankle had been patched up and plastered, he was refusing to answer any of the questions put to him.

'But I thought you said you'd charged him, so why do you need us?'

'Well, the thing is, he was cooperating but now he's not.'

'As I say, it could be one of them, but I can't really be sure,' said Latimer.

'Well, if that's the best you can do.'

'Can we have our tape back now? All this is causing a great deal of tension in my life, you know.'

'I'm afraid not for the moment, Mr Latimer,' said Jenny.

39
Breaking News

Nick had tapped in Jimmy Collins' number; his uncle knew by the tone in Nick's voice that the news he had been almost expecting had now arrived.

'I knew it would end with something like this.'

'I really am so sorry, Uncle Jimmy.'

'And you say he left a note. What kind of a note, and who to?'

'Well, basically it just said he'd had enough and couldn't see things getting any better after he was released. It was addressed to me, Uncle Jimmy. He had a bit of information for me about a case I'm involved with, so I can't really show it to you.'

'So, my lad's a police informer, as well as a failed robber. First your mum and now this. I tell you lad, this will see me off. Never should have outlived either of them.'

'Look, Uncle Jimmy, I know you don't approve of what I do, and to be honest, I'm not that proud of my family's history, but we are what we are and if there's anything I can do, you'll let me know, won't you?'

'Well lad, thank you for that and look after yourself. I suppose we will have to wait for the coroner's report before we sort out the send-off. Reckon I should have got shares in that undertaker's business. They're doing a roaring trade, thanks to our family.'

Oh Jimmy, thought Nick, if only you could have been a little less successful as a thief and a hoodlum, you might still have a son.

Alexei had, as planned, spent the night with the well turned out woman he'd met at the hotel. She was the kind of female he despised: self-assured and instructional in what he was and was not to do during their lovemaking. She told him she was married and he both pitied and despised her husband. She was a real cow and he felt her disdain for him, even as they writhed amongst the scatter cushions on the bed. He left her room with her still asleep, taking with him her expensive looking jewellery, partly as a little insurance, as his funds were running a bit low, but also as he knew she would not call the police, as things might get embarrassing for her. He needed to get back to Lincolnshire, where he had some unfinished business.

Stella Kingsley did what she would often do when one or more of her cases was frustrating her: focus on another, namely the Rimmer Farm murders. Was it a jealous lover who'd throttled Lizzie, having first force fed her ibuprofen and vodka? And why were all roads seemingly leading to Killpeck Farm and this Wilkes character? She was going to have to be up front now with the anti-terrorist boys, and they weren't going to like it.

She was still trying to get her ahead around the various investigations, when Idris Perks popped his head around the door.

'Come on Stell! I thought it was about time I took you out for lunch again.',

'What do you mean, again? You've never taken me out to lunch!'

'Haven't I? Well, I've thought about it before. I thought we'd go to that new place. If we hurry, we can get an early bird deal.'

'You sure know how to treat a girl, Idris, I'll give you that,' said Stella. 'Don't wait up: I'm having lunch with Doctor Death!' she called out to her team, as she and Perks made her way out of the office.

At his house in Stamford, Nigel Osgood was getting cabin fever. All he wanted was to be left alone and go about his business. Riddell was having none of it, however, and even when he was allowed a short walk down to the paper shop, Osgood would be accompanied by an anxious Keith and Riddell, the latter with a very obvious bulge just below the breast pocket of his smart suit. The looks he got from the locals were for the most part sympathetic. One or two, however, looked at Osgood as if their town had had a visitation from the angel of death. Osgood had told no one of his terminal diagnosis as he felt no one needed to know. But he was tempted now with all this fuss and that poor misguided boy gunned down like that. It did, however, give him quiet satisfaction that he had got under the skin of the far right so much that they felt the need to bump him off. Although Riddell seemed to have his doubts, he was still going on about Markovich and the Russians being behind it. Osgood wasn't going to worry about it now. If he had been in Markovich's position, might he not have sought vengeance in the same way? Believing in turning the other cheek and actually doing it were two very different things. Anyway, thought Osgood, what will be will be, and then he turned his thoughts to the more parochial.

'Keith, what did we win?'

'What do you mean, win, Bishop?'

'By coming top in the quiz?'

'Well, I don't know whether it counts. We hadn't finished when that crazy came in and tried to chop you to pieces.'

'Well, I still think it counts as a moral victory, at the very least,' said Osgood.

'What, that you weren't decapitated?' said Keith, who often had the feeling the Bishop was not quite twelve to the dozen.

'No, that we won the quiz, silly boy,' said Osgood.

'Oh Mr Riddell, could we have a word? Something has been troubling me.'

'Of course, Your Grace,' said Riddell.

'Keith, I'd like a few minutes with Mr Riddell alone.'

'Right, you are, Bishop. I'll go and help Penny in the kitchen. She's making you one of her famous casseroles,' said Keith, bustling back from whence the three had come.

'Infamous, more like,' whispered Osgood, under his breath.

'Now, Mr Riddell, what I want to know is what exactly you have done with my laptop?'

The Ravenous Magpie didn't have a lot to recommend it, if you were not a sports fan; there were television screens everywhere one looked, with a variety of sports available for the aficionados of such things. Idris Perks pulled a chair out from under the table for Stella to sit down on.

'Well, thank you, kind Sir,' said Stella teasingly.

'This is nice, isn't it. Good to get out from the workplace, get a bit of peace and quiet,' said Perks.

'I wouldn't have thought noise pollution was a huge problem in a morgue,' chuckled Stella.

Despite, or perhaps because of the banter, Kingsley and Perks had been firm friends for many years. Marjorie, Idris' late wife had been one of Stella's greatest friends, and when Marjorie died, Stella had made sure that Idris, who was not the most self-reliant of men under normal circumstances, cooked for himself and organised for a cleaner to come in three times a week. It was three years since his wife's death and Idris and Stella had got out of the habit of meeting up. The shade of Marjorie had begun to cause a slight awkwardness, so both were glad to have the opportunity to ease the little bit of tension that was there between them when not involved professionally on some case or other.

'I still miss her dreadfully, you know,' said Idris.

'I know Idris, and believe me, so do I.'

'We had been together since med school.'

'Yes, my dear, I know. Your marriage was a rarity in this day and age.'

'She was so alive!' said Idris.

'Must have made a nice change from the path lab.' Stella leant over and grasped his hand. 'I think we had better order; I need to get back to the office. It's absolutely mad at the moment. Crimes are like London buses; you wait for hours for one to come along and then suddenly you have three murder enquiries on your patch.'

Indira and Shani Chowdry had got as far as the door of Lincoln police station, but seemed on the point of losing their nerve, when Nick Mycroft came across them.

'It's Mrs Chowdry, isn't it?'

'That is right.'

'Won't you come in? We'll put the kettle on and have a chat, shall we?'

'You must understand, this is all very difficult for my daughter and I.'

'Yes, of course. We are very grateful for any help you can give us. As you know, we are doing all we can to provide answers to the grieving parents in this awful case.'

'Oh god, this is all my fault,' said Shani, bursting into tears.

'Nick led them through to a vacant suite of rooms, usually reserved for victims of crime. He rang upstairs and asked that Jenny join them.

'Okay, would you like a cup of tea or coffee before we get started?' said Jenny.

'No, thank you. Shani has something to tell you… this will not be easy for her… it will not be easy for me. I have always known my husband was a bully and a dreadful snob, but this… this is too much… that is why we decided to come back home. Now Shani, when you are ready, tell the Detective Inspector what you know.'

'Me and Hanif met at college,' explained Shani in a barely audible whisper.

'She'd had to fight her father over that, mind you,' said Indira.

'I had started a creative writing course and Hanif was so sweet and encouraging. But there were so many fights at home that I had to give it up.'

'Go on, when you're ready, Shani,' said Mycroft gently.

'But I could not give up Hanif.'

'Her father knew nothing to begin with. But I... I knew something had changed. A light had come on in my daughter, Inspector.'

'So, what happened when presumably your husband found out?'

'He became incandescent with rage, out of control. Even in the bad times of the past, I have been able to pacify him, but I've never seen him like that,' said Indira.

'It was just bad luck. Hanif and I had had a lovely day out and as usual he was dropping me several streets away, in a very quiet part of town, when to my horror, my father came down the road. Apparently, there were roadworks on his usual route and this little street had become, what do you call it... a rat run? He did nothing at the time, but I knew he had seen us.'

'She was grounded Inspector. I was instructed to lock her in her room. Only to allow her out for meals and to go to the bathroom,' explained Indira.

'It was terrible for my mother. No one outside of home knew what he was really like.'

'Oh, darling, I think some of those who worked for him knew him for what he was.'

'So, what happened then?'

'Well, I was not prepared to imprison my daughter indefinitely, Inspector. We were very careful to ensure Shani was at home when he left for work and when he returned home at night.'

'It was then that my darling Hanif did what he did,' said Shani.

'And it was eventually to cost him his life, Inspector,' said Mrs Chowdry.

40
Reign of Terror

DCI Stella Kingsley had enjoyed her lunch with Idris at The Ravenous Magpies and had agreed to pop over to his house that evening to help him at last sort out his late wife's clothes for distribution to charity shops or disposal. However, her mood darkened when confronted by Terry Tomms' determined martyrdom.

'Mr Tomms, the only thing I can think of charging you with is wasting police time.'

'Do what you will, Inspector, I am ready for whatever sanction your corrupt judiciary have to throw at me. I would go on hunger strike should New Glory require it of me.' Tomms was now sweating profusely and hardly in control of his emotions. 'We will be heard one way or the other, Inspector Kingsley.' At previous interviews, he'd been all in favour of the forces of law but now like some dyspeptic Don Quixote, he was leading a charge against them.

'Well, from a health point of view, you probably could do with losing a few pounds, so I don't think we need to worry about any hunger strike,' observed Kingsley.

'Well, be that as it may, do you want to cuff me?'

'No, although I do see there have been a few misdemeanours along the way, mainly tax fraud.'

'Mere misunderstandings. And not germane to the issue.'

'Look, Mr Tomms, you have told us all we need to know, and we shall be passing it on to the security forces in due course, but for the moment you are a free man. Just ensure we have your address, in case MI5 require it.'

'MI5,' said Tomms, 'now we're talking.'

In despair, Stella rang downstairs for assistance. Sergeant Hedges came up.

'Ah, Sergeant Hedges, can you please escort Mr Tomms from the police station? He has completely finished helping us with our enquiries.'

As Hedges was seeing the still protesting Tomms out of the police station, they were passed by the Chief Constable and a small man in a beautifully cut Savile Row suit.

'Ah, DCI Kingsley, a word if we may?' said Chief Constable Poulson coolly.

All Saints church in Stamford dates back to the thirteenth century. It is an impressive building with an imposing spire and Nigel Osgood was looking forward to officiating there, while the incumbent was being separated from his gall bladder. He had decided to preach his sermon that Sunday on his favourite parable, 'The Prodigal Son.' If he had still got his laptop, he would have, of course, been using that. Instead, he was working upstairs on his cranky old PC.

Osgood had always been intrigued by the whole concept of redemption and how and why it actually occurred, and where in the story did this leave the other brother, who'd stayed at home and worked hard and now felt usurped? He'd had his favourite alb professionally cleaned and was hoping for a reasonable congregation. Osgood knew that he was not everyone's cup of tea, but also thought he would get a few extras, who would come along out of curiosity, given recent events. He'd not been surprised when Riddell had categorically denied involvement in the disappearance of the laptop. He was a very cool customer indeed; it wasn't like the old days, when any Tom, Dick or Harry could get into the service providing they had been to the right school. Keith had done sterling work in keeping the press at bay. As ever, they wanted to make a meal of it. All Osgood wanted was what was left of his life, however long, to have some normality in it. There was talk of a government minister wanting to pop in and have a chat, to make sure he was alright, and also, Nigel suspected, to make sure the government was seen to be taking all 'acts of terrorism' seriously, from whatever quarter they might have come.

Back in Lincoln, Indira and Shani Chowdry had now accepted cups of tea from Jenny James.

'Okay, when you are ready to continue.'

'Hanif wrote to my father explaining that he loved me and wanted us to be together as man and wife. He wrote that he understood my father's misgivings on inter faith marriages and would not expect me to adopt any of his family's religious practices. This only served to infuriate my father more, particularly when he made enquiries and found out Hanif's father was a car mechanic. That's when the harassment began.'

'I could not bear for them not to meet, so when I was instructed to lock Shani in, I disobeyed my instructions.'

'My father became totally obsessed. He suspected that something was still going on and that is when he must have decided that the only way was to... murder the man I loved. He arranged a meeting, supposedly to come to some kind of agreement. Instead, he sent some of his men to kill him.'

'And forgive me,' said Nick, 'are you saying you have proof of that Shani?'

'Well,' Shani hesitated.

'I can confirm it, Inspector,' said Indira Chowdry. I have his mobile phone. You see, I think you will find enough information on it to help you convict my husband. I just feel so dreadfully sorry for the parents.'

'But why was he so opposed? Was he very strict in his interpretation of Islam Mrs Chowdry?'

'No, my dear... he was, is, and always will be a dreadful snob,' replied Indira.

The question going through Alexei's head, as he drove up the motorway, was how this job was now to be accomplished, given that security around Osgood would be tight twenty-four seven and undertaken by crack professionals from the British Intelligence services. It was the kind of puzzle he would have liked solving in his younger days. But now, well, it was all about making a statement: nerve agents and plutonium were simply not his style. The problem for Alexei, was in order to get near to Osgood, he would need to hide in plain sight. He still had his high-powered rifle with him. But again, he was not in the business of getting into a shootout with some swot team. This fashion for people to get themselves shot or blow themselves up seemed so futile. He was neither a believer in heaven nor hell and had no desire to find out just yet if he was right. He was also aware that it was quite likely that the intelligence service had cottoned on to the fact that the attempt on Osgood's life was not instigated by New Glory.

The hire car handled very well in the torrential rain. He switched the radio on to catch the BBC local news: the media were running with the notion that the attempt on Osgood's life was a right wing assassination plot. There was also an update on the Rimmer murder investigation, which really wasn't much of an update. The police were still appealing for any information people might have. If he had felt any guilt over killing Lizzie Rimmer, it had now completely dissipated: the blonde at the spa hotel had turned him down flat when he'd offered to bring a bottle up to her room. He was not used to women using him as that stuck up English woman had: the bitch had treated him like a piece of meat. He felt a rage inside him, a killer's rage, and one he would need to channel carefully.

41
Intelligence Test

'DCI Kingsley, can I introduce Mr Brown. He is on an attachment from Chatham House as Senior Threat Strategy Director.'

'How do you do,' said Kingsley.

'DCI Kingsley,' said Brown superciliously.

He was a somewhat unremarkable man slightly greying at the temples but otherwise of indeterminate age.

'Mr Brown is here to facilitate mutual professional practice at the interface of crime and terror activity,' said the Chief Constable.

'The fact is, DCI Kingsley, we are responsible for national security and you, dear lady, are standing on our toes and stopping us from dancing, as it were,' said Brown, sitting on Stella's one comfortable chair, sprawling across it as if this was his office rather than hers.

For a moment Stella Kingsley thought about playing hardball but then looked at Poulson's face and decided in this case it might be prudent to take a different tack.

'Forgive me, Mr Brown, the last thing we would ever want to do is queer the pitch for you. However, as you will be aware, we have been dealing with a number of highly sensitive cases.'

'Yes, DCI Kingsley, I am aware of that and I hear you've had a spot of bad luck, if that's what it was, with the Rex Priday case going for a retrial. I was surprised you couldn't get that to stick.'

'The retrial will go our way, I'm sure,' said Kingsley. Brown was the kind of Englishman Kingsley despised: clever and entitled and snidey with it.

'Well, that's by the by,' said Brown. We are more concerned regarding that fact that you're not exactly tippy toeing around this Jason Wilkes business.

'We are investigating a double murder in which there is a possibility that Wilkes may well have been involved, Mr Brown.'

'Well, that's as may be, but it's our belief that Wilkes is merely a pawn in the game with regard to the assassination attempt on Bishop Osgood, and I'm concerned that one of your plods may...'

'Well, of course, that is none of my business. However, what I would say is this New Glory outfit couldn't organise a shag in a brothel,' said Stella, who was beginning to feel her temper fraying badly.

At this Poulson gave her a hard stare.

'There we would agree,' said Brown. 'Terry Tomms is, of course, known to us, but as far as we are concerned, New Glory pose a threat only to themselves.'

'Look, I'm really not getting a clear picture here of who you are saying is running the show,' queried Kingsley.

'Well, let's just say forces are at work in this country at the moment, closely aligned to a potential enemy state i.e., we think there is a cell still active and out to disrupt our political discourse, pitting left against right in a way we haven't seen since the 1930s,' Brown expounded.

'Well, I'm sorry but all this sounds a little above my pay grade,' said Kingsley. 'Besides, some of us think this present government is doing a pretty good job of that all by itself.'

'That's quite a revealing comment. Of course those of us entrusted with national security would feel it wholly inappropriate to make such an observation.'

Stella felt her face colour. She had never been fond of mansplaining, but this windbag was testing her patience to the limit.

Poulson took a comb out of his pocket and combed what was left of his hair.

'Stella, I know that now we've had this little chat, you will rein in any of your team who might need it,' Poulson said.

'I'll be briefing the Home Secretary on our discussions. So, I do hope we all understand each other,' said Brown. 'Well, nice to have met you at last, DCI Kingsley, and I hope you have more success on your outstanding cases. Clear up rates are so important to the public's confidence, don't you feel?'

As Brown got up, he knocked Stella Kingsley's large bag to the floor. It doubled up as both her bag and briefcase. He picked it up disdainfully and placed it back on her chair, which he had just vacated.

'Yes, as is not having to use lethal force in one of our village halls, which tends to give the locals the jitters. Good to meet you too, Mr Brown.'

Poulson gave her another withering look as they left. Stella could hear him fawning all over Brown. She switched her intercom on for the general office.

'Well Cosmo, you must come over for a round of golf at my little club. We will have a bite of eat afterwards: my shout of course.'

'Well, that's very good of you. That Kingsley woman, is she always that bolshie?'

Stella smiled. She wasn't sure whether there was anything she liked better than rubbing the top brass up the wrong way.

Bob Coombs sat down at the table opposite Lomax, whose brief sat alongside him, a sallow faced man, who had the expression of someone who would much rather be elsewhere.

'Mr Lomax, there is a new matter which we would like your help with. We understand a man named Jason Wilkes was for some time in your employment at Killpeck Farm.'

'And what's that got to do with the price of fish?' said Lomax.

'May I remind you, Mr Lomax, that you are already facing very serious charges, which could result in a very lengthy prison sentence. It is in your interest to assist the police where matters of national security are concerned.'

'You've lost me.'

'Have you not seen the newspaper, Sir?'

'Not since you incarcerated me in here, no.'

'Mr Wilkes died while attempting to assassinate a senior member of the Church of England.'

'Well, it can't be the same little shit I had working for me. He was as thick as the proverbial two short planks.'

'So, you can confirm Mr Wilkes was in your employ?'

'Well, yeh, but he did a runner after I had a little word.'

'What was the problem?' queried Coombs.

'Someone had taken one of my vehicles without permission. Here, you're not trying to say I had anything to do with trying to top no clergyman?' asked Lomax angrily.

'No, no. At the present, that's not what we are saying. However, all roads at the moment seem to lead us to Killpeck Farm. What kind of vehicle was it that was stolen?'

'It was a pickup.'

'And who exactly do you suspect was involved in this theft?'

'Well, look a lot has happened. It was about a fortnight ago. I get all sorts coming to pick for me, you know.'

'Mr Lomax, if you can cooperate with me over this matter here and now,' said Coombs, 'I may not need to hand you over to our security people, who are not – shall we say – as polite as me when it comes to the crunch, and believe me, we are coming to the crunch.'

'Are you threatening my client?' said Lomax's solicitor.

'Oh, I wondered when you might join the conversation, and no, I'm not threatening your client, just explaining a few of the facts of life,' said Coombs.

'Now, Mr Lomax, have I clarified the situation or shall I make that phone call to the intelligence services.' Coombs reached for the office phone.

'Well look, there was this Bosnian Serb, I think he were. Bit of a tear away, but to be fair, he was a good picker and then there were this other bloke called himself Alexei. A bit too clever for his own good if you ask me. Anyhow, they both scarpered, although to be fair Alexei came back for a couple of days, but he was always asking for time off.'

'Okay, Mr Lomax: that will do for now,' said Coombs.

42
Remembrance of Times Past

'Well, it's very good of you, Stella, but I would have thought you'd have had better things to do on a Friday night,' said Idris Perks.

'Oh, look at this dress! I remember her wearing it when you went to get your OBE,' said Stella, smoothing out the floral dress which she had just retrieved from the wardrobe and which had belonged to the late Marjorie Perks.

'Yes, that's right. We all had a bit of lunch together that day, didn't we, before going to the palace?'

'That's right and you christened your honour, "Order of the Body Examiners."'

'Yes, we had a laugh that day, didn't we, and to think that was only a couple of months before she got the diagnosis,' said Idris wistfully.

'Wonderful memories,' said Stella, as her eyes moistened.

'Oh, I'm sorry: is this upsetting you?' said Idris.

'No, it's the dust from the wardrobe getting in my eye,' lied Stella.

'Now let's have a break. I'm cooking us something to eat, so would you like chilli con carne, or... chilli con carne?'

'Oh, Idris, I don't want you to go to any trouble.'

'It's no bother but I'm afraid chilli is my signature dish, i.e., it's the only thing I know how to cook.'

'Well, that's very good of you. I'll get started on the shoes, shall I?' said Stella, looking in amusement at the rack upon rack of her late friend's shoes.

Later that evening and after sharing a bottle of wine with their meal, both started to reminisce about their younger lives. Stella told a story about a boyfriend from her first year in the Met. They were on the same beat, but she dumped him when she found out he was being unfaithful, when the fire brigade was called to cut him out from his own handcuffs attached to the bedstead of a florist from Pimlico.

Idris was recounting gory tales from med school, where a certain skeleton used for training purposes would be taken over to the nursing halls of residence and placed in some unsuspecting nurse's bed, with a cheeky message attached.

'I know we've talked about this before, but Rex Priday, I mean knowing what we both know now, do you think he might have...? Stella asked.

'Been offending then... do you mean was he hacking people to death, when we all shared a house?'

A certain awkwardness descended on the meal.

'Oh, come on, you know what I mean,' Stella probed.

'Oh, I'm sorry. I accept that people don't just become psychopaths over overnight. He was a bit of a queer fish alright but then you get all sorts at med school. You see, Stella, I've always been better at reading what's going on with the dead, as opposed to the living.'

'Forgive me being curious, Idris, but to be honest, I'm still racking my brains to see if we've missed anything because I'm telling you now, if we don't get a conviction and justice for Betsy Mulligan at the retrial, that's it, I'm handing my badge in and retiring to the Isle of Skye.'

'Very nice too. Alright for some. Pension pot must be overflowing, then,' said Idris.

Alexei had found it easy to blend in with the media circus that had now installed itself in Stamford. There were crews from many different countries. In the bars in the town, if asked, he would say that he was covering the Osgood story for Russia Today television. Some of the media people gave him funny looks, but their tongues soon loosened after he'd bought them a few drinks. One such reporter was Ernie Parslow, a small, round individual dressed in good quality clothes bought a long time ago.

His thorn-proof jacket had leather patches and sleeves with frayed cuffs. Ernie had worked on various East Midland, local papers, and because he was seen as Johnny on the spot, enjoyed being the font of all knowledge. He told Alexei, when on his third large scotch, that he'd heard Osgood intended carrying on much as normal.

'He's even taking services, on Sunday, while the vicar is on holiday. What's your angle, then Alexei, if you don't mind me asking?' said Ernie.

'None, just here reporting events,' said Alexei.

'I suppose you're interested because old Osgood's what you might call, a bit underdone.'

'Excuse me?' said Alexei.

'You know, pink, red under the bed, one of your lot, by all accounts.'

During the evening a plan began to formulate in Alexei's head. Like all good plans, it appeared simple enough. The last church he had set foot in was in Moscow for his mother's funeral. The state, of course, didn't approve of such things at the time, so the place was full of the homeless and people at the back of the church sleeping off their vodka binge of the night before. However, Alexei was well read. He knew a little of the eucharist service in Anglican churches and how things were done, and so he could see that this might provide an opportunity, one that he didn't intend to miss.

There was no way Nick could get time off for Brodie Collins' funeral, which had been arranged for the following week, but he felt he needed to speak with his uncle, and pop in and see his father, who by all accounts was coping with his own grief admirably, with the help of his new girlfriend. For Jimmy, though, Nick was fearful, now the two people his uncle cared for most were gone. As one of the Collins gang, Jimmy had seen his share of violence, even meted it out on occasions, but now his world had crumbled. He'd always looked out for Nick's mother, Nellie, in their younger days, while Nick's grandfather was serving a life sentence for manslaughter. Frank Collins had overseen the family's dodgy businesses and their growth in the thirties, and then for a time after the war, there was money to be made in all sorts of ways: building on bomb sites, providing loan shark services to war widows, and black-market goods during post war rationing. His life sentence came about after a botched wages snatch, in which one of the security guards fell through the open doors from the back of their van, with Frank at the wheel. He narrowly avoided being charged with murder, due to having an excellent barrister. If convicted of murder, in those days the noose awaited him. Frank's son, Jimmy, now lived in sheltered accommodation in Braintree and when Nick arrived, he was already standing outside in the car park. Despite being in his mid-nineties, he was still erect, and in his black frock coat and with his tied back, long white hair, Jimmy still made an imposing figure.

'You know, if there was any way I could make it next week, I would,' said Mycroft.

'Oh no sweat, Son. I know how busy you crime fighters are,' said Jimmy, smiling grimly, displaying his few remaining shark-like teeth.

'Is there anything I can do, Uncle Jimmy, anything at all?'

'Nah, Son. You're alright,' commented Jimmy, taking a long draw on his cigarette.

'I'm not happy about what happened for Brodie, not happy at all,' said Nick.

'Listen Son, prison is what it is. It goes with the territory. But there is something I need to talk to you about.'

'Well, you know I'm here for you, Uncle Jimmy.'

'The thing is, there's a bit put away.'

'I'm not with you.'

'Well, you know, from the business.'

'Oh, right!'

'It's legit, you know. We diversified after Dad died: shops, property, offshore accounts.'

'Look, I'm glad, of course, but what's that got to do with me?'

'Well Son, with Brodie gone, it's only right it's kept in the family, so when I curl up my toes... well, if you excuse the pun, cop the lot.' Jimmy took a long draw on his cigarette and then stubbed it out defiantly on the *No Smoking* sign outside the building.

'What are you saying?'

'You now become sole beneficiary, Nicholas. We are talking around four mills in ballpark figures. Not all in readies of course.'

One of the carers in the sheltered accommodation looked out suspiciously from one of the windows. Jimmy nodded and gave her a somewhat goofy smile back.

'She hates me, that one,' said Jimmy. But I'll bring her round. You never lose it, Son.'

As he drove away, on his way to see his father, Nick was struck by Jimmy's forced cheerfulness in their last few exchanges. Was he just trying to lighten the mood? All that stuff about the money, was that some kind of sick joke? Jimmy had been a practical joker in his youth. The story went that during one turf war encounter with another gang, he'd posted one of their member's digits back to them, in a Cadbury's box of chocolate fingers.

43
An Unexpected Turn of Events

'Well Idris, I've had a lovely evening,' said Stella Kingsley.

'But this wasn't it,' said Idris.

'Sorry,' queried Kingsley.

'Groucho Marx,' Idris explained. 'How about I drive you home?'

'Idris Perks wash your mouth out.'

'Oh gosh, I hope you don't think I was...'

'No, my dear, I'm just aware that I would be over the limit, and so, therefore, I suspect you would be too. Besides, I've ordered a cab. Now I just want to check I've got my house keys.'

'What did you say?' said Perks.

'I always put my keys in the same place in my bag.'

'How you find anything in that great sack, god only knows. It must play havoc with your back carrying that thing around all day,' he said distractedly.

Idris suddenly stood up.

Stella was a little taken aback.

'What's the matter my dear. Are you unwell?'

'That's it! I knew there was something at the back of my mind.'

'Idris, what are you on about?'

'That bastard, Priday.'

'What about him?'

'Well, I'll know it, if I see it.'

'You're not making any sense.'

'Can you get another warrant to search his house?'

'What? You mean, where that poor girls' bits were found?'

'No, no. Not his flat in London.'

'Well yes, but we've already turned the whole place upside down.'

'Let me know and I'll meet you up there. I'll know it if I see it.'

'Okay. I haven't the foggiest what you are on about, but I'll call you first thing.'

Nick was shell shocked by his conversation with Jimmy Collins, and drove across London's gridlocked streets in a daze. Was he really going to inherit a fortune? How could he be sure the money was legit? Well that was a ridiculous notion in itself. Even if the family had gone straight, his grandfather's reign of terror over the East End had set the whole thing up. But how responsible are we for our antecedents' misdeeds? How many respectable people had had their lives smoothed along by their slaver great great grandfather making a fortune in the early nineteenth century. Posh money could be equally tainted. With all these thoughts floating about in Nick's head, the journey seemed to fly by, and he arrived at his father's just before ten.

'Hello Son, we were starting to think you weren't coming,' said Jake.

'Yeh, we were thinkin' of turning in, wasn't we, hun?' said Carly.

'I'm sorry. It's been one of those days. I went to see Uncle Jimmy, you know because of not being able to make the funeral and that.'

'How was the old rascal? I haven't seen him since your mum's funeral. Anyone would fink he didn't like me.'

'Oh, you know Uncle Jimmy. He isn't a great one for the human race at the best of times, and this business has knocked him right back.'

'Well, we are all stuck in this vale of tears, as they say. Jimmy and I were never the best of pals but, well you know how fings were Nick. I mean well... families eh, who really understands them?'

His father had a habit of leaving his thoughts in mid-air, with trite rhetorical questions.

'So, you're alright Dad, are you?'

'Yeeees, Son, I'm fine,' said Jake.

Nick had to admit his father did look well. He seemed to have lost a bit of weight.

'That was a shocker, poor old Brodie topping himself like that. Absolutely tragic, I know, but... well life has to go on.'

His father's penchant for the hackneyed cliché used to drive Nick insane. It was a kind of post war patois, but it was so at odds with the modern world, where everyone had to express exactly what they were feeling, that Mycroft had almost begun to admire this linguistic cloaking device.

'Talking of which, we've got a bit of good news, haven't we Jakey,' said Carly.

'A little birdie tells me it might have done you a little bit of good,' said Jake, touching his nose like a character from a Dickens novel.

'How do you know?'

'It's business, Son. I always make sure what's on the cards, as it were. Here's the funny thing, though. It would mean that if I still had the shops, you'd have become my boss. Funny old world sometimes, eh?'

'Here, Jakey, are you going to tell him or not?' said Carly impatiently.

'Well, I suppose the lad needs to know. Show him your finger, Carly.'

There on Carly's finger was a ring of old gold with rubies and sapphires surrounding a large diamond. It was gaudy and over the top, like something you might get in a 'Lucky Bag' but worst of all, for Nick, was the fact it was his mother's engagement ring.

Nick got up and mumbled his congratulations.

'Yeh, well I'm happy for you.'

'We didn't see the point of waiting. I know Nellie would have given it her blessing. With her gone, she'd have wanted me to be happy, don't you think, Son?'

'Yes, well anyway, I have to get back. It's all hands to the pump at work at the moment.'

Nigel Osgood awoke in a grumpy mood; he was in pain, which didn't help. The bitterness that he'd felt all those years ago at Julian's death had returned with a vengeance. Whether this was a delayed reaction to what had happened in the church, he was not sure. He had been with dying parishioners and had seen bodies being prepared for burial in various parts of the world, but his Julian and the Wilkes boy were the only two people who he'd witnessed actually being killed.

Riddell was in his kitchen making himself a cafetière of coffee.

'I'm sorry but I must insist that you leave my house,' said Osgood imperiously.

'That's not a good idea at all, Sir,' replied Riddell, pushing the plunger down deep into the glass.

'Look, unless I am under house arrest, I think I have the right to say who is in my property.'

'But we cannot be sure that your life isn't still under threat.'

'If you are not gone in the next twenty minutes... I swear...'

'Well, Your Grace, I have to advise you in the strongest...'

'Young man, this is a civil liberties issue, and I have friends in the media who would be very interested,' said Osgood, half bluffing, his face turning a deep shade of puce.

'Sir, I think you are forgetting that had I not been there that night, you might not be here now,' said Riddell, coolly sipping his coffee.

Nothing seemed to phase this young man, Osgood thought.

'And it's not that I am not grateful, but I feel suffocated.'

'Very well, but I must make you aware that you may still be in considerable danger. I will vacate the property, but I intend being a presence in the village, while investigations are ongoing and I'm afraid a uniformed officer will still be charged with guarding your front door. You have to understand, Bishop, that it is not just about your life, but about reassuring the local population. What happened has come as a terrible shock to people.'

'You really think having intelligence goons and PCs barely out of nappies with Tommy guns outside my front door means the people of Stamford will feel reassured?'

'We have a job to do, Your Grace. You minister to your flock; think of us as sheepdogs, keeping you safe.'

'I just want to get some of my old life back, that's all, Mr Riddell.'

'But...'

'British Intelligence ruined my young life. If I see you hanging around, I shall report it to my friends in the press that I am being harassed over something that happened forty years ago. I just need some peace and quiet in the ti...' Osgood stopped himself just in time. After all, the fact he was terminally ill was nobody's business but his.

44
Getting a Head Start

Rex Priday's flat was in one of the less fashionable streets of Bayswater, but even so would have commanded a two-million-pound price tag on the open market. It was set out over two floors, in Adam style. Most of the property looked hardly lived in. The kitchen was all clean lines, a place for everything, and everything in its place.

Stella Kingsley had had little difficulty in securing a second search warrant. She was struck by the fact that it was a light and airy property, very unlike the house in which the remains of Betsy Mulligan had been found. There were several expensive pictures on the walls. His tastes in this area were eclectic and ranged from a preliminary George Stubbs pencil sketch to ultra-modern abstract works by up-and-coming artists.

'So, what exactly are we looking for, Idris?'

'I'll recognise it when I see it,' said Idris enigmatically.

'Look, I don't mean to be ungracious, but I have got so much on my plate just now.

'Study, where's his study?' said a distracted Perks.

'Upstairs, third on the right, if I remember correctly,' said Kingsley.

'The Book of Ezekiel, chapter 37, verse 3 "Can these bones live again?" or something along those lines.'

'Oh, you're not going to go all religious on me now are you?'

'There! There! The display case.' Perks could hardly contain himself.

On the back wall of the study was a large glass cabinet with various antique medical teaching aids. There was a plaster mould of a heart, parts of the human skeleton and various pieces of early surgical equipment.

'Bless my soul!' said Idris. 'It's there.'

'What?'

'The skull is the key to everything. That's what he used to say.'

'Who used to say?' asked Kingsley.

'Priday, of course!'

'So, what we are looking for is that skull,' said Kingsley uncertainly.

'Inside it, actually, with a bit of luck,' said Isaac, his eyes twinkling with excitement.

Nick had just fed Bodkin Adams and had put his feet up to read the Saturday papers, when he got a message from Jenny on his mobile, inviting him for Sunday lunch the next day after she'd finished singing in church, and suggesting they take Ratface for a walk. This sounded good to him. He'd find it easier to resist her in daylight hours, so he agreed. He was still trying to process what had happened when he'd gone back to London. What was he to do about Uncle Jimmy and his will?

There was no way he could accept being the beneficiary and stay in the force, knowing that – however watered down – the money came from crime. He would need to make this clear to Jimmy, but he knew it wouldn't go down well and then there was his father, who really wasn't much of a father, but you only really get one. He was infuriated at the man's insensitivity and Carly, who Nick had been quite sweet on at one time, had sat there smugly wearing his mother's engagement ring. It all felt yucky, like a Greek tragedy, almost oedipal in fact.

He was just about to call his uncle, and say the whole thing with the will was impossible, when the call came from Stella Kingsley.

'Hi Nick, sorry to ring you at home, but I just wanted you to know, looks like we may really have nailed Priday this time. I'll tell you about it later, but first I've got a real big favour to ask. Would you supervise Lomax, i.e., escort him to the morgue? I want him to have a look at the unidentified stiff in

Idris' lab and see if he can identify him. There's a possibility he's one of the pickers from Killpeck Farm.'

'Right, Ma'am, will do,' said Nick. He wasn't usually keen on escorting members of the public to identify bodies, but Lomax deserved having his life made as unpleasant as possible, after what he'd wanted to do to Jenny.

'Scumbag,' he said under his breath. Bodkin Adams gave Nick one of his looks, as if he'd never seen Mycroft in his life, and returned to his tuna in jelly.

Bob Coombs came into Kingsley's office with coffee and an iced bun.

'I've just heard the news about Priday, Ma'am. What I don't understand is how the SOCO boys missed it first time round.'

'The key to the house, where we found Betsy's body, was extremely well hidden, Bob,' explained Kingsley. 'Apparently, when Idris Perks and he were students in the shared house, they used to keep the key in a skull by the back door. The skull had a false eye and the door key was kept behind it. Seems Priday used it for the same purpose for the house in Lincoln, to which he has always maintained, he had no key. He claimed that the only key was with the letting agents in London. They confirmed the fact they had a key but had been waiting instructions. Priday had been paying them a retainer but had kept on putting off a joint site visit with them.'

'Why hadn't they been up front with us at the beginning of the investigation, Ma'am?'

'Well, they didn't want to admit to just taking a fee, and also having body parts in one of your letting properties isn't probably the best advert. Their relationship with Priday involved several other properties, you see, so they were making a mint from him.'

At that point, Mr Brown from the intelligence services arrived at Kingsley's door.

'I think we have a problem, DCI Kingsley?'

'Do you, Mr Brown, and pray what that might be?'

Bob Coombs tried to suppress a chuckle as he left them to it.

In the path lab, Dr Perks was going about his work humming a Rossini overture to himself, when Nick Mycroft arrived with Lomax handcuffed to Dick Hedges.

'Gentlemen, gentlemen, do come in!' said Perks cheerfully.

'Morning, Idris.'

'I have our unknown friend all ready for you, over here. Do you know, I can't remember having to show so many people around one corpse!'

'Ah, Sergeant Hedges, how are you and all your little saplings?'

'All well, thank you Doc, growing up fast though, you know. All this overtime couldn't have come at a better time.'

'And who have we here?'

'This is Mr Lomax, who is helping us with our enquiries.'

'Sensible man. So now, let's get down to business.'

'I take it, it is Mr Lomax, who is going to see if he can identify who we've got here.'

'That's right,' said Nick.

'Well, just a couple of tips: when I draw back the sheet, try not to close your eyes or squint, as if looking at the sun. Take your time and drink in what you see.'

'Can we get on with it?' said Lomax.

Idris Perks, who was in an exceptionally good mood that day, drew back the sheet covering Drac's corpse, rather as a conjuror might.

'Well, I'm not really... wait a minute... yes, it's him, that Serbian nutter. Sorry, don't mean to be disrespectful... Drac that was his name... or the name he gave us,' said Lomax.

'So, you've got details, addresses, next of kin, that kind of thing?'

'Well, no not really. You see, our turnover of staff made that a bit difficult.'

'You mean you couldn't be arsed to keep records, being more interested in that little weed growing side line of yours?' said Nick.

'Look I have come of my own free will to help you, on the understanding from your bosses that such assistance would help me, if I were to be looking at a prison sentence for events at Killpeck, which, may I remind you, I was involved in under duress.'

'Oh, pipe down, Lomax, and tell me what else you know about this Drac character, and why, for instance, you didn't report him missing?' said Nick in a rare display of emotion.

'Look, if I reported everyone who came and went at Killpeck, I'd be on the phone to you lot all the time,' said Lomax.

'Okay, what I need you to think about very carefully is when was the last time you saw Drac alive? Your help so far adds up to about one night less at Her Majesty's pleasure in my estimation.'

'Look, I can't remember exactly. Maybe three weeks ago, about the same time Jason left and that Alexei went soon after.'

'So, they worked together this Drac and Jason Wilkes?'

'Yes, of course they worked together.'

'Were they friends?'

'Well, I don't really know. They seemed to hang about together a lot, you know as foreigners tend to do. But to be honest, I try not to have too much to do with the pickers.'

'Why? In case you get too attached?' said Nick sardonically.

'No, army taught me this stuff.'

'Ah yes, you were a major, weren't you?'

'That's right.'

'Dishonourably discharged from what I read,' said Nick trying to ignore his burning hatred for Lomax.

'Totally trumped-up charges. Some toffee-nosed colonel, pen pusher type had it in from me from the word go.'

'Gentleman, if you could continue your conversation elsewhere? I am expecting an intake from a hit and run up near

Scotch Corner, at any moment. We are the overflow lab for the whole of the east coast. It never rains but what it pours,' said Idris cheerfully.

45
Black Ops

Chloe Whiting needed to get out from the Trubshawes'. She was finding the B & B terribly claustrophobic after one night, and besides, her brief from Goldwing had been to see what she could dig up about how people viewed Osgood in the town.

She knew how the Trubshawes felt about him but wanted to get more of a feel from other townsfolk. She thought she'd start with a mini pub crawl. Beginning on the edge of town and working inwards, her first pub was a sports bar full of television screens, with it appeared, three different premier league matches being screened at the same time. Chloe ordered a large glass of white wine. The place appeared unpromising, filled as it was with young men in their teens and early twenties staring intently at their chosen game. Most of the media circus had already left town, so at least they'd be mostly locals but would probably only now know Osgood lived in their town from the 24-hour news strapline running across the TV screens. The shooting at the quiz night had, after all, been the biggest event to hit the town since the Vikings last invaded.

She was on the point of moving on when a man in a thin rimmed sleeveless jerkin approached the table.

'Excuse please. I just moved to here. Wondering what time church is. For me very important say my prayers.'

'I'm sorry, I'm just visiting myself but there is a lovely church here.'

'I love your English churches: Westminster Abbey, Sainsbury.'

'I think you mean Salisbury.'

'Oh yes, sorry.'

Chloe was struck by the man's chiselled features and sad soulful eyes.

'Look, I'm sure someone behind the bar will know. The Great British pub and the church often go hand in hand in places like this. I'll go and ask at the bar, if you like.'

'Okay, but you so kind, may I buy you drink as thank you?' said Alexei bowing his head courteously.

Poulson and Brown were in Stella Kingsley's office. Mr Brown had sat himself in her chair. He had his hands together tapping his fingers together in the same way the headmaster at Kingsley's school used to when he was displeased by some minor misdemeanour of her and her friends.

'Well, let me cut to the chase, DCI Kingsley, our friend the Bishop is getting paranoid about the protective surveillance we have been providing since the assassination attempt. We are not able to offer him close protection, as he says it is violating his human rights. All, of course, quite extraordinary but given Bishop Osgood's high profile within certain quarters of the media, we need to be seen to obey. Hence I'm pulling my man out from a personal protection role to a peripheral watching brief.'

Brown moved on from fiddling with his fingers to rearranging various things in Stella's office: walking over and straightening a mirror, repositioning her desk tidy, then picking up her book on 'mindfulness' and flicking through it with a disdainful look on his face.

'And you think there may still be a threat?' said Kingsley.

'Well, let's just say, we have information that suggests that the Reverend Osgood could still be in real danger,' Brown replied.

'And so... er... you won't want us plods involved in any way... that would be unthinkable.'

'Well, the thing is, the whole situation is extremely tricky politically. I have had to withdraw our man, Riddell, and place him on other duties. What we need is a discreet presence, someone who can blend into the background.'

'Surely that's the thing your department is expert at?' sneered Kingsley.

'I think we can find an officer to fit the bill,' said Chief Constable Poulson, 'Don't you Stella?'

'Well, Sir, we have been stretched to the limit in the last couple of weeks. But I could spare DS Coombs.'

'Needs must, DCI Kingsley. There we are, Mr Brown, your problem is solved, after a fashion,' said Poulson.

Nick hadn't managed to get a lot more out of Lomax as they drove back from the path lab. 'So, there's nothing more you can tell us?'

'Look, there is something, but it might not be important. Anyway, I told the other fella, Coombe was it?'

'Detective Sergeant Coombs, you mean.'

'Well, it's probably not relevant.'

'Let me be the judge of that.'

'It pissed me off at the time.'

'So not all bad news then,' said Nick.

Lomax didn't seem to hear him.

'Well, the pickup was nicked around the time Drac disappeared.'

'Any idea by who,' said Nick, trying to regain his professionalism and putting the image of this slob leering over Jenny in the greenhouse at Killpeck Farm to the back of his mind.

'Well, it was that Alexei and Drac, and I'm pretty sure that Jason was involved, though he denied it.'

'And you're sure that was the night Drac disappeared.'

'Yes.'

'And that they were driving a pickup?'

'Yes.'

'And do you know where they went with it?'

'Well, there are two possibilities. There's only two things to do around Killpeck at night: go to the pub or do a bit of rough shooting.'

'Where would you go for that?'

'Well, if they took the pickup, probably somewhere like Nipton Wood, which is very good for rabbit shooting but they could have been down the pub for all I know.'

'This pickup; where is it now?'

'Well, as far as I know, unless you lot have commandeered it, it's in the yard at Killpeck.'

'By the way, I hope you lot are bearing all this in mind, when it comes to my situation.'

'You keep cooperating with us, Mr Lomax, and I'll see what can be done.'

'Right.'

'There is, however, the little matter of you being in cahoots with Mr Yui, who will be charged with attempted murder of several people including a police officer.'

'I have told you that man intimidated me into allowing him to use my place to grow his filthy weed.'

'Oh, the fact your business had been going down the pan for several years, and you just saw the chance for extra money is the relevant point here.'

'I tell you, that man is one scary individual, as are the people he works for.'

Nick, encouraged to find Lomax in such a loquacious mood, continued his questioning.

'So, what happened?

'Well, they just drove in a big posh people carrier one day, four of them there were. They told me that they were after renting a bit of space in the area. Well, I was a bit dubious, but things haven't been going that well, with not having enough pickers and there being a glut of fruit, it was difficult to make any money.'

'So, you knew that they wanted to grow cannabis commercially.'

'No, I swear, I thought it was kosher. They said it was chillies and peppers what they wanted to grow,' said Lomax.

'Presumably you know the difference between marijuana and pepper plants?'

'Listen, when they arrived with the plants in the middle of the night, it was all well... so bloody intimidating.'

'So, they made you an offer you couldn't refuse,' said Nick wearily.

'I feared for my life. I tell you these were the type who'd slit their own mothers' throats for getting a week behind in the rent.'

Unbeknown to Lomax, Nick had met one or two such people as a child, but to him they had seemed avuncular and indulgent and were often honoured guests in his family home. It was only with the benefit of hindsight and police records that he had come to understand fully that there was another side to them.

'So, what was the deal? How much did they pay you?'

'Nothing up front, but I was to get a cut once the crop was harvested. Yui was left to ensure I fulfilled my part of the deal.'

'I will need you to make a full statement when we get back to the station.'

Stella Kingsley couldn't help but feel quietly satisfied with the way things were turning out. The vital evidence found at Priday's house must surely help secure a conviction at his retrial. The bravery of the Chowdry women in providing information meant that Hanif Singh's parents would evidently see justice done, and Colin Chowdry and his thugs would be given long, long sentences, and now there was the supercilious Mr Brown having to eat humble pie. She was also pleased with seeing Idris, and that their friendship was becoming easier. She was sure that this was something Marjorie Perks would have approved of. On the way home from work, she decided to treat herself and had popped into the off licence near the station to pick up a bottle of gin. She'd parked down a quiet little side road, as she was a little self-conscious about buying booze so close to her place of work. It was irrational, she knew, and something her male counter parts would think nothing off. She even thought the man in the shop gave her a funny look but she intended to go home, order a takeaway and pour herself a stupendously large gin and tonic. However, as she returned to her car, on opening the door, she felt something being shoved roughly over her head, and then everything went dark.

Nick Mycroft was up bright and early and busy feeding Bodkin Adams, who was slaloming his way between his owner's feet. As Nick predicted, the cat just about tolerated Ratface's presence in the house, but you could tell he was having trouble reigning in the desire to swipe the dog with one of his substantial claws, and the temptation was becoming increasingly difficult to resist.

For his part, Ratface seemed very much at home, sprawled out in front of Nick's woodburning stove.

When the phone went, Mycroft hoped it might be Jenny confirming dog walking arrangements for today, but it was Bob Coombs.

'Nick, sorry to bother you at home, but I'm a little concerned. The boss hasn't got in yet and she's usually here by eight, or before, as you know, and before you ask, I know it's the weekend, but she told me that because it was so hectic at the minute, she'd be in as normal.'

'Well have you rung her?'

'Well of course, but nothing on her mobile and her landline just goes to the answerphone.'

'Look, I'm quite sure there's nothing to worry about,' said Nick.

'Well, you see it's a bit awkward, Nick. I've got that Mr Brown here; you know, the hush hush one up from London,' whispered Coombs.

'And?' queried Nick.

'Well, he's asking about what arrangements have been made for Bishop Osgood's protection.'

'And?'

'I haven't got the foggiest,' admitted Coombs.

'Well, you'll just have to stall him,' instructed Nick.

'I don't know if I can.'

'Okay. Look, I've got to go up to Stamford anyway.'

'What for?'

'It's not in work time, so Bob, it's not really any of your business.'

'Okay, okay.'

'Keep in contact and if DCI Kingsley doesn't come in, I'll liaise with

Brown. Okay?'

'Right, you're the boss.'

'Yes, at the moment in absentia, I am, Bob.'

'Oh, you mean while the gaffer's away.'

'Yes. Now, is there anything else I should know?'

'No Sir... sorry yes, there was something. Dr Perks phoned. He asked if the DCI or you could ring him.'

'Okay, thank you, Bob, and remember can you ring me if or when DCI Kingsley comes in?'

'Will do.'

'Sir,' prompted Mycroft.

'Sir,' said Coombs.

46
Order of Service

At All Saint's Church, Bishop Osgood was getting robed. There's something about putting on the old best bib and tucker, as he called it, that always cheered him up. He thought it was rather akin to armour in that he felt somewhat guiltily invulnerable once in his cassock and alb. He had got to the church early, in order to ensure he knew where everything was. The only fly in the ointment was that he thought he'd spotted that Riddell character lurking in the churchyard, when he'd specifically asked them to leave him alone. But as his sermon was to be on the art of forgiveness, he thought he'd better lead by example. The congregation was beginning to dribble in. There were several familiar faces, one or two members of the press following up on the 'Attempt to Slay The Red Bishop,' story, and a few curious out of towners coming to see what all the fuss was about.

Jenny James and the other members of the choir were also getting changed and gossiping cheerfully about church life, the weather, and their infamous guest celebrant.

Meanwhile, Nick and Ratface were making their way from Shappington to Stamford. The dog was sprawled out on the back seat. Nick had received a written response to his letter expressing disquiet around the circumstances of Brodie's death.

Dear Mr Mycroft,

First of all, let me again express my deepest sympathy for your loss in such tragic circumstances, especially when Mr Collins was coming towards the end of his sentence. We will, of course, be reviewing our policies and procedures around safeguarding 'At risk' prisoners and thank you for your input.

Nick scrunched the letter tightly into a ball and tossed it out of the car window.

He was not about to leave the matter at that. He meant to ensure that something be done about the rate of suicides in prison, particularly among younger men, although it couldn't help Brodie now.

He rang into the station to find out if Stella Kingsley had appeared but there was still no news.

'Well, I tell you what Bob, if you're that worried, just pop over to her flat and see if there's any sign of life.'

'I'm not sure that's my place?'

'Sir,' Nick corrected Coombs, hoping this time that Coombs would get the message. Normally, he accepted Coombs and, his slap dash approach to some aspects of policing, but the death of Brodie had made him peevish. Why couldn't people just do things properly?

'Sir,' said Coombs.

'Look, just do it, okay! If she's not there, call me, as then there's just the possibility we might really have a problem.'

There was something vaguely familiar about the voice of whoever it was who had taken Stella Kingsley against her will.

'Right, out you get, Madam!' Stella couldn't help being reminded of her father, a shopkeeper from Mansfield, who was the archetypal, small man with something to prove and who having had a day being obsequious with his customers, could turn into a proper little martinet with his own children.

'But I can't see where I am going,' said Kingsley.

'Well, I'm sorry, but it's a bit late in the day...' said her captor.

'For what?'

'I mean if you had had the decency to take us seriously from the beginning.'

'So, what do you intend to do now? Mr Tomms, isn't it?' Kingsley had recognised the inclinations in the accent.

'That's to be decided by the committee,' said Tomms, his face (which of course Kingsley couldn't see) was becoming more florid by the minute. Beads of sweat ran down his forehead. He appeared incandescent with rage.

'That's you and...?' queried Kingsley.

Stella's response didn't improve Tomms' mood.

'Never you mind.'

'Terry, I think this has gone a bit far now don't you?'

'People will sit up and take notice now, I'm telling you.'

'I'm sure they will, Terry.'

Tomms had taken her onto what appeared to be an old airfield. At the back of what had once been living quarters, was a row of lock up garages.

'New Glory will take back this country and if it takes direct action to do it, that's what it will have to be.' Tomms took hold of Stella's arms and manhandled her out of the car.

'But why kidnap a police officer, Terry? I thought you were all for law and order?'

'You've all gone soft, you have. Look at those taxi drivers, still going free some of them, and then that Hanif or whoever he was. And you lot blaming us, when it was one of his own what done it.'

'Your organisation claimed responsibility, Terry,' said Stella.

'I tell, you this country has gone to the dogs,' said Tomms.

'Anyway, Mr Chowdry isn't one of their lot, as you put it, Terry, and he's been charged.'

'Well, whatever, things are going to have to change. It strikes me all us whites are expected to do is apologise for everything, when it was us what civilised three quarters of the world. It's diabolical, I tell you,' said Tomms, turning his head round towards Stella as he spoke.

'So, what are you going to do now, Terry? Try and get a ransom for me?'

'No, it's not about money. It's about changing the drift to bleeding heart Marxism.'

He arm-wrestled her to the door of the lock up.

'I shall demand the release of any of my "brothers from the right" in return for your release.'

'Well, that's not going to be agreed to, where acts of terror are involved.'

'We're not terrorists, Detective Chief Inspector, we are Freedom Fighters,' said Tomms, shoving Kingsley firmly to the back of the space, securing her hands behind her back to the remains of an old car engine and slamming closed the garage door.

'Freedom Fighters, I tell you! That's what we are.'

Nick Mycroft parked his car in Stamford town centre and decided to make his way to the church on foot, to make sure that there was nothing obviously untoward going on in the car park or approaches to the church. This Brown character from MI5 or whoever, had given the local police very little information to go on. He checked the back of the church before going in to take his seat near the door. There was already quite a large congregation: the servers were lighting the altar candles and the church wardens were handing out service sheets and hymn books. There was a cold wind blowing in from outside and most people were keeping their coats on. An elderly woman in a wheelchair was being pushed into church, with some difficulty, by a younger woman, possibly her daughter. Nick could see they were struggling and went over to help. It was while he was doing this, that he saw Jenny sitting at the back with the rest of the choir preparing for the service. She smiled and waved. As he waved back, he failed to notice a cadaverous, dark haired man slip into a pew on the other side of the church.

In the vestry, Bishop Osgood was rereading his sermon, highlighting in yellow which section he wanted to put most emphasis on. Everyone had been very sympathetic and supportive, apart from one anonymous letter, pushed through his letter box: *GAY COMMIE VICAR HOPE YOU ROAST IN HELL*, signed *A regular communicant.* These Christians can be tough eggs, Osgood had thought to himself.

In Lincoln, at the front desk, Sergeant Hedges was resigned to another Sunday shift. His planned fishing day out was postponed yet again.

'Hello, can I speak to the senior officer in charge?'

'And you are?'

'My name is Riddell.'

'Well, Mr Riddell, can I ask, is the matter urgent?' asked Hedges.

'Well, it depends on what you class as urgent?' Riddell replied sarcastically.

'I'm afraid we are very pushed at the moment, Sir.'

'Look, I'm not sure, but I think your governor may be in trouble.'

'Who do you mean, exactly, Sir?'

'I think DCI Kingsley is being held against her will, and that her life could be in peril.'

'And what leads you to believe that, Sir?' queried Sergeant Hedges.

'I work for the security forces; we were tracking your governor and our information suggests she may be in danger. Here's my ID...'

'One minute, Sir. I'll phone upstairs and get someone down here right away,' said Hedges.

When he got the message from Hedges, Bob Coombs raced down the stairs three at a time.

'This is the gentleman in question, Bob,' said Hedges.

'Right, Mr Riddell, what information have you got for us?'

'Well, your DCI has been under surveillance by means of an audio tracking device.'

'Hang on, do you mean without her knowledge or consent?' said Coombs.

'That's hardly the point right now,' said Riddell coolly.

'What the hell were you bugging her for, for Christ' sake?'

'We had suspicions that her actions might put one of our investigations in jeopardy and be a further threat to national security.'

'What? You mean you think she's a spy? You all must be out of your tiny little minds.'

'I'm sure your boss thought she was just doing her job, but we needed to be sure our operation wasn't being compromised.'

'Well, do we know whose got her, or where she's supposed to have been taken?'

'We don't know who. The audio connection is weak and muffled but the tracking device has given us an idea of where.'

'So, what are we standing here for then?' said Coombs impatiently.

'Can you think of any reason she would be being held?'

'Look, we haven't got time for any of this,' said Coombs. 'Are you coming or what?'

'For all we know, this may be criminality and not terrorist related.'

'Okay, whatever! Just supply me with the information and slip back into your smoke and mirrors world,' sneered Coombs.

Chloe, unlike some of her girl friends, believed she was a good judge of character. Alexei was charming and attentive and alone in a foreign land, all the things her married lover, 'Mr Upstairs,' was not. She had felt taken for granted and now this striking young man was paying attention to her and was actually interested in what she was saying. So, it had felt easy and natural to go back with him to his hotel room. She was surprised at the urgency with which he made to love her. There appeared no expectation on his part for her to initiate anything in bed, unlike Mr Upstairs, who had an inflexible list of requirements in that department. She'd ring Barry Goldwing in the morning and tell him she was making good progress in making connections in Lincolnshire.

47
Sacrament for the Dead

'And on the night, he was betrayed, he took bread and blessed it and said, this is my body which is given for you.' It was a line Osgood had recited countless times over his long life. It resonated with him now, in the same way it always did. '*On the night he was betrayed*, as he had betrayed Julian, all those years ago. He was brought back from his guilt trip by a quiet satisfaction that his sermon had been quite well received, even his line about Jeremy Corbyn having been welcomed by the Labour Party, as their own Prodigal Son.'

Every now and then, Jenny would glance down to the congregation in an attempt to catch Nick Mycroft's eye. It was on one such occasion, she thought she recognised the middle-aged man sitting towards the back of the church as one of the pickers from Killpeck Farm. Yes, she was sure it was Alexei. What was he doing here? It wasn't his kind of scene, she felt sure.

The service continued: first the choir sang an anthem and then the congregation began filing up towards the altar to take communion. The front few pews emptied on the nod from the church warden.

Stella Kingsley heard a gurgling noise coming from the other side of the garage door.

'Terry, is that you? Don't you think this has all gone far enough?'

All she could hear was laboured breathing and more gurgling.

'What's going on out there?'

'Somebody, please help me!' gasped Tomms.

'Open the garage door, Terry! I'll get you help.'

But now there was only silence.

Stella attempted to wriggle from her bonds, some kind of nylon bailer twine, but Terry had tied them well. She was reduced to banging her foot against an old oil drum, as she was beginning to lose her voice.

Riddell and Coombs were approaching the airfield when the signal from the tracker in Stella Kingsley's handbag went dead.

'Damn it,' said Riddell.

'What's up?'

'I've lost the signal'

'Oh great! So that's it. How the hell do we find her now? By the time we find her, god alone knows what might have happened.'

'Hey, look, this whole area is like a prairie back home. There can't be that many places to look.'

'I'm calling for back up. She could be miles away by now.'

'I doubt it. We were closing in on her location when we lost the signal.'

'Right, well there's the haystack. Where do you suggest we start looking?' said Coombs.

In Stamford, Alexei was sat with Chloe, watching as the congregation filed their way up to the altar rail. He could feel the small vial of strychnine in his jacket pocket. This, of course, was not how he had planned it to be. If that idiot kid, Jason, had not made such a cock up, Alexei would now be back in Moscow and his bank account would look a whole lot healthier than it did now.

Jenny James could not be sure, but the bloke sitting at the back of the church certainly seemed familiar. She had returned to the choir stalls having taken communion.

'Receive the body of Christ.'

Nigel Osgood was placing the wafers in the hands of those kneeling in front of him. Behind him Ralph, the elderly server, held the chalice from which members of the congregation were taking sips of wine.

Alexei approached the altar rail, making sure he was the last in the congregation to take the bread from Osgood. Then, with great theatrics, in what appeared to be a show of reverence, Alexei took the cup from Ralph. As he did so, he trickled a little of the strychnine into the chalice, pretended to take a sip and then handed it back to the old man. He returned to his seat in the belief that the next man to drink from the chalice would be Osgood and this would see his mission accomplished.

It was Coombs, who first heard the muffled shouting. They had looked in all the hangars on the air base; some still contained the remnants of aircraft, others were in poor repair with the wind blowing through what remained of them like a seaside storm whipping through the bones of long dead whales.

As they got closer, they could see something lying against one of the lock up doors.

The noise was coming from inside the garage.

'It's Tomms... Terry Tomms!' exclaimed Coombs.

'What? The fascist from New Glory?'

'It's him alright.'

Riddell pulled a handgun from his jacket.

'What the hell! This isn't America, you know.'

'I don't like the way this feels.'

'This feels like a fat, deluded, old twat, who's about to expire.'

'Bob Coombs, I've never been happier to hear that voice,' said Stella Kingsley, who had managed to free her mouth from the duct tape that Tomms had gagged her with.

'Are you okay, Ma'am?'

'Yes. What's happened to Tomms?'

'Not sure he's still breathing.'

'Okay, can you hear me, Mr Tomms? I'm just going to take a look at you,' said Riddell.

Tomms roused himself on one elbow. He was not a good colour and was breathing heavily.

'I'd prefer it if your colleague did,' said Tomms. I've nothing against you personally, but each to their own, don't you think?'

'You've got to be kidding me?'

'Right Mr Tomms, I am arresting you on suspicion of false imprisonment.'

'And if you won't let Mr Riddell help you, you'll have to wait for the bloody ambulance. This is not a multi-coloured swop shop, you know.'

Alexei was nearly back to his pew at the back of the church when he realised things were not going exactly to plan. Once he had turned from the altar rail, he had expected Osgood to consume the remaining wine in the communion cup. Instead, a hale and hearty Nigel Osgood appeared to be following Alexei down the centre aisle of the church. What the hell was going on?

Nick Mycroft, on the other side of the church, had been busy gazing at Jenny through most of the service. She looked nothing less than angelic in her chorister robes. His feelings for her were not particularly pure, however, nor was his daydreaming that there was some way it could work between them, even if it meant him leaving the force. He could then look after them both, on the money from the criminal he was set to inherit from. Jenny would go from being chorister to gangster's moll.

It was then that he saw Alexei running up the aisle towards the altar and Osgood.

Ten minutes after Coombs had radioed for help, an ambulance arrived on the airfield and Tomms was loaded aboard. Two patrol cars escorted it as it drove off into the night. Stella Kingsley had refused entreaties to go to hospital and was sat in the back seat of the car, sipping from a whisky flask, which Bob Coombs just happened to have in the glove compartment.

'You had us really worried there, Ma'am.'

'Tomms is a pompous little shit, Bob, but let me tell you, when you've been in the same interview room as Rex Priday, you know what real evil is. Anyway, what's been happening while I have been out of commission?'

'Not a lot, Ma'am.'

'And who's your friend?' Stella said referring to Riddell, who was standing a little way away from the car, talking into his mobile phone.

'One of that Mr Brown's goons. He's the one who shot that boy the other day, trying to carve up that old bishop.'

'So, what was he doing with us plods?'

'Well, he's the one who knew you were in trouble.'

'How come?'

'They've been tracking you electronically. You'd been discretely tagged, Ma'am,' said Coombs, with relish.

'Who the hell does he think he is?'

'Don't get worked up, Ma'am. Now, let's get you back to the station.'

'Yes, where I'll be having a few words with Mr Brown. What the hell do these security people think they are playing at bugging senior police officers? I mean, the worlds gone mad, mad, I tell you. As if we hadn't got enough to worry about with multiple murder enquiries?' Her relief appeared to have given Stella a case of verbal diarrhoea.

'Well, who knows what would have happened? You might have been a goner, without Riddell, Ma'am.'

'Thank you, Bob, but when I want your opinion, I will give it to you.'

Alexei hadn't factored in that when a member of the congregation was unable to reach the alter rail due to infirmity, the officiating priest and server would come down to the congregation and give the eucharist there. Ralph, the elderly server, was bending down to the woman in the wheelchair, who

Nick had helped get into the church. Jenny jumped out from the choir stalls aware that something was very, very, wrong. Her first instinct was to put herself in between Osgood and Alexei, who she saw had a blade in his hand.

Nick Mycroft, too, was out of his pew, but he was panicking. Jenny was just a few feet from some nutter with a knife.

'Armed police!' he bellowed, when all he had in his hand was a copy of 'Hymns Ancient and Modern.'

For a moment Alexei hesitated, looked squarely at Mycroft and then diving between Ralph and the woman in the wheelchair, he grabbed the chalice.

Time stood still for Alexei and he was transported back: to the small, third floor flat in Moscow and his mother, with the life being strangled out of her by her condition, to how he would help her down the steps to the stairwell on the ground floor, where her wheelchair was kept, and how in this most egalitarian society, few people in that part of the city would go out of their way to help her.

'Alexei, put the knife down,' said Jenny.

'My dear, whoever you are, you must stay out of this,' said Osgood.

'I am a police officer, Your Grace.'

'Well, I thought I made it quite clear, I do not require protection and I certainly won't have a young person like you losing their life on my account.'

Then turning to Alexei, Osgood said: 'Now young man, having desecrated this house of God, may I ask what your intentions are?'

'It's nothing personal, Bishop, business that's all.' Alexei moved slowly towards Osgood.

For a moment, the elderly woman lifted her head off her chest, and with some difficulty in a clear and somewhat fruity voice said, 'What on earth do you think you are doing, coming into the house of God as if you owned the place? Now be a good boy and return to your pew.'

Alexei looked at her, then at Jenny, and then at Osgood, while turning towards the back of the church, where Nick was standing.'

'So, where's your gun Mr Policeman?' He smiled and looked once more at the woman in the wheelchair. Then he put the communion cup to his lips and drank the contents.

48
Nunc Dimittis

Alexei died on the way to hospital, despite the best efforts of the paramedics. Nick had gone in the ambulance with him, but Alexei could not, or would not speak. Although circumstances pointed to Alexei being responsible for events at Rimmer Farm, The Chief Constable, when he spoke to Stella Kingsley, felt it best for the Crown Prosecution Service to keep the case on file for the present.

'Now Stella, are you sure that you're fit enough for duty?'

'Well, I won't be taking part in the Great North Run this year, Sir.'

'Oh, I'm sorry. Were you planning to?'

'It's a joke, Sir.'

'Oh right. By the way, Mr Brown sends his regards and... um... thanks for what we did vis a vis Bishop Osgood. Strange kind of chap to be a cleric, but I suppose it takes all sorts.'

'Yes Sir, and a good result being able to charge Chowdry with Hanif's murder.'

'Yes, good work there. I always thought him a bit pompous.'

Pot and kettle, thought Stella.

'Give your crew a slap on the back from me?'

'Will do, Sir!'

'Oh, and Stella,try and get the budget under control. The overtime bill this month was far too hefty.'

'Right, you are, Sir,' said Stella.

'We live in straitened times, you know.'

'Absolutely, Sir. By the way, how's that place in France coming along? Got the pool in yet?'

'Very droll, DCI Kingsley. Now run along before I remember to remind you that your fly tipping arrest targets for this year are far from being reached.'

'This place has seen better days,' said Jenny, as they sat in The Black Hart, a rundown city centre pub.

'We haven't though. Well done everyone. Several results this week,' said Stella Kingsley. Here,' she said to Bob Coombs, handing him several notes, 'Can you get the drinks? It's my shout.'

'Over my dead body,' said Idris Perks.

'You're not at work now, Idris,' said Kingsley.

'I know, but I tell you, to get that poor soul identified in the lab and to hopefully finally finger that bastard Priday! I haven't felt this good since Wales last won the Triple Crown.'

Bob Coombs arrived back with the drinks.

'I have spoken to the Chief Constable about putting you forward for a bravery award, Jenny,' said Stella Kingsley.

'Oh gosh, Ma'am, it was a team effort. If Nick hadn't been there, I don't know quite what I would have done.'

Jenny had quietly slipped her hand under the table into Nick's. He seemed somewhat distracted.

'How about that unpleasant little man from New Glory?' asked Jenny.

'Tomms? He's still in hospital, of course, but will be charged with false imprisonment.'

'The tabloids will no doubt make him into some kind of anti-establishment hero,' said Perks, sipping at his half of bitter.

'Well, that's as maybe, Idris. All I know is I was glad to hear Bob's voice at that airfield.'

'God, I don't like to think about it, Ma'am,' said Jenny.

'He hadn't got the bottle to really hurt me, but if Bob and that chap from Brown's department hadn't found us...'

'We aim to please, Ma'am,' said Coombs, in between contented sips of his pint.

'And how about the Bishop?' asked Jenny.

'He maintains that this was all some deep state put-up job, but thankfully hasn't implicated us.'

'It says in the papers that the Kremlin is suggesting Alexei was poisoned by British Intelligence,' said Coombs.

'Well, there's a surprise,' Kingsley replied.

'Ratface, come here,' said Nick. The old dog who had been trundling an old crisp packet round the bar with his nose lolloped over to their table.

'Oh, sorry boy. Have we been ignoring you?'

'What you going to do with that dog?' asked Bob Coombs.

'Well, Lomax doesn't want him back. Besides, I don't think you're allowed them where he's going.'

'We are going to dog share him permanently, Ma'am,' said Jenny, looking over at Nick with ill-concealed affection.

'Is that right, DI Mycroft?' said Kingsley.

'Apparently so, Ma'am,' said Nick looking down at a text message from his father.

It read: *Sorry to be bearer of bad news. Your Uncle Jimmy passed away in the night. Gone to a better place, no doubt.*

Nick was not surprised at this news. Jimmy, the hard man, had been broken by Brodie's death. His feelings, like those for all his family, apart from his mother, were complicated. His uncle had known no other life than that to which he'd been born. He might just as well have been a Roman legionnaire, so anachronistic was the thinking he'd grown up with. Men were judged by how good they were with their fists. A woman's place was in the home. Respect was earned on the street and by the size of the wad of notes in your wallet. And yet, Nick pondered that you can't choose who you love. Although part of Nick pitied and had at times feared Jimmy, there was no doubt he cared for Jimmy more than he had ever been able to love his father. On a more mundane level, what was Nick going to do about his career now he was a rich man? And more importantly, how much of it could he keep in good faith, and even more importantly, how much of all this was he going to tell Jenny, (whose hand was now gently stroking his thigh)?

In the office of Janus Films, Barry Goldwyn was in an ebullient mood.

'So, it turns out The Red Bishop wasn't so much of a pinko as he made out.'

'How do you make that out?' said Callum.

'Well, it appears he sold his commie boyfriend down the river all those years ago.'

'And your point is?' said Callum. 'Osgood never tried to hide this stuff from us.'

'No, but all his bleeding heart malarkey about the evils of capitalism was hogwash.'

'I think he's suffered enough, don't you,' said Chloe.

'Talking of boyfriends, you had a bit of a narrow escape our Chloe, with old Alexei the assassin, wouldn't you say?'

'At that moment, there was a knock at the door and Phyllida, Barry's secretary came in.

'Sorry to disturb you, Mr Goldwing.'

'If that dress were any shorter, you'd do more than disturb me,' said Goldwing.

'I thought you'd better see this,' said Phyllida.

Barry gave a kind of grunt.

'What is it?'

'It's just come through from Lambeth Palace. *The Archbishop of Canterbury is saddened to learn of the Right Reverend Nigel Osgood's death. Our brother in Christ passed away peacefully in his sleep last night.*'

'Oh. that's very sad,' said Chloe.

'Right, Callum. Get onto all the news channels; tell them we've got a glowing tribute to a great church man feature just about ready to rock and roll.'